Elvis
has Left
the Building

SCEPTRE

Also by Tania Kindersley

Goodbye, Johnny Thunders
Don't Ask me Why

Praise for Tania Kindersley:

Goodbye, Johnny Thunders

'Kindersley writes convincingly of the delirium of falling in love, the refusal to accept the blindingly obvious, and the lengths to which seemingly sensible people go when an affair ends . . . Nancy's heights and depths are painfully real, and the evocation of a hot London summer is such that you can almost smell it'
The Sunday Times

'The writing is fluent, snappy and contemporary, but the mood is elegiac and deeply romantic. Death, despair and self-destruction hover in the background and the novel brilliantly catches the insubstantiality of young, doomed love and that moment in life when nothing is so intense or so agonising ever again'
Mail on Sunday

'There are no over-dramatic twists, no elaborate conceits. What it does have is real atmosphere, a portrait of a young woman living in Nineties London that rings absolutely true'
Express

'*Goodbye, Johnny Thunders* lets you feel the rush of love and danger. Thrilling, poetic and sexy – a top class talent'
Cosmopolitan

'Brilliantly captures the pain and desperation of fallling in love. Eloquently written and utterly believable, *Goodbye, Johhny Thunders* is a real triumph'
Company

'The book almost reads itself. The bittersweet story of wide-eyed Nancy . . . is wry, funny and immensely appealing'
Big Issue

'A bittersweet, atmospheric love story'
The Times

Don't Ask me Why

'A serious and reflective novel of friendship and growing up
. . . the novel has a hypnotic quality and an aching sadness
and wisdom that all will recognise. It is very good'
Elizabeth Buchan, *The Times*

'A cool, class-act tale about female friendship'
She

'Love, lust, dreams and the meaning of friendship are woven
into a sensitive, tragic tale . . . All becomes clear and worth
it in the end. And, like Kindersley's last novel, it's hauntingly
written'
Company

'Kindersley's language is acute, discomforting and scalpel-
sharp'
Independent

'Achingly nostalgic, the author conveys the rapture and
yearning of youth – and the anguish of bidding it farewell'
Mail on Sunday

'Eloquent, witty tale of college sex, friendships and bust-ups'
Marie-Claire

'This book works as an Oxbridge novel – which, highly
unusually, portrays a mixed university where students actually
work – as a lament for a youth we all thought would never
pass, and as an exploration of friendship. It is quite brilliant'
Daily Telegraph

'A well-written, sharply observed love story about a passionate
friendship between two women . . . a good weepy'
Sunday Express

'The novel has heart'
The Sunday Times

Elvis
has Left
the Building

TANIA KINDERSLEY

SCEPTRE

First published in 2000 by Hodder and Stoughton
A division of Hodder Headline
A Sceptre book

A CIP catalogue record for this title is available from the British
Library.

ISBN 0 340 68586 7

Typeset by Palimpsest Book Production Limited,
Polmont, Stirlingshire
Printed and bound in Great Britain by
Mackays of Chatham plc, Chatham, Kent

Hodder and Stoughton
A division of Hodder Headline
338 Euston Road
London NW1 3BH

To my sister.

1

I met Fred when I was twenty-one.

It was a Sunday at the end of May and the sun was shining out of a flat blue sky. I walked down to the river and along to the Tate. I had a feeling for the Tate and I thought I'd have a look at some of the things I liked that hung there. There was a Calder mobile at the end of a dingy corridor that you could walk right past if you weren't looking out for it, and a red Rothko, which sent me every time. It could have been any gallery on any day, but it was that one.

There is always a point in any museum when you have seen enough, when your senses get hit by aesthetic overload and you have to walk very quickly to the exit with your head down and your eyes front so you don't see another single painting. I got to the cut-off point just as I was passing the Turner room, which was fine by me, because I had never liked Turner, even though I knew I was supposed to. It was all too lush somehow, the way I saw it, too opulent; it made me think of money, not art. I walked fast through the marble lobby, filled up with the murmuring Sunday crowd, and out into the day, which was a shock after the regulated amber light of the high rooms inside. I sat on the white steps and looked out over the river, which was flowing fast in the wrong direction. It was dark pewter and the sun was glancing off it in thin shooting points of light.

After a moment I realised that a man was standing in front of me. I looked up and I had to squint a little because of the light.

He said, 'You look like a photograph.'

I mean come on, it was a line. It was something. No one had ever said anything even remotely like that to me before, not even my friend Stella, who said some stuff, when the mood was in her.

I put my hand up to shield my eyes, and all I could see was a tall dark man, in silhouette against the sun, with an upright figure and straight shoulders. His hair was combed down and perhaps even slicked with some pomade or hair oil, which gave him the look of someone foreign from an old film, and he was wearing a thin-cut black suit and a white shirt, and I thought he was the one who looked like something out of a photograph.

'Did you just come out?' he said.

'Yes,' I said.

'Do you want to get a cup of coffee?' he said.

Afterwards, I thought it was curious that he should just come up to me and ask like that. At the time I didn't think it was strange at all. Maybe it was because he didn't show any embarrassment or reticence; there was nothing affected or stilted about him. He just asked me for coffee as if that was what people did to strange women every day.

'My name is Fred,' he said, as we walked along the Embankment.

'My name is Iris,' I said. 'My name is Iris Spent.'

'That's a name,' he said.

We had coffee in an unmemorable café in the back-streets of Victoria. It was an anonymous place where people didn't look at each other or talk to each other; there was linoleum on the floor and smeared glass in the windows.

I can't remember what we talked about.

I remember staring at his face and having to stop myself.

I remember thinking that his skin had a fine sanded sheen to it that I hadn't seen on a man before; I thought it looked like Irish skin, something Celtic about it. I wondered if Fred was an Irish name; I wondered if he would turn out to have a great-grandmother still living in Killarney. His eyes were so dark they looked almost black. I thought that I had never seen anyone with eyes like that before.

I remember that every time I looked up he was looking straight at me, so I had to look away again, at his ear, or the red Formica table.

He took my number and said he would call, and then he walked away.

On the way home, I wondered about what he said, about looking like a photograph. There is a picture of Lee Miller taken by a Russian called George Hoyningen Huene; I saw it once when I was seventeen and remembered it ever since. She has her back to the camera with her feet, dressed in white rope soled shoes, planted wide apart. She's leaning into her right hip and looking out over her left shoulder and she has the merest smile on her face as if she knows the camera is there but she doesn't care.

The smile makes you wonder if she is sleeping with Huene and torturing him with take it or leave it. She is brown and white and sheer and sleek and perfect and the picture is static except for her shadow running away across the length of coir matting she's standing on, as if it is trying to escape the frame. Her hair is short and slicked close to her head and the sun is shining on it and she is impervious. Later, I read in a book that this perfect untouched girl would go through war and drugs and loss and drink and despair, and it made me sad and I always thought of that photograph afterwards.

The reason I thought of it then, that Sunday I first met Fred, was that I had a profile a little like Lee Miller – just a little, a long nose with the face sloping down on a plane, and I was wearing my hair very short then. I wondered if that was the photograph he was thinking of. (Straight on I didn't look like her at all: my face is small and square and covered in freckles; I have slanting grey eyes that go blue in the light and straight eyebrows without any curve in them, and all I ever wished for was that golden Lee Miller beauty, but I don't have it and there is nothing I could do about that.)

Years later, I thought of it again, and I asked Fred whether that was the photograph he meant and he said he had never seen it in his life.

For two days nothing happened. I found myself remembering how he had looked when he first spoke to me, his face indistinct in the back light. I couldn't sleep at night and I lay in bed thinking of the details of our meeting, trying to read between the lines. I had only yearned for someone once before: when I was nineteen, I worked in a bar and I had a crush on the barman. He was ten years older than me, sure and polished, and we became friends because we laughed at the same things.

I was haunted with thoughts of him; I wanted him to fall in love with me so badly I could feel it hurting in my body; this desire, this wanting, turning into a heavy physical ache behind my shoulder-blades. I kept thinking: I'll say something, I'll tell him, and then at least I'll know. Anything, I thought, would be better than this uncertainty. I thought: It's the eighties now, I'll ask. I pictured it in my head, I ran the scene: I could see the kind sympathetic look on his face when he said I just don't think of you that way. I could see the furrow of concern in his forehead when he said: It's not you, it's me. (It's not you, it's me; the newest lie on the block.)

I carried the want and the ache around with me, and one

day when I came into work they said he'd been offered a job in Glasgow and quit. I went home that night and cried in the bathroom, and the next day I felt a vast relief because it was finished and I didn't have to ache all over my body any more.

And then there was Fred, this strange man whose surname I didn't even know, and I was aching for him, and it made me remember the last time as if it had never gone away (my body saying Oh no, not this again) and it made me so angry I didn't know what to do.

I refused to think about it and I didn't check my answering-machine and I pretended I didn't care at all, because he was only a man and I had better things to do, and then on the fifth day, when I had convinced myself that I would never think about him again, never again in my whole wide life, he called and asked me out, and we've been together ever since.

We were together until one Friday night, nine years later, in March this time, the beginning of spring, the beginning of official summer time, the Friday when he told me he couldn't see me any more.

I couldn't even say why or how or what. He said it so normal and reasonable and downbeat that I just sat and stared at him, and before I could shout or cry or call him names, he left the flat with a bag under his arm and said that he would send round for the rest of his stuff. And that was the end of Fred and me: after nine years, he walked out of the door with a bag in his hand.

I suppose this kind of thing happens every day, but it hadn't happened to me and it felt entirely without pre-cedent or form. I didn't know what to do or where to go; I didn't know what happened next. I thought I must have seen this at the pictures, I must have read this in a book, there must be a stock reaction I could use. Did I start smashing china now, or get stumbling drunk, or call up an ex-boyfriend and sleep with him?

For a week, I didn't do anything. I sat in a state of nothingness, a condition of dull limbo, waiting for something to happen.

It hurts so badly when you love someone and they don't love you back that you can't feel it or think about it all at once. And the worst is that while you're trying to take in the shock and comprehend the feeling of having been in a car wreck, while you have a pit in your stomach as if someone's shoved a hand in there and started pulling, and your head aches like there's a vice on it, and you're not sure you have full control over your motor functions, while all that's going on, as if it wasn't enough, there's a voice in your head, going round and round on a loop, saying How could you be this stupid, how could you be this dumb, what's wrong with *you*?

There's another voice that says What are you making such a fuss about? You are an intelligent, independent female at the end of the twentieth century, and thousands of women fought for you not to feel this way. You got liberated so you wouldn't have to feel this way.

And you tell yourself that it's just a man, and there are people out there with cancer and hepatitis C and diseases they don't have a name for yet; you tell yourself that in Russia there is a strain of TB that has become immune to antibiotics; you know that there is ethnic cleansing in the Balkans and El Niño bringing flash floods to Poland and forest fires to Mexico. And you have all your faculties and a roof over your head and you are not HIV positive (are you?) and you have good friends and a job and you are not living in a cardboard box or dependent on methadone.

And you count all these blessings, over and over again; and it doesn't make any difference.

I counted them, all my blessings. In that first week, I sat up one night and made a list of them, every single one I could remember.

I sat until the dawn broke, and I listened to a sad album called *Pink Moon* recorded by a boy who killed himself when he was twenty-six because no one ever bought his records, and I counted my blessings, one by one.

At six in the morning, as the birds were yelling outside and the morning light was already growing dusty with the dirt of the city rising up from the tarmac streets, I read through the list, all the wealth of blessings that I held, and I knew that, just now, none of them made any difference at all.

There's something horribly hackneyed and used about being left, because you know it's happened to so many people before you and it will happen to so many after. It's so familiar and known, and at the same time entirely dark and new.

Neither of us believed in marriage, we always agreed about that. Fred had a horror of the bourgeois, although he was one, that was where he came from; he was reacting against his parents – that was why he was so good at his job. We didn't think of churches and white dresses and elderly relations and people in hats, we didn't want to sign anything legally binding. We dismissed all that because we were free spirits, of course we were, it was the nineties: it was the end of the millennium and there were no rules any more. The personal is political, that was what people said (women said), and I believed them. But it was more than that, for me: it just wasn't the way my mind worked. I never wanted someone to sign on the dotted line, to stay because of a piece of paper or a social obligation or a sense of shame. I wanted them to stay because they wanted to; I never wanted to put salt on anyone's tail. (People who thought they knew said this was unrealistic.)

But I did think that it would go on for ever, even if we hadn't said so in front of a crowd. I thought it would go on for ever because I wanted it to, as if sheer wishing made things happen the way you planned.

We carried on together, in this unspoken accord, through our twenties. I spent most of my twenties changing my mind; Fred stayed just the same. That was what I liked in him. I had never known stability before: it was all new to me and I found I liked it. Fred was four years older, but it didn't seem to mean that he knew things I hadn't learnt yet. He had travelled more, was all. He had taken a year off after school and gone round the world with a backpack, just like everyone except me. (I stayed in London and worked in a bar and did my Ph.D. in unrequited love.) He had stamps on his passport from Indonesia and Easter Island, from Sri Lanka and Guatemala, from Nepal and the Philippines. He had some pictures he had taken blown up and put on the wall of his bathroom, sunsets over water and street children begging for dollars. It was his only overt display of vanity.

I thought we were together for ever because no one had said any different. I thought we were together till the end of it because it felt like we fitted, two pieces in a tumbling jigsaw; because when I was with him I got a sense of belonging, of some kind of certainty.

Afterwards, when he had walked out with his bag in his hand, I sat in my room and wondered how I could not have seen it.

Does everyone say that? I'll take a bet they do. I'll bet they sit on their sofa, suddenly their sofa for one, and put their head in their hands and wonder, How could I have been so wrong? How could I have been so blind? How did I not see it coming? How?

And why, of course. Because there never is a good answer to that question. Even if Fred could have told me why, spelt it out, put it into words, into the ABC of excuse, it wouldn't have explained.

In the week after he left, I sat in my room and ran it again in my head, hoping for clues, hoping for comfort, hoping for something.

The first night, that Friday night, when everything changed, out of a clear blue sky:

He came home late. Fred ran a gallery selling contemporary art in an obscure dead-end street just the wrong side of the tracks, in the lost hinterland north of Oxford Street, the wandering maze of streets before you get to Marylebone, before you hit Harley Street and the expensive quacks and the double-parked Mercedes, that dingy no man's land that doesn't have a name. But for all that, the Bond Street fold trekked there willingly every time there was a show, because it was where the wild boys were, it was where the talent was. That was Fred's gift: he could sniff out the Next Big Thing faster than you could say money in the bank.

We worked together. People said you shouldn't mix business with pleasure, but it had turned out fine, in our case. Or at least, up to then it had.

I went home early that night and waited; he said he would be back at six but he wasn't. He was later than that, two hours later, but still I didn't think anything of it.

The first strange thing was that he didn't come and sit down. We lived apart, but we used each other's places so much they were like our own. So when he came to mine, he always walked in, went straight to the fridge, got a beer, and came and sat down on the green sofa. My flat was small, it was famous for being small, that was its thing; there were two sofas and a low table with a lamp on it and a translucent yellow glass bowl from Bermondsey market and one blue picture hanging over the fireplace.

That night, I heard the door go, I heard his footsteps sounding on the wood floor, but he didn't go to the fridge and he didn't sit down.

Oh, it's so fucking banal, isn't it? (Remember Humphrey Bogart in *Casablanca*? Remember him so weary and cynical and seen-it-all, saying to Ingrid Bergman how all stories are the same, how they all start 'See, mister I met a man,' how they all go along to the tune of an old piano from the back parlour.)

Fred came and stood in front of me, and because there was a skylight behind him and the last of the light was running in from the west, he had a limpid aureole of sunlight around his head and I couldn't see his face clearly, just like that first time we met, and suddenly I was back on the steps of the Tate again, I was that twenty-one-year-old girl in the photograph, knowing nothing except what was in black and white.

I hadn't guessed anything till then, but when he didn't sit down I knew instantly that something was wrong, because you do. I never read a book or saw a film when this scene came and the girl didn't know, just know, in her blood and her bones and the very guts of her, that there is something wrong when they come and stand in front of you and look at you with that look. You know the one, you've seen it. It's hesitant and bullish at the same time, it's impatient and reticent, slightly baffled and almost angry. It's the paradoxical look that gets handed down, from generation to generation, just so that whoever sees it knows instantly that something is wrong.

I had a strange feeling that I'd read this script before.

I said, 'What is it?'

He took a small breath and let it out and said, 'I can't see you any more.'

Even though I'd known there was something wrong I didn't know what it was, not until he came right out and said it like that, so bald and unadorned. There was nothing, nothing, that let me see this coming. We hadn't been fighting or sniping; we hadn't been reduced to no sex and long silences and small barbed sideways remarks in public places. I had seen other couples do that. We didn't do that.

In my head, I said: I don't understand. I said: This isn't right, you must have got the wrong apartment, the wrong woman. In my head, which suddenly seemed to be filled with traffic, I said, You should go out and come back in again and start over.

Out loud, I said nothing.

A small look of relief crossed his face. I wondered if he had been planning this, if he had been trying to time it right. Perhaps he had wanted to tell me for weeks. We had gone to Barcelona for the weekend in February; we had sat up late and eaten tapas and taken baths together in a white-tiled hotel bathroom. As he stood there in front of me, his face clearing with the realisation that he had done what he came to do, I wondered whether he had been thinking all that time, figuring when he could break the news to me. It must be hard, telling someone you don't want them any more.

'Well,' he said, 'I'll get my stuff.'

He went to the cupboard by the door, and took out a small bag he used to carry clothes and overnight things with him, between our two places. He carried it into the bathroom and shut the door.

That was when I almost lost it. It was the door closing like that. He never shut the door, usually.

When there isn't very much left, pride seems to be the last to go. I didn't want to let him see me cry, so I swallowed it down, and when he came out of the bathroom and crossed over to the bookshelves and took down his books (E.H. Gombrich, *The Story of Art*; John Richardson on Picasso; Norman Davies, *Europe – A History*; David Sylvester, *About Modern Art*; no novels, non-fiction only; Fred didn't believe in fiction) I was sitting still and calm, watching him.

Inscrutable, I thought, be inscrutable. Who was it who was inscrutable? Was it Buddha? Was it the Sphinx?

Fred said, 'I'll get the rest of my stuff later.'

I wondered what he meant. He hardly kept any things here. Was he going to come and go through the record collection to check that I hadn't got his copy of *Abbey Road* by mistake?

I nodded. I couldn't speak. I had a horrible conviction that if I opened my mouth I would vomit all over the floor.

He turned to go. He stopped. He looked back at me. Not right at me, actually – he looked around me, at my elbow, my left ear, at the wall just behind my head. He frowned, as if something had just occurred to him.

'I'm sorry,' he said.

And then he walked to the door, three steps across the wooden floor, three neat, quiet steps, and he opened the door with his left hand, walked through it, and closed it with a small double thud, as if to make sure it was absolutely shut.

It took a minute. I had a feeling of being pinned to a hard surface. Actually, I'm not sure that's true. It wasn't a feeling so much: for a moment, I wasn't feeling anything. It was as if all capacity for sensation had been wiped from me with a sponge. Then a really bizarre thing happened. My head snapped back on my shoulders as if something, some blast of air, had hit it, and I felt a shock as intense as when you see a car smash with the bodies still in it.

I took in a hard breath, a sharp intake of air, and I made

a noise, a horrible alien noise, like a groan. Then I cried. One minute my face was dry and my chest was still, and the next there was water all over my cheeks, dripping down on to my shirt, and I was sobbing like a child. I felt crazed and panic-stricken, as if I was out of control, as if I had started something I could never stop.

But I don't know why I'm bothering to tell you all this, because you probably know it already. Because it's probably happened to you.

2 ∫

At the beginning, the first night, it was mindless pain and shock. The week after, it settled into a nothing, a limbo, a blank space.

I didn't cry again. Perhaps it had frightened me too much. It was so primal and violent. I'd never cried like that before, except when my mother left.

I sat at home, because I didn't know what to do. I found myself baffled and without recourse to ideas.

I couldn't go in to work because I worked with Fred, and obviously we couldn't go on like that any more.

I called Michael, who worked at the gallery, at home, because I didn't want Fred picking up the telephone, and said that I wouldn't be coming back in. 'Fred probably knows already,' I said. 'What else would he expect? But I thought I should let you know. Just so you know,' I said. 'I thought I should let you know.'

Michael was embarrassed. There was sympathy coming through his voice, but I could tell there were people in the room. 'He told me already,' he said.

I felt as if everything I knew and believed in was being washed away from me, like water spiralling down a plughole. What did he mean, 'He told me already'?

'There will be a cheque,' Michael said. 'Severance pay,

that kind of thing. There will be money.' As if that made everything better.

Someone slammed a door in the background. I could hear voices coming down the line, garrulous evening voices, out there in the city, where people were having a good time.

'I'm sorry,' he said.

'Yeah,' I said. 'That's what they all say.'

I stayed at home with the blinds down, afraid of the light. I took a lot of baths. Then my friend Paco came home from Paris, where he had been for the last year, and the first thing he did when he got back was come round. He didn't trust the telephone.

I opened the door.

'Hey,' said Paco.

He was dressed in black trousers and a creased blue shirt; his hair was longer than when I had seen him last, and he had a little bit of a tan, as if he'd taken a weekend somewhere hot, and he was wearing green sunglasses and two days of beard. He was balancing a long canvas bag on his back, like the ones sailors used to bring home on shore leave in the forties.

I realised that I was shocked that it wasn't Fred, back to say it was all a terrible mistake, that he was the one I had been expecting. I stood and stared at Paco, taking in the minute details of his appearance, as if to give myself time to recognise that it wasn't the scene I had played so fast in my head. His trousers had a tear in the left leg, and there were thin lines of tiredness around his mouth.

'What happened to you?' he said. 'You look like a train wreck.'

He kissed me on both cheeks and put his arm round my shoulders and gave me a hug and then he walked in and put down his long canvas bag and looked around.

'Can I stay for a couple of nights?' he said.

'Yes,' I said.

'So,' he said.

He went to the fridge, took out two beers, gave me one, kept the other for himself, sat down in one of the two sofas, waited till I had sat in the other, smiled at me, showing his gold tooth, drank at his beer, put it down, pulled out a pack of cigarettes, a foreign brand I didn't recognise, lit one up, sucked at it a bit, settled back in his seat, and looked right at me.

'So,' he said. 'Do you want to tell me?'

'Fred broke up with me,' I said.

My voice came out flat and dull, as if there wasn't any life left in it. The words sounded unknown and strange, as if I should be using them about someone else.

Paco raised up his eyebrows and grimaced with his mouth and let out a sigh.

'Oh, Iris,' he said. 'That's not fair.'

'Ha,' I said. 'I don't know what it is. It's horrible. It's strange, mostly.'

'Yes,' said Paco.

He ran his hand through his hair. He had long fingers with fine pink nails. His nails were always very clean and well-kempt, which was surprising, because he never looked groomed in any other part of him. He wore his clothes anyhow, often barely ironed, and his hair was sometimes needing washing, and he usually could do with a shave. But he had beautiful delicate clean hands, like a pianist. I remembered that, and suddenly I was overwhelmed with gladness to see him.

'Oh, Paco,' I said, 'I don't know. He just came in one night and said it was over.'

'Just like that?' said Paco. 'After nine years?'

'Nine years,' I said. 'And now I'm left with an empty space. I spent the last seven days not moving, not speaking. The only thing I could do was sit in the bath.'

'Like in *The Bell Jar*,' said Paco. He loved Sylvia Plath; he knew her poems by heart. 'There might be things,' he said, 'which aren't cured by a hot bath but I don't know what they are. Something like that.'

I stared at him mutely, as if he were speaking Russian.

'I was in love once,' he said.

I looked at him again, this time in surprise. He always had girls floating around him, but I'd never thought they got that close.

'I was,' he said, seeing my look. 'It was a long time ago. It was a girl I met in Mexico City. She never looked at me. It was like I didn't exist, as if I had imagined myself. She was a rich girl and I was a poor boy, so maybe she was bred not to see me. That made me cry.'

'Oh, Paco,' I said, 'I'm glad you're back.'

We sat up very late. We drank some more beer and then a bottle of fierce brandy Paco had bought at Charles de Gaulle. We listened to *Come Fly With Me* by Frank Sinatra, one of the albums he recorded for Capitol Records in 1953 with Billy May conducting his orchestra and arranging the songs the way he liked them. Billy May was born in Pittsburgh and played the trumpet; he moved to Los Angeles in the middle forties and worked with Glenn Miller and Alvino Rey; then he went on the road with his band, and when he came home, Capitol got him and put him in a studio with Frank and they took three recording sessions to make the album and, oh it's a beauty. There's 'Come Fly With Me' by Sammy Cohn and Jimmy Van Heusen, and 'Autumn In New York' by Vernon Duke, and 'Isle Of Capri' by Will Grosz and Jimmy Kennedy. They are the kind of songs that old people mean when they talk about them not writing songs like that any more.

It was Paco who first introduced me to Sinatra, when I was sixteen. We had run into each other in a coffee

bar in Soho one sultry weekend. I was looking at the
juke-box, searching for Duran Duran and Adam and the
Ants, because it was the age of the new romantics, but
there was only puzzling stuff by people like Tony Bennett
and Bobby Darin and I was looking about, unsure what to
choose, and Paco came up beside me and said, 'I would try
5A,' and I thought What the hell, let's see where the road
takes me, so I pressed 5A and it was Sinatra singing Johnny
Mercer's 'One For My Baby'.

It starts out with a distant plaintive piano, like you're
in a bar in the middle of nowhere and some tired player
who's maybe had one too many bourbons and one too
many Lucky Strikes is letting his hands slide over the
keys because he's got nothing better to do. Then the voice
comes in, and it's low and resigned and late-night blues, it's
every lonely drinker you ever saw in every black-and-white
film, where the dame let some hoofer down and he's all by
himself with only a silent barman for company.

And then these swoony strings come in, so subtle you
hardly notice them, and the piano is still going, and Frank
starts singing louder, so you know he really means it, but
there's nothing this man can do about the empty night, and
even though there's something defiant in him, you know he's
beat; and when you think you're left with that voice and the
old piano, the saddest sax blows in, out of nowhere, a lonely
gusty old saxophone, and the strings fire up and die away, and
it's just Frank and the piano again, and you can see him, sitting
in the dark empty bar, waiting for that woman who isn't
coming back, and it's one for my baby, and one for the road.

I'd never heard music like that before. I hadn't been raised
with it: my mother listened to Joan Baez and Joni Mitchell
and Bob Dylan, because that was her era and her politics,
and once I was old enough I listened to Radio Luxembourg,
late at night under the covers, and they didn't play anything
like Frank. They played young music, not this oldster's stuff.

I mean, Sinatra was just some lounge singer, a Vegas guy, like Sammy Davis Jr and Dino Martin and all those other old soaks, that was all I knew. I knew about New York New York and I did it my way, because didn't everybody?, but that was as far as it went.

And then Paco came along and guided me to that song on the juke-box and I felt something shift in my stomach, a sort of recognition, like when you see the sea for the first time after a long journey.

So that was how we became friends, Paco and me. And whenever we're together now, we always listen to Sinatra, because that's one of the shorthands that keep us together; we don't have to say anything, but we remember that first time and all the times in between, when it's just been us and Frank, and all the other stuff doesn't matter so much.

I woke late the next morning. The light was far into the room and I felt disorientated and strange, as if someone had laid me out the wrong way. For a moment, I thought there were people in the flat, but then I realised it was the radio. I sat up in bed and looked out through the open door into the sitting room. Paco's stuff was spread about the sofa; the cushions were dented where he had slept the night.

He was up at the end of the room, where the kitchen counter ran along the far wall. There wasn't a kitchen, as such: there was a wall of shelves for pots and pans, and a sink and a gas cooker and a counter that pulled down so you could work at it. Paco was standing there, with brown paper packages laid out in front of him and a knife in his hand, his sleeves rolled up above the elbow to show his strong compact forearms. I sat on the edge of my bed and watched him. I thought that if you didn't know, if you walked in now, you would think we were the couple who had been together for nine years, you would think this was domesticity and contentment. You would think there were roses coming up all over and cherries without any stones.

Paco looked up and saw me watching him.

'Hey,' he said. 'You slept.'

'Yes,' I said. 'I did.'

'It's lunch,' he said. He picked up a package from the counter and waved it at me. 'I got a sea bream,' he said. '*Dorade royale*, you don't get those every day. So I'm going to cook it, Portuguese style.'

Paco always said everything he cooked was Portuguese style, which was strange, because he wasn't Portuguese and he had never been there. He was a mongrel dog for sure, a hybrid cross: his grandparents were Mexican, Irish, Jamaican and Spanish. But he always cooked Portuguese. All it meant really was that everything got baked in the oven and he used a lot of olive oil and potatoes.

I didn't feel much like fish, but I supposed I should eat. I took a shower and got dressed and went out and sat on a stool by Paco and watched him slicing up potatoes too fast.

'You put the potatoes like this,' he said, laying them out in rows in a flat pan. 'And then you put onion on top, and then you sprinkle over the secret green sauce,' he said, showing me. He had any number of secret green sauces; I couldn't always tell the difference between them. 'And then,' he said, taking out the fish, which was fat and silver with a black sign like the mark of Cain just behind its head, 'you put the fish in, and you pour olive oil over and some sea salt, and then you bake it.'

So it all went into the oven and we drank a cup of coffee and waited for it to cook.

'Stella called,' said Paco. 'She says she can't take New York any more. She's coming home too.'

'That's good,' I said. 'It's not the same without Stella.'

Stella Parker was our other friend, from the old days.

She's famous now, people know her name, but back then, when we first knew her, she was just Stella, and no one knew quite what to make of her.

I met her when I first moved to Soho, when I was seventeen. My mother left England when I was fifteen, and for two years I lived with my aunt Ursula and my cousin Pansy in a small room in their house on Primrose Hill. I never felt comfortable in north London. I didn't want space and charm and gardens and rambling Edwardian terraces: I wanted asphalt and neon and hard pavements and hookers and pimps and dealers and junkies and rock and roll.

I hated Primrose Hill because of its bogus village-green thing: it sat on top of its hill, looking down on everyone else, so superior about its chi-chi restaurants with their white lace curtains and their exorbitant prices, and its cramped boutiques that sold olive oil from Umbria and five different kinds of coffee bean, and its old-style bookshops where you could buy anything except a book you actually wanted to read. I was fifteen, what do you expect? Primrose Hill is death to a teenager: it is middle-aged and middle class and if you were dropped there by an alien you would think that all anyone cared about in the world was stripped pine and climbing roses.

I sat on the hill and dreamt of the city. I spent my life on the Underground, on the Jubilee Line from Finchley Road, past St John's Wood, Swiss Cottage (Why? Why? What was that grotesque cottage all about, stuck in the middle of the road like that?) to Bond Street. Sometimes I got out there and walked, past the shops with their wide glittering windows and the auction houses and art-dealers with their small discreet doors, all the way to Piccadilly, where I took a left past the grand arch of the Royal Academy and crossed the Circus and walked up Shaftesbury Avenue, where the traffic was always jammed up, whatever the time of day, streams of double-decker buses, nose to tail, going nowhere fast.

Sometimes, I changed at Bond Street on to the Central Line, the lovely red line that went through the heart of the town like an arrow, all the way from Ealing Broadway to Theydon Bois, in a soaring scarlet arc. (Someone told me once who designed the Underground map. I don't remember his name, but he was a man of unsung genius: to take a confused tangle of subterranean tunnels and make it into a beautiful diagram of bisecting coloured streams, a work of art in its own right, and recognisable as a brand name, something that says London Town the minute you see it, whether you are from Minnesota or South-East Asia.) On impatient days, I took the Central Line two stops along to Tottenham Court Road, and then it was only a block walk and I was in Soho, which was the heartbeat of the city as far as I saw it.

I liked Chinatown, with its secret doorways and windows of wind-dried duck, the flayed carcasses hanging red and helpless against steamed-up glass for anyone to see; I liked the grocery stores and supermarkets with bright unforgiving lights and signs all in Chinese, so if you did ever buy anything there you had no clue what it was until you got it home and tried to figure it out by touching it and tasting it and sometimes even then you still didn't know. I liked the close-faced Chinese women, always talking and looking straight ahead; they never let their eyes wander for a moment. I liked that it was so foreign, it smelt different, not English, it smelt of fish and ammonia and something unidentifiable, as if you had stepped into a back-street in Peking just for a moment.

I liked Mayfair, in a different way: there was something alluring about those mysterious backwaters the other side of Regent Street. I liked it because it was closed and still and secret, and there were places you could walk that made you imagine what it was like in the eighteenth century, when women drove around sitting on the floors of their carriages because the feathers on their heads were three feet high.

But really, the only place for me then, in my green days, the place I truly loved with every beat of my yearning metropolitan heart, was Soho. I loved it because it was dirty and illicit and cramped and urban. There were no trees in Soho, apart from a token effort in Soho Square, where people sat in their lunch-break and read the newspaper. There were illegal drinking dives and blatant strip-clubs, dodgy after-hours venues and beckoning peep-shows. In Soho, all the outcasts could go and be on the inside, right at the centre of things; the drunks and the poets and the transvestites and the queer boys and the prostitutes and the dancing girls and the people who only came out at night. When I was a baby my mother had done one practical thing for me. She had started an investment fund. It wasn't much, but even when she was flat broke and busted she somehow managed to pay in the monthly fee, and when I was seventeen she wrote to me from Tasmania, which is where she had fetched up, and said that if I went along to the bank, they would give me my money.

It seemed like the world to me then. It was the world because it was freedom.

So I said goodbye to my aunt Ursula, and I paid the deposit on a room to rent in a small street just off the main drag. It was a sagging Georgian house in black brick, and there was a room and a bath on each floor, and the landlord had fixed the dry rot and rented them out for not too much money, because back then, before the council cleaned it up, no one wanted to live there except the lowlifes. There was too much sleaze on the streets for the respectable element, who preferred the lily-white streets of Kensington, where you could catch a cab without being molested and you were never far away from a good department store.

I got the top floor. On the floor below there was an old man who coughed all night and drank a bottle of whisky a day: his name was Frank Mitchell and he was a playwright. He had white hair and a yellow face and he looked about eighty, although the landlord said he was not a day over sixty-six and was very handsome and full of sex appeal in the fifties and had girls running about after him like headless chickens.

Stella lived on the ground floor.

I met her the day I moved in: she was the first person I saw. I opened up the front door with my brand-new key and found her sitting on the stairs.

'Are you the new one?' she said. 'I've been waiting for you. The landlord said you were coming at eleven.'

She looked at her watch, as if I had kept her waiting on purpose. It was eleven thirty-four.

'Hello,' I said. 'I'm Iris.'

I had a thought that she was going to welcome me to the building, offer me a cup of sugar or a loan of some tea-bags. I smiled at her, but she didn't smile back. She stood up and she looked me all the way up and down and then she walked round me.

'Hmm,' she said. 'My name is Stella. I live on the ground floor. I live in number one.'

I felt as if I was being put to some kind of test and I wasn't sure if I had passed. Stella looked at me with flat brown eyes. She had dyed red hair cut very short to her head and thin white skin stretched tight over her bones. I never saw anyone with such white skin before. It was absolutely smooth and pale without any mark on it at all, except under the eyes, where it was shadowed violet in two small smudges. She had a clear direct look, and although she was very tall, maybe six foot, I guessed, from looking at her, she carried herself straight, without the apologetic stoop that tall girls often held. She was my age, maybe a year older. I was acutely conscious of the fact that she had got here first.

'Watch out for Frank,' she said. 'He lives upstairs and he'll pinch you if you let him.'

And then she walked along the corridor to her door and went inside without saying anything else. I stood for a moment in the small hall, astonished. But I was thrilled too. This was why I had come to the heart of the city; this was the whole point. You didn't get girls like that in Primrose Hill.

'I miss Stella,' I said to Paco now. 'I speak to her on the telephone and she sends postcards but it's not the same.'

'Does she know about all this?' he said. He made a gesture round the flat, as if I had been redecorating or moving furniture.

'About me and Fred?' I said.

'Yes, you and Fred,' said Paco. 'What else is there?'

'No,' I said. 'I didn't tell her. I didn't tell anyone. I didn't know what to say.'

'You just tell her,' he said. 'What are you going to do? She's your best friend.'

'I know,' I said. I felt dumb and inexplicable, now he said it like that. 'It's just, it's . . . I don't want to talk about it because it's all been said before. I was with someone, and he left, and it happens all the time. You love the wrong person or you love them the wrong way or the time runs out because some things don't last for ever. And it's been written about in a million books and films and poems and pop songs and there's nothing original about me.'

'Iris,' said Paco, looking at me very straight, 'you're not a picture on the wall. You don't have to be original. No one is original. Everyone makes mistakes and gets the blues and has their heart broken. It's not boring, it's what happens.'

'But I feel boring,' I said, and I could hear the words

come out in an explosive wail, the way that children shout illogical slogans in the face of their rational parents. I was scared of flying, had been since I could remember. I knew that I had more chance of being run over by a bus, I knew that engines didn't tumble off aeroplanes, I knew that they didn't drop out of the sky like stones. But every time I got on a plane, I was convinced in my deepest heart that this lumbering metal tube wouldn't make it; it wasn't meant to be half a mile up in the air with three hundred fat people in it; it would surely plunge to earth, punished for trying to defy gravity. I knew this, right in my bones, so I spent every flight tensed for instant death, and I was always surprised when I found myself getting off at the other end, euphoric with another death cheated.

I felt the same now, about Fred. I knew that what Paco said was true. But all the same, I felt what I felt.

'This feels,' I said, 'like life is imitating a shoddy television soap. All he has to do is tell me that there is another woman and the whole tawdry scene will be complete. I feel like something that should be on the TV just before the news.'

Paco laughed. 'I don't know,' he said. 'I don't know what I'm going to do with you.'

He stubbed out his cigarette and went and looked in the oven. A smell came out of some herb I couldn't identify, one of the secrets of his green sauce. It smelt hot and cooked and foreign.

He took the dish out and looked at it with pride.

'I can cook for you at least,' he said. 'It's a start.'

3

The next night Paco suggested we go out for a drink, a walk, something to eat. He said I should get out of the house. He said that he hadn't seen a lick of the city since he got back, except for the drive in from the airport. He said it was time we got ourselves a breath of open air.

I didn't want to. I wanted to sit and stare at the wall. I thought that if I sat still for long enough it would pass; I would wake up one morning and find that I didn't care, that these feelings of loss and abandonment and dislocation would have dissipated, dissolved, leaving me clean and clear and empty and ready to start again.

I said I couldn't go out. Anyone else might have gone and left me there, sitting in the corner with my face to the wall, but not Paco. The way Paco saw it, once he was there, he was there for the long haul. There had been times when I wondered why I had never been in love with him, the way you wonder with your male friends; the love is so easy and so durable, you don't know why you can't translate it into something sexual and then everyone gets to live happily ever after. But life doesn't work like that, although I couldn't tell you why.

We sat and talked instead, just like we had been doing since Paco arrived. We didn't talk about Fred. We talked about old times; we talked about the past. There's something necessary and reassuring about the past when the present has just undergone some kind of seismic upheaval that you don't understand very well.

When it was time to eat, Paco cooked macaroni cheese because he said I needed comfort food.

'I can comfort you,' he said. 'It won't make it much easier to bear, but it's something. I can cook you good food and watch you eat it.'

What he didn't say, but what I knew he meant, was that was what mothers did. That's what is supposed to happen, isn't it, between daughters and their mothers? The heartaches come, the let-downs, the disappointments, the casual daily betrayals, and you call Mother, because that's what she's there for. And she comes right round, and cooks you something she used to make when you were a child and you fell off your bicycle or your hamster got sick and died, and you know that everything is all right because your mum is there, cooking for you.

Except I never had a mother like that. My mother wasn't a bad mother, I couldn't say that about her. It was just that she never thought of herself as a Mother. She was a woman who happened to have a baby. She had me by mistake, because it was the sixties, and even though it was the time of the pill and sexual liberation and free love, people hadn't really got the hang of it yet, and accidents kept happening. She was seeing three men at the time, and she didn't plan on having a child with any of them. She didn't know which one was my father, and she didn't bother to find out. It was the kind of thing that meant nothing to her, knowing where you were from. She could count out one of the three, because he came from Grenada and I was white as snow (or rather wild pink and howling) when I arrived, a week early, catching her by surprise.

All I knew about Grenada was that it was known as the

Spice Island, and I always thought of that island with its fragrant winds and wondered if the man who could so easily have been my father had gone back there and was looking out over the blue Caribbean sea and smelling the scent of salt and cloves in the air.

The other two possible fathers were a pianist from Folkestone called Louis Winter and a loafer called Peter, my mother didn't know his last name. She never talked about them as I was growing up; after she had me they drifted away, and for a while there were no men, it was just the two of us. We lived together for the first twelve years of my life in a high room with a pitched roof and three square windows looking out over a garden in Kensington. Kensington wasn't a swell area then, this was long before million-dollar houses and American oil tycoons and Far Eastern business supremos; Kensington was respectable and dowdy and, most important of all, cheap.

We had the top-floor flat in a white four-storey house, and the floorboards were bare and smelt of turpentine and pine needles and age, and you could see the tops of the trees and the sky from the windows, which were squat and sturdy and looked out to the west, so we got the sun in the afternoons. One of the strongest memories of my childhood is lying on the wood floor in the long summer evenings, in a shaft of dusty sunlight that came in, thick and yellow, through the high windows. I remember the feeling of heat and stillness, I remember the aromatic smell of the wooden floor as it was warmed by the sun, I remember watching the dust dancing in shafts of light.

I always wondered how anyone could live low down, near the street. I thought the only way to live was near the sky. I've always lived on the top floor, ever since.

Men didn't come to that flat. My mother made jokes to her sister that the five flights of stairs were the best contraceptive you could ask for. One time, when she said this, my aunt Ursula, thinking I was out of the room, said in a harsh unguarded voice, 'Well, it's a bit late for that, isn't it?' I didn't realise then that she was talking about me, but I worked it out later, and that was the first idea I had that I wasn't wanted, that I was in the way, an encumbrance, that I shouldn't have happened.

It's a strange thing to know that you weren't meant to exist, that you were unwanted, something that came into being through the merest shimmy of chance. Sometimes it makes me feel as if I don't really exist at all.

When I was fourteen, I asked my mother about the men who might be my father. She was distracted and irritable: she seemed to resent being asked to dredge through distant memories. But I was insistent, and in the end, this is what she told me.

Louis, the pianist, used to play lunchtime concerts in the Wigmore Hall. He had a gentle face and wore his hair long, which made the girls swoon. People went to his concerts like they were rock gigs, to hear him play Scriabin and Rachmaninov. The respectable patrons of the Wigmore Hall, the middle-aged office workers, the liberal bourgeoisie and the elderly Eastern European refugees, were startled to see their imperturbable vaulted hall turned into an upmarket version of the Cavern Club.

He had a violent burst of celebrity: he recorded for the BBC, was interviewed for *Bazaar*, had his photograph taken by Stephen Shift, who was the most keenly desired of the new breed of photographers. Everyone wanted Stephen Shift because instead of chasing after dolly-birds or hanging around with crowned heads and pop stars he was a recluse. He lived alone in a large brick house on the river at Chiswick, which he had bought from an impoverished marquis, and people who had been there said there was no furniture or paintings or decorations of any kind, just wide perfectly proportioned eighteenth-century rooms painted in pale Wedgwood colours, running one into another, in an extravagant parade of space.

Louis Winter, the man who might be my father, drove down to the river one bright short winter day, and sat in an empty Regency room and had his photograph taken.

When my mother told me this, I felt violently excited. There was evidence, there was a record: I could see, at least, what he looked like.

'Can I see them?' I said. 'Can I see the photographs? Why have you never shown them to me?'

'I never kept any,' my mother said, as if the thought wouldn't have occurred to her. 'There was only one, in any case,' she said. 'It was quite famous. It was in *Vogue*.'

'I could go and look it up,' I said, and my voice was unsteady, with the weight of this unaccustomed emotion. 'I could see if he looks like me.'

'It won't do you any good,' said my mother.

'Why not?' I said. 'Why not? Why won't it? Why?'

My mother sighed and shook her head.

'Iris,' she said, 'it was a photograph of his hands. That was all. That was all Shift took. He wasn't interested in the face. He just wanted the hands.'

I managed to find a copy of the magazine. There is a cramped corner store near Raymond's Revue Bar that sells vintage magazines and old fashion pictures, and I asked them if they could find me a copy of *Vogue* for the spring of 1966, and they made a note of it and took my number.

They didn't call for several weeks, and in the end I gave up hope; I thought it was a sign, that I wasn't supposed to see the hands of the man who might be my father. I felt demoralised and deflated, and then, after three months, the telephone went, and a bored voice asked if I had ordered a back copy of *Vogue*, because one had arrived with my name on it.

I took a taxi all the way, and it cost me five pounds, which is a lot of money when you are fourteen, and it was another fiver for the magazine, which cleaned me out completely so that I had to walk all the way home, because I didn't even have the bus fare. We were living on the fourth floor of a mansion block behind the Grand Union Canal. It was a long walk from Brewer Street, across Oxford Street, through Manchester Square and all the way up the grey unremitting length of the Edgware Road, then left into Clifton Road and right into the red-brick heart of Maida Vale.

They had given me the magazine in a brown paper bag, the way that pornographers hand over copies of their triple-X-rated publications, the ones where people are doing it with animals or amputees. (I knew about this: I had already spent too many Saturday afternoons in Soho.) For some reason I wouldn't look at it until I got home, although I was dying with impatience to see the picture. But I wouldn't allow myself, not even a quick snatched look, so I walked and walked, over the hard unforgiving pavements, past the second-hand furniture marts and neon amusement arcades and Persian carpet stores that line the Edgware Road, carrying the package so tight that my hands grew hot and slippery against the brown paper.

When I got home the flat was light and silent. The road where we lived was a backwater, on the way to nowhere, so there was no traffic in the daytime. It felt as if someone had turned the city off.

I sat down and pulled off the brown paper, checked the date on the front cover, which had a photograph of a girl with big black eyes and teardrops balancing on the end of improbably long eyelashes.

I opened the magazine. It smelt musty, as if it had been stored somewhere damp, and the pages were thicker and duller than they are now, not shiny and glossy and inviting but deadpan and flat.

I missed it the first time – I was leafing through too fast, past pages of dense black and white print and dark fashion spreads of curiously ordinary girls in shift dresses and high boots and tight belted raincoats. For a sinking moment I thought my mother had made a mistake. I went back, past the book section and the restaurant reviews ('I find the waiters at the Boulestin very frightening indeed'), past profiles of Tom Wolfe and Margaret Forster, advertisements for PLJ and Pace Setter hairspray and the Tao clinic for facial hair, until I found it.

It was one entire page. It was a grainy black-and-white picture, the hands very big, with elongated fingers, stretched out improbably by the angle of the camera. The light and focus were so acute that you could see every vein and whorl and mark on them. They were totally unrecognisable.

I looked at my own hands and could see no relation or frame of reference, because my hands weren't blown up in black and white in some old fashion bible from the sixties. My hands were small and pale and insignificant compared to these iconic objects, these disassociated things. I thought furiously that it was typical of Stephen Shift with his reclusive habits and his empty house to have taken a photograph like this, that didn't tell you anything, that didn't connect anything with anything.

On the page opposite there was a short paragraph about Louis Winter, who had transformed lunchtimes in W1 with his stellar playing, who had screaming teeny-boppers clutching their white patent handbags mixing with music teachers and civil servants on their lunch-break. Louis Winter, it said, was clearly destined for greatness. Louis Winter, with his long hair and his velvet jackets, was emblematic of the new breed of British youth: talented, iconoclastic, dynamic, beating the world for fun.

Well, they were wrong about that. My mother told me that a couple of years after the photograph was taken, bitter and disappointed that the offers had never come for the Proms or the Festival Hall, that finally the deals with Deutsche Grammophon and EMI had come to nothing, Louis Winter had emigrated to Canada, and the last she knew he had settled into a new life in Toronto.

I asked about the other one, the man with no second name, and my mother said that she didn't know anything about him at all, because they never had that kind of relationship. She said she had never seen him since. She said that he could be dead by now, for all she knew.

When my mother was telling me all this, about these men, these possible dads, I felt sad and unreal, but there were moments when I felt furious, as if she had purposely deprived me of something that other people have, as if I had some right to expect more from her than vague memories and no excuses.

'Why,' I said, 'didn't you find out which of them it was? Why didn't you go for a test? Why didn't you keep in touch with them, in case this time ever came, when I would start to ask questions? Why didn't you?'

She shrugged her shoulders. My sudden fury rolled off her like summer rain. She didn't see that my happiness or my life were much to do with her. She believed that you made your own luck, and that to go around blaming other people for your life was futile and short-sighted.

'Do you want to talk about it now?' said Paco.

For a moment, I thought he meant did I want to talk about my mother, because that was what I had been thinking about. It was curious. I didn't think about my mother very often, not now. She was part of my past life, another life, one that sometimes didn't seem to have anything at all to do with the one I lived now.

When we were teenagers together, running round Soho

and scoring speed off dodgy men in dark basement clubs, Paco and I went through one hot summer when we talked fiercely about nothing except our mothers, or so it seemed to me afterwards, looking back. We were seventeen, and I had just moved into the flat above Stella, and Paco and I were becoming proper friends. Before then, we used to see each other mostly by chance. We hung around in the same area, went to the same places, so we used to run into each other and go for a coffee and a smoke, but we didn't become genuine friends until I moved into Soho for real. It was as if, up to then, I had just been a visitor, a tourist, because I always had to go home to the hill.

On the first day I moved in, Paco came and banged on the door and said he was going for a sandwich and did I want to come.

'How did you know I was here?' I said, pleased with surprise.

It felt astonishing that he should know but also completely fitting and right. This was what happened when you were in the real city, in the deep dirty beating heart of it.

'Heard,' said Paco. He gave me a cryptic look, as if he was just sat there in the middle of the grapevine, as if every piece of information had to go through him first before it could arrive anywhere.

'Yeah, right,' I said.

He laughed.

'Frank Mitchell was talking about it,' he said. 'He drinks every afternoon in the Colony Room, and I was in there yesterday, and he said there was some chicken moving into his building, some peachy young thing from north London. He was pleased about it. He had to give up trying to pinch Stella years ago, he knows she would give him GBH if he tried it on with her.'

'And I wouldn't?' I said.

Paco put his head on one side and looked at me from under his eyebrows.

'I don't know,' he said. 'Would you? Maybe you would. Me, I don't think so. I think you'd ask him nicely. I think you'd ask him to desist.'

I gave him a real fuck you look.

'You think I'm a nice girl?' I said. 'You think I mind my Ps and Qs?'

'Maybe,' said Paco. 'I'd say you were contained, anyway. Stella isn't. Everything hangs right out in the open with her.'

I wasn't sure if I was pleased or not. I liked the idea of being contained; I never agreed with that line about no man being an island. I thought most of us were islands, to tell the truth, cut off from the mainland at high tide. I liked to think that I was complete, a drawn circle. So I smiled at Paco, and let the part about the nice girl go.

Maybe he had a point. I was polite anyway, I don't know why, it wasn't something my mother or my aunt had ever taught me. They didn't give a shit about manners, but I did, had done since I was a child. It was always me in shops or on the bus who would say please or thank you, while my mother waited impatiently to be gone.

'Do you?' said Paco. 'We don't have to. We can talk about something else. We can talk about anything you want.'

I realised he meant Fred.

'I don't know,' I said. 'I'm not sure what to say. It feels unreal, as if it's happening to someone else. I think I took it for granted that Fred and I were together, the way you take it for granted that you're a woman or you have dark hair, that it's not so much something you're doing but something you are.'

'Yes,' said Paco. 'I think I thought of you like that too.'

'I don't feel we were ever so joined at the hip as to be

indissoluble,' I said, 'but there is a sense of rupture, as if the order of things has changed in some fundamental way, and I can't adjust to it.'

'It's a shock,' said Paco, nodding his head. 'Nine years to nothing at all.'

'This morning,' I said, 'I suddenly wondered if I really did love him. I got so used to the idea that I loved him, because why was I with him if I didn't love him? Of course I loved him, we laughed and talked and we worked together and we had good sex. That's love, isn't it?'

'I don't know,' said Paco. 'I don't know what it is.'

I drank some of the wine he had given me and lit a cigarette. I had given up smoking five years ago, but I didn't care; I didn't feel my lungs mattered, just now. I didn't feel anything mattered. I felt as if I had been cast adrift from my moorings and I was floating out to sea and I didn't care as the horizon receded behind me.

The smoke tasted rank and bitter and reassuring.

'There was the girl in Mexico City,' I said.

'Yes,' he said, 'but it never happened. It was just a feeling, that's all. I don't know what it's like in real life.'

'I should know, shouldn't I?' I said. 'I should be able to tell you, because I was with someone for nine years. Nine years, Paco, do you know how long that is? And we saw each other every day, and we went on trips together, and I've seen him naked and I've seen him sick and I've seen him drooling in his sleep, and all at once I'm thinking, Did I really love him, was that what love was? Was that what love is?'

'Well, what did it feel like?' said Paco.

'I don't know,' I said. 'I should be able to tell you, but I just don't know.'

I sat back in my chair and looked round my place. It looked different to me, as if I'd been looking at it from the wrong end of a telescope, and now someone had handed me the glass the right way round and everything had come into a closer focus. It was so clean and light. There were two long skylights in the vaulted roof, and the blue evening light came streaming down from them. It was my place; it had been mine for the last ten years. It felt to me that this room was where my adult life had started, when I left the dirty streets of Soho for the muted grandeur of Bond Street. If you stand at Conduit Street facing south, Bond Street runs up a gentle incline and swerves to the left so you can't see the end of it. At Grafton Street, Asprey takes up half a block with its arched black windows full of useless silver baubles and there is a blue plaque on the wall of number fifteen that says, Sir Henry Irving, actor, lived here 1872–1899, and on the corner the bronze allies sit on their bench, Sir Winston and FDR, looking healthier than they ever did in life.

It is a street of banners, incongruous and gaudy coloured cloths advertising Chanel and Bulgari, Bentley fine jewels, Philip Antrobus and Graff, Clough jewellers and pawn-brokers. It's a street of suits and builders, I never knew a time when there wasn't construction of some kind, a street of hard hats and skips and rubble, alongside the expensive cars with smoked windows. It's a street of foreign languages: walk any block and you will hear Spanish, Italian, Dutch, American; you will hear languages you can't recognise; you will hear things that might be Armenian or Pashto, Tamil or Slovenian. It had been an atelier, originally, this room. The building had belonged to a couturier, a Frenchman called Monsieur André, who was all the rage before the war. He sewed elaborate dresses for society women who changed clothes three times a day; he survived the forties and cloth rationing, but then the sixties came along and turned everything on its head. The business limped along, running on residual loyalty and old half-dead women who still needed one cocktail frock a year, but by the end of the seventies the debts had piled up and the bank was no longer patient and forgiving.

It was the end of the old era, the company went into receivership, the last of the clothes were auctioned off in a humiliating garage sale, and Monsieur André walked along Waterloo Bridge one bright April morning, with his pockets stuffed full of stones, and jumped.

After they fished him out and identified him, they found out that he wasn't French at all. His name was Sidney Arthur Pleat, and he was born in Sandwich in a small terraced house set back from the sea, born in 1908, the year that Winston Churchill became president of the Board of Trade and Elgar composed his first symphony and Austria-Hungary annexed Bosnia. I thought of that sometimes: 1908. While Sidney Pleat was born into a dingy back-street in sleepy Sandwich, just across the Channel, Georges Braque was painting the landscapes in L'Estaque that were to launch Cubism and set Paris on its ears. Picasso had outraged sensibilities the year before with the *Demoiselles of Avignon*. He was living in a sordid studio in the Bateau Lavoir, with a beautiful and indolent mistress called Fernande (three subjects for conversation: hats, perfume and furs), a large friendly dog and a small tame monkey. Leo and Gertrude Stein had come to town and were buying every painting they could lay their hands on. That was the year that the famous banquet was thrown for Rousseau, where all the painters and poets and Bohemians gathered together and dined off piles of rice because the local grocery shops closed before Fernande got there and rice was all she had, and André Salmon ate a cake of soap and simulated delirium with foaming mouth and rolling eyes to shock a pair of starched Americans.

While creative turmoil ran through Paris like a virus, in a grey back-street in Sandwich, Sidney Pleat was born. And when he was old enough, Sidney developed a French accent and a taste for expensive frocks and dowager duchesses and gave himself a new name.

Anyway, the end of the story is that after he died, the

building was bought by a twenty-one-year-old boy called Jem Starling. Jem talked fast and plausibly, and for some reason had always wanted to own a building. He wanted to be able to drive down a London street and look up at a stone front and say, That's my building. He liked Bond Street because it was where his mother had brought him to shop for luggage when he was a small boy. It was as random as that.

So he silvered the bank into giving him a loan, and he bought the building and leased out the ground floor to a shop selling Swiss watches, fountain pens and other small foreign luxuries; the two middle floors went to a travel company selling cruises to the Far East, which went spectacularly bust in suspicious circumstances and had disgruntled cruisers rattling at the doors to get their money back for phantom holidays. On the top floor, where the walls sloped in and the thin building narrowed, and Monsieur André had his atelier, Jem put in some rudimentary plumbing and a false wall to make a bedroom, and it was there that he lived.

In the late eighties, he bought another building and then another, and land besides, plots out beyond the docks in the East End, some marshy acres on the Suffolk border; he had grown rich from the boom, so he bought himself a large flat-fronted house in the suburbs, and he decided to let the top floor of his original Bond Street building. But the people who lived in Mayfair were rich people, and rich people expected a minimum of two bedrooms and marble bathrooms and kitchens gleaming with modern appliances; no Mayfair person worth their salt would be seen dead in an atelier room with two skylights for windows and a bedroom with room only for one bed and some hooks on the wall to hang clothes from.

It was Paco who heard about it, of course (it was Paco who told me all these stories, like I was a child at bedtime, because Paco knew everyone in a square-mile radius from Golden Square and their business and he'd always tell you, if you asked). The lease was running out on my Soho flat, and the rent was being hiked up and I couldn't afford it any more.

We went and had a drink with Jem, who was six foot five and had a face that seemed as if it was smiling all the time, and we drank pints of Guinness in a dark pub off Berkeley Square, and by the end of the evening it was agreed and arranged and we shook hands on it, and the next day there was a formal lawyer's letter through my letter box ('What's this?' said Stella, who always got to the post first. 'I thought about *steaming* it open.') and I signed on the dotted line, and the top-floor room was mine, subject to contract.

Paco and I didn't talk about love any more that night. We drank some more wine, and listened to *Only The Lonely*, another of those seminal albums that Sinatra made for Capitol Records, and then I was too tired to do anything any more, so I went to bed, even though it was only ten o'clock. It was barely dark. But I felt drained with sadness and bafflement, and there didn't seem to be anything else to do.

I didn't sleep much, in the end. It was hot and airless, and I lay pinned to the sheets with torpor and heat, my eyes dry and open, staring at the ceiling.

I had never had a serious relationship before Fred; I wished now I had. I wished I had had my heart smashed up before, so I could look back and say Oh yes, this is what happens now, I remember this. But I hadn't. I was twenty-one when I met him; I had barely made it out of the house, let alone round the block.

I didn't know anything. I didn't know what to do with the pain of separation, because it had never happened before.

I was happy with Fred, I thought; I was, I was. That was happiness, wasn't it? I liked being in a couple, a unit. I had never had a family; there was my mother and me, and then one day there was just me. There was a distant dream of a possible father; there was the vague presence of my aunt

Ursula before she met a man and went to live with him in Catalonia. (She still sent me a card at Christmas.) And then there was Fred, and I felt that I was part of something, that there were two of us, us against them. It felt good that there was someone who knew every small quirk and detail of my character, because I didn't bother hiding any of it from him, not after nine years. He wasn't the kind to judge or get shocked; that was part of his fight against his bourgeois upbringing. His parents were proper and decent. They didn't go to church on Sundays but they believed in the principle. They lived clean straightforward and sober lives. My upbringing had been anything goes; there was a secret part of me that hankered for the order that Fred had known when he was young.

Stella said boring, sometimes, when she was in that kind of mood. She and Fred never saw the point of each other and I didn't mind; I kept them in two separate parts of my life. Stella didn't understand about wanting something solid to put your feet on; she said push it all the way and so what if you tripped up and fell on your face. But I wanted security; there was a regularity to Fred, despite his profession. He was wild when it came to art, but steady as stone when it came to life, and I liked it that way. It was everything I had never known.

We didn't fight much; we never went to bed angry. We didn't seek to humiliate each other or put each other down. Sometimes, when I watched other couples, all the sound and fury, I thought it was because we lived apart. Sometimes I thought it was just the way we were.

I thought it was love, and I thought it would last for ever, and I was wrong.

The next day, Paco and I went to collect Stella from the airport.

Stella had gone to America two years before. She went

through a spasm of disgust with England; it was too small too petty too parochial for her. She said everything was happening elsewhere, away in the wide-open spaces of bigger countries, while English life pursed its lips and hid behind net curtains. So she cashed in her savings – she actually had a post-office account, with a blue savings book, and she had been salting away small lumps of cash since she was a teenager. By the time she came to draw it out, there was £10,879.21 waiting for her.

'Tips and typing money,' she said. 'Ten grand for getting my bottom pinched.' And she bought an airline ticket to New York City, and flew away.

That time, Paco and I took her to the airport on the red airbus from Hyde Park Corner.

'Don't come,' she had said. 'I'm shit at goodbyes.'

But we went anyway. I couldn't believe she was really going: her life seemed so central to mine. I followed her to the airport and waved her off, and for two years, as she wandered round the 50 states, from Seattle to Miami, Fla., she sent me letters and postcards, charting the rise of her fame.

She got published in the first year, with the novel that all the English publishers had rejected, and because she was young and tall and crazy-looking, with her thin white skin and angry scarlet hair and her flat brown eyes, and because she lit right up whenever the gleaming red light of a television camera was directed at her, she became famous, with a rushing overnight-sensation fame.

Then, because America had taken notice, the English scrambled to keep up. She got offered deals by the publishers that had rejected her first time round. Most people would have taken pleasure in telling them to take a long walk off the end of a short pier, but Stella wasn't like most people. Stella, really, wasn't like any people at all. She took the publisher which had spurned her most thoroughly, the one which had ignored her manuscript until she sent several letters reminding them about it; the publisher which suggested, in its rejection letter, that she might be best advised to think about another line of work. It was not just rejection, it was personal. It was offensive.

So they came crawling back, as surely they must, because a novel that sold 800,000 copies in America couldn't be ignored any more. And she was young, and she was female (same sex as the Future), and she was great-looking in a twisted kind of way, even if she did insist on dyeing her eyebrows black, like Groucho Marx. She was sexy, Stella; she looked as if she knew about sex. Why, the publishers said, as they went out to lunch in long yellow restaurants in Charlotte Street, did we miss her the first time round?

Her plane landed at 8.45 a.m. and she was first out. Stella never travelled with luggage; she hated standing about those chugging carousels, watching mesmerised with the other fish-eyed travellers. So even when she was coming back from two years in America, she still had one bag slung over her shoulder.

'You fucks,' she said loudly, when she saw Paco and I waiting for her. 'Trust you two.'

Two middle-aged women turned round, shocked and curious, then puzzled when they saw it was Stella. Had they seen her face somewhere before? Was she a television personality?

That was the sort of fame Stella had here. Within London, the chattering classes, the people who lived in Islington and Notting Hill and knew that brown was the new black, they knew about Stella. Outside that, people who read contemporary fiction, who believed in Tom Paulin, who listened to Radio Four, who looked at the arts pages, they would know. And then a few net surfers, because there was a site devoted to Stella on the web, set up by a boy in Washington State. So out of a population of 60 million, maybe a million at the outside. It's not a household name, not the kind of fame that stops you walking down the street or through the supermarket.

It's perfect fame. Not enough to escape the fickle nature of it, because those million will forget you fast as greyhounds if you produce something they don't want to read; they know what they want, and if you don't give it to them they are unflinching and unforgiving. Stella couldn't escape that, because no one can, but she had acknowledgement without constraint. She didn't have to think about what she could do next: there weren't fans camping outside her building. She had two pervs writing to her (Do you suck cock? Do you mud-wrestle?), one offer of marriage from a twitcher who lived in Weston-super-Mare, and a hate-mail campaign from a white supremacist in Tallahassee. Homosexuality is a DISEASE, the coloured races will rise up and OVERWHELM us, he wrote: Stella had a character in her first book who was black *and* gay *and* female, so that was all the bigots up in arms in one go. 'Lucky to only get one,' she said laconically.

She got written to by people asking for advice about advances and help with finding an agent ('I have written a novel about a smallpox epidemic in thirteenth-century Poland'). Occasionally she got stopped in the street. It happened more in America, where she was known in a different way: she wasn't just famous there because of what she had written but because she was a Briton abroad, and a girl, and crazy-looking, and she would say the first thing that came into her head, and they went nuts for that kind of thing on *Letterman*. They loved her because she thought the Queen of England was a transvestite and she believed that men should pay more taxes because they made up 93 per cent of the prison population and it cost more to keep one person in jail than to send them to

Eton College, choice of royalty and aristocracy and the aspirational rich.

She had been back to England for one fleeting visit since this fame-trip hit: to get published and do the tours, talk to the nice people at Radio Four, do a little mild daytime TV ('It's so far out, it's in,' she said, to three million bemused viewers), sign some books in a warehouse near Didcot power station, which were sent out all over the country ('Get your signed copies HERE'), give a reading at the ICA as part of a female-power season, attend a couple of free parties and get her picture taken by heavy-set bearded men with two-foot lenses ('Do all you paparazzi have tiny dicks?' she said, in a genuine spirit of enquiry).

So this was what happened to her in England; she got the puzzled do-I-know-you? looks more often than not, and sometimes she got the looks anyway, just because she was the way she was.

It was two years and she hadn't changed at all. She didn't look any older or any wiser; she didn't have lines of age on her face or that apologetic I-know-better look that people get when they give up the ghost of their twenties and admit that they are over thirty now and everything is different.

Stella had always been unashamedly and unambiguously herself, and she never apologised for that. I could see instantly, looking at her in the flat neon corridor of the airport arrivals hall, that was still there, and I was glad for it. You never knew what time away could do to a person. They could come back reassembled upside-down, as if the pieces were still there but someone had put them together in the wrong order.

'Iris,' she said, folding herself round me. I could feel her spare strong arms clasped round my back. 'Iris, goddammit. It's good to see you.'

I wanted to cry. It was a sentimental wish; it was two

old friends meeting after a long time in an impersonal whispering airport hall. But I didn't want to start crying now because I would stop thinking about Stella and start thinking about Fred and I wouldn't be able to finish the crying and we had a train to catch.

Stella let go of me and grabbed Paco and kissed him on his face.

'It's a welcoming committee,' she said. 'Did you just stay at the airport since I left?'

We took the fast rail link into Paddington. It was only the second day it had been officially open and it felt like science fiction.

'This fucker is new,' said Stella, looking around the underground platform with its globe lights set into the floor and its beautiful sanded concrete blocks.

The train glided in like something out of *Blade Runner*, and fourteen minutes later we were in Paddington.

'This fucker is slick,' said Stella. 'Fancy the British coming up with something modern and efficient and sleek like that. That's not what we're famous for. What about the battle of Waterloo?'

'I thought the British won that,' said Paco.

'It was a shambles,' said Stella. 'Chance, that's all. Haven't you read Victor Hugo? Don't you know about the sunken road?'

'No,' said Paco, with dignity, 'I don't.'

Every so often some magazine or media hypester or television pundit came up with the notion that there still was a Great in Britain; that because we had the best pop music in the world and we had street style we still counted for something, as if the fact that the kids on the streets knew how to dress and play a guitar made up for fifty years of industrial decline.

Stella never bought that for a single moment, none of

us did: we were children of the eighties, we had watched the miners strike, we knew that they no longer built ships on the Tyne, we had seen Brixton burn. We were a small island with an inflated past; Great Britannia was a nostalgic tear in post-war eyes, outdated and obsolete as the last night of the Proms and Land of Hope and Glory. So the sleek futuristic rail link felt like an alien thing to us, not something you would expect to bring you to the centre of such a crumbling old town as London was. (Don't get me wrong, not that I don't love London with every beat of my heart, but tomorrow's world is not part of the deal, that's all.)

We took the tube back to my place. Stella slung down her bag. She yawned and stretched her arms and looked at the second sofa out of the corner of her eye.

I saw her looking, and she saw me seeing.

'Can I?' she said, raising up her eyebrows. 'Just for a couple of nights.'

'Of course,' I said. 'You know you can. Paco's here too, just for a couple of nights.'

'Oh,' said Stella, sitting down abruptly. 'It will be like old times, won't it? Just the three of us together.'

She smiled her blinding smile at us both, and then a thought occurred to her and she turned back to me.

'Will Fred mind?' she said.

Paco and I looked at each other.

'What?' said Stella. 'What?'

'He's not, he isn't . . .' I said. I stopped and cleared my throat and started again. 'He's not in the picture any more,' I said clearly.

'What?' said Stella. 'Why? Am I being dumb? I didn't sleep on the flight. Am I missing the point?'

'There is no point,' I said. 'We split up. We, well, he didn't, couldn't, wasn't.'

I sat down on the other sofa and put my chin in my hands and looked at Stella, who was staring at me intently.

'I don't know,' I said. 'He left and it's nine years down the drain and I don't know why.'

'Fuck,' said Stella. 'Do you hate him? Should I hate him with you? Was he a bastard?'

'No,' I said. 'I don't think so. He just stopped. Whatever it was, he stopped, he didn't want me any more. I don't think you can hate someone for that.'

'You can,' said Stella, in a fierce voice.

It made me laugh suddenly because I remembered that voice, from when we first met and all the years after that.

'Maybe you should,' said Paco.

'No,' I said. 'No. I don't want to be bitter and twisted.'

'Why not?' said Stella. 'Get bitter and twisted, you should, it's your biological prerogative.'

'Yeah, yeah,' I said.

'I'm serious,' said Stella. 'You're a woman, so chances are you're going to get fucked over, and now you have and you have the right to get bitter about it.'

'You could get drunk,' said Paco. 'You could just drown all those sorrows.'

'You great nancy,' said Stella, with disdain. 'Butch up. She should get bitter and ponder on it and wreak havoc and revenge.'

'I don't know if I've got it in me,' I said. 'I just feel hollow and bewildered.'

'Oh, Iris,' said Stella. She rolled off the sofa and came over and sat down beside me and leaned her hard shoulder against mine and put her arms round my neck. 'We won't leave you, anyway. You know that.'

5 ∫

There was a party the next week. It was Stella's idea to go. I didn't want to go anywhere, and Paco didn't care either way. Paco was entirely philosophical about life: the way he saw it, it didn't matter whether you went to the ball or not; if the prince was going to come he would arrive when he was good and ready.

Stella said we should go.

'What do you mean, there's a party?' she said.

Paco had told her. He had seen the invitation sitting on my table and asked me about it and I had told him. It was April now; March had slid away from under us and the blossom was out and the sun was shining and the trees were turning green and gaudy after their bleak winter brown and the art parties were starting, which would run through the summer. This was the first one, and I had been looking forward to it, until everything changed and now I didn't want to go anywhere ever again.

'A party,' Stella said, her eyes lighting up like someone had thrown down a gauntlet at her feet. 'That's what we must do.'

'But you're just off the boat and I am catatonic with misery and Paco would be just as happy to stay in and make us gnocchi with secret green sauce,' I said.

'That's no good,' said Stella. 'You can't just sit here in

the roof waiting for your life to end. You've got to see him sometime. This is the smallest town I know, you're going to run into him sooner or later and you're not going to be prepared and it'll shred you apart like tissue paper.'

'Thanks,' I said.

'This way,' said Stella, 'we put makeup on you and a fuck-you frock and we make an entrance and then you've seen him and you haven't died from it and after that it's never going to be so bad again.'

'I don't know,' I said.

I felt a nebulous terror building somewhere under my ribs. I didn't want to see him, I didn't want to see anyone. I wanted to hide. Why did I have to go out ever again? Why couldn't I be like one of those old women who keep cats and collect stacks of yesterday's newspapers?

'We know,' said Stella. 'I know. I'm right, aren't I, Pac, aren't I right?'

Paco shook his head and shrugged his shoulders, like we'd seen him do a thousand times before.

'Maybe,' he said. 'Maybe not. Couldn't do any harm anyway.'

'See?' said Stella triumphantly. Coming from Paco that was like a ringing endorsement. 'And might do much good. Will do much good. Come on, Iris, say you will. I'm going to paint your face so pretty and every man in that room will want to go to bed with you and Fred will stand there all night regretting what he's done.'

I knew she wouldn't give up till I said yes. I knew also that she was right. I would have to see him sooner or later and the best way to do it was when I was prepared and surrounded by allies. But still I wanted to hide.

'All right,' I said.

'That's my girl,' said Stella happily. 'You'll see. That stupid fucker isn't going to know what hit him. I never did like him anyway.'

*   *   *

So we went to the party. Once Stella made up her mind, that was it. I could be mulish on occasion, but Stella was like some elemental force, the kind of thing that people track with delicate machines that can detect a shudder a hundred miles away.

She took some little black New York dress out of her bag and shook it out and gave it to me and told me to put it on. We were the same size, almost. She was two inches taller and longer in the waist: she had long sloping flanks, like *La Serpentine*, that Matisse sculpture of a leaning figure with an elongated torso and stretched athletic legs. (She's almost two feet high, cast in bronze, and if you want to see her you have to go to the Baltimore Museum of Art. I only ever saw a photograph, a postcard someone sent me once from somewhere, and I looked at it and it made me think of Stella.)

I put on the dress, and it looked sharp and urban; it curved out over my hips to make a sweeping bell shape; there was some hint of the thirties to it.

'It's Visconti,' said Stella. 'No?'

Stella's references were not always literal. I got the idea. And she was right, there was something cinematic about it, something drama-queeny about the black against my pale face and flat black hair. I had had magpie blue streaks put into my hair a couple of months before, they were fading now, but every so often, if the light was coming in the right direction, you got a sudden flash of sapphire.

'Hey,' said Stella, seeing it. 'That's hair. What have you been doing, going downtown for your hair?'

'This is London Town,' I said. 'There's no downtown here.'

When we were young and first friends, tentatively testing each other and seeing whether we would love each other for ever, the way girls want to, we went through a phase of acting jaded and blasé; we decided London was small and dismal and provincial, with its early closing and sixties pre-fab, its boys in blue and theme pubs. We wanted hard city things, we wanted all-night delis and yellow cabs and steam issuing from the pavements. We wanted gangster patois and Brooklyn accents, second-generation Italians and all-night coffee bars. We didn't want fish and chips and come in for a cuppa, we wanted pastrami on rye and hold the mayo. So we started talking what we thought was New York talk.

In those days we only knew what we saw in the cinema and heard on the radio, any time they managed to get some genuine New York hero to come and be interviewed; we learnt where we could. We chewed gum and drank Diet Coke (which we called soda). We talked about going downtown and the bridge-and-tunnel set coming into the West End for the weekend. This, we knew, was how people in Manhattan disparagingly referred to those who tripped in from the boroughs in their polyester drip-dry clothing and their safari suits.

In London, people came up west from the suburbs, they came in over the bridges and through the tunnels, just the same. They wore vivid blue eyeshadow and Spandex; the girls looked like they were auditioning for page three (Mandy likes collecting stuffed toys and picking wild flowers when she's not getting her tits out for the lads) and the boys went for that horrible suburban-soul-boy rig, grey slip-on shoes and white socks and a gold chain round the neck. It made Stella and me shudder. We would hang around Leicester Square tube station at eight on a Saturday to watch the specimens emerge, blinking into the neon night, like underground creatures who are not fully equipped for our atmosphere.

We would stand, drawing on our US import cigarettes, squinting through the smoke and talking in our ersatz Manhattan cant.

We grew out of it, after a while. When Stella went to America, to seek her fame and fortune, she sent me a postcard with one line on it. It said in thick black letters: THEY DON'T UNDERSTAND A WORD I SAY. I laughed about that for a long time.

'Sit still while I do your lips,' said Stella, staring hard at my face.

I hadn't once looked at my face since Fred left. I hadn't bothered with makeup or grooming, because what was the point? Neglect, I thought, that's what happens to the mad old sad old women; they stop doing their hair and their faces and they get that crazed haywire look and people start looking away from them in the street and refusing to serve them in shops because they look too insane.

I was suddenly overcome with gladness that Stella was going to do my lips, as if this was the sea wall between me and the sliding slope down to lunacy and loss of social graces. With Stella back, I knew that nothing could get so bad because she wouldn't let it. She understood all about misery and loss of reason: her family was riven with it. Her mother had lived on pills for years before she died, variously diagnosed with manic depression, endogenous depression, clinical depression, and once, by a particularly aggressive psychiatrist, contiguous depression.

'Whichever way you look at it,' Stella said to me once, 'that woman was *depressed.*'

The doctors agreed that it was due to chemical changes in the brain; pills, they said, were the answer.

'Get that woman on medication,' said Stella. 'That's what those boys in white coats want. Get those crazy chicks on some nice blue pills quick as horses, and we won't hear another worry out of them.'

Stella was angry at doctors in general and psychiatrists in particular. She should know, she'd seen enough of them.

Valerie Parker spent Stella's childhood loaded down with enough barbiturates to sedate a small pony. Sometimes the diagnosis changed and the doses shifted. On one occasion, they experimented with a new pill, which led to hallucinations and advanced paranoia, with Valerie standing on a roof-top at eleven o'clock at night, screaming that she was going to jump because MI5 were out to get her.

'You have to laugh,' said Stella. 'It has a certain picture-book quality to it.'

That was when they said Valerie was manic and put her on a cocktail of lithium and a few other charmers, which got her a notch above catatonia; she walked and talked, but no one was ever quite sure who was pulling the strings.

'There was a cloud over her eyes,' Stella said, when she told me these stories. 'As if there was a veil between her and the world. That's no way to live,' she said. 'That's no fucking way to treat a lady.'

Then there was the trouble sleeping, so it was pills to sleep and pills to wake and pills to keep calm, Valium and Ativan, Seconal and Librium and Halcyon, blue ones and yellow ones and pink ones, pills for every eventuality. No one thought to ask her any questions. No one thought to ask why.

Stella's mother was brought up by parents who would rather die than express an emotion; you put on a good front, because the show must go on, even when the theatre was crumbling to dust.

Valerie Parker was taught that little girls didn't laugh out loud or make a noise, little girls sat with their ankles genteelly crossed, little girls spoke when they were spoken to. When Valerie's uncle died in a train smash, no one in the house cried because these things happen and what about the children starving in Africa?, they really had something to cry about. Valerie did cry, in her bedroom, when she thought no one could hear; and her mother came in, white and furious in a pink quilted dressing gown, and beat the child with a thin leather belt, for letting the side down. She beat her until Stella's mother stopped crying, and she never cried again.

'And they say it was a chemical disorder,' said Stella, in disgust. 'They said it was to do with her neurotransmitters. If you weren't allowed to laugh or cry on pain of *beating*, don't you think you might develop a bit of a disorder?'

One day, when Stella was fifteen, her mother gathered her pills together and took them all in one go.

'That really is the way to treat a chemical imbalance,' said Stella. 'How happy are you going to be if you swallow them all in one shot? That's *happy*. That's a one-way trip to heaven and no mistake.'

Stella's mother, they said afterwards, had been failed by the system. Stella's father, who remained dry-eyed and stoic through it all, was killed six months later by a stomach cancer that ran through his body with ruthless efficiency.

'They never felt a thing,' said Stella, 'and it killed them.'

Stella felt everything. She said it was because she wanted to stay alive. I sometimes thought, when I watched her feeling everything so keenly, expressing every thought that came into her head, that she was driven, haunted by the picture of her mother, sitting silent and ladylike and numbed in the corner of the room, but I never said so. I wouldn't have her any other way than the way she was. She was more alive than anyone I ever met.

'Look now,' said Stella, holding up a mirror for me to see.

I shied away instinctively. I didn't want to look. I wanted to disappear.

I took a hold on myself and turned back and looked. I couldn't believe that nine years had gone up in smoke and I looked the same as I had before. There was maybe a darker shadow under my eyes, and I was pale, but I

was always pale. I had a slight yellow cast to my skin;
I sometimes wondered whether my mother had ever had
any starlit nights down in Limehouse in the year before I
was born, but then she had it too, a slight foreign texture,
Mediterranean maybe, or further east.

Stella had painted my lips such a dark red they almost
looked purple. My mouth was long and slightly lop-sided,
clownish, I thought. Stella said expressive. 'It's an artistic
mouth,' she said. 'It's a creative mouth.' She had put black
lines round my eyes and lilac shadow on them and bright
spots of rouge high on my cheekbones so they looked like
something out of a decadent foreign town in the twenties.

'It's going to be a wild night,' she said. 'I want you to
look like one of those girls in Paris at the turn of century,
the ones who sat for artists and turned a trick or two when
they had to make the rent.'

'You've been reading too many books,' I said, but I was
pleased in some part of me. I looked like a woman again
anyway, even if it was one on the game.

'Fuck-me frock and fuck-me lips,' said Stella.

She was really enjoying herself, I could see.

'I am glad I'm back,' she said.

The party was to be held in Mayfair, in some old, forgotten
Whig mansion, one of those houses that you couldn't
believe still existed in the fervid rushing nineties. (Stella
liked the nineties, she liked the sound of it; but she worried
about what they were going to call the next ten years,
after 2000: 'What?' she said. 'Think about it. What? The
zeros?')

There were a lot of art parties at that time; there was
confidence back in the market. The Sensation boys and
girls had given everyone a shot in the arm: people were
talking about Britart in the same way they spoke of Britpop
and Britlit. People were buying art again, in a way they

hadn't since the crazy eighties bubble had burst so spectacularly.

Stella and Paco and I had been in New York the day they sold the portrait of Dr Gachet at Christie's; the very apex of the boom.

Stella had won a premium bond for £5,000. It seemed an unreal thing to happen; Britons always talked about winning a premium bond or winning the pools, but I never believed it happened to a real person. Stella got a businesslike white envelope, with a short letter and a fat cheque. The cheque was bigger than normal size and printed on pink paper so it looked like Toy Town money, not something you could convert into cold hard cash. But the bank didn't murmur; she took it in and passed it across to the teller – My name is Brian Jones, his badge said, here to serve you – and although he looked barely old enough to shave or vote or have legal sex, he looked up and smiled with some composure when Stella said she'd like the cash straight away.

'Certainly, madam,' he said. 'And how would you like your money?'

We took the cash round to the local travel agent (COSTA DEL SOL, self-catering holiday campsite, £99) bought three tickets to New York on Air India, which was the lowest rock-bottom you could go in those days, and spent a merry flight eating yellow rice and drinking Drambuie and listening to a voluble Keralan called Albert talk about Spinoza.

We had never been out of the country before, not even Paco with all his scattered relations. We had taken a trip the summer before to the Isle of Wight, which almost felt like abroad because it involved a sea voyage. But this was crossing the Atlantic on a big bird, a Boeing wide-bodied jet. This was the city we'd dreamt of and read about and watched on the silver screen and aped in our speech and mannerisms.

We tried to persuade Stella to keep the money. She was always short of cash; any time she had any she spent it all on books and shoes and long-playing records, and even though she never paid for anything that wasn't second-hand and knocked down to half its original price, although she haggled in the back-streets of Soho as if she were in the bazaar in downtown Cairo, it still added up to more than she earned, every month, without fail.

She didn't want to keep the money, whatever we said about it.

'It's fairy-tale money,' she said. 'It's all phoney, this cheque. It wouldn't feel right to bank it. Let's take it to New York City and spend it on bagels.'

So we arrived in a big yellow taxi and checked into a faded flea-pit hotel downtown, which pleased our sense of rock-and-roll history: it was the kind of place where Sid Vicious and Lou Reed might have stayed; the kind of place where Janis Joplin would have had dirty drunken sex with a man whose name she never caught.

We spent a lot of time walking, up and down those long shadowed canyons, astonished by the scale of it. We knew everything was bigger in America, we weren't born yesterday, but all the same, we weren't prepared for it. Manhattan might be a small island, but the men who built it knew all about monumental. As we wandered gaily along streets lined by skyscrapers so tall that the sun couldn't reach the pavements, leaving them in atmospheric monochrome shadow, we wondered how it was that such a thin plot of land could physically support such a weight of concrete and glass and people and cars and expectation.

'It's one of those things,' said Stella, 'that shouldn't really exist, that isn't really possible. It's one big paradox of a town. It's a floating contradiction.'

We went to Chinatown and ate dumplings and chop

suey, we walked round the Village, we drank beers in the White Horse Tavern. We saw the house where Henry James lived and the studio where Edgar Dime had worked in the fifties, when he painted the *Harlem 50* series and got everyone talking.

One night we went to a swanky uptown hotel to have a drink in the bar. We ate pizza mostly, or damp, steaming frankfurters from gleaming metal carts parked up on the sidewalks; hotel bars were our extravagance.

It was Stella who had this tic, this love. In London, she would make us dress up and take us for a martini at the Ritz or a gin fizz at the Savoy. Paco and I had been reluctant at first: to us it was money to burn. But gradually we came round. There is a slow seduction to hotel bars. It's not, curiously, about money, although everything else in those days was; that was the era of money, money's finest hour. People who had never dreamt of it had it, it was spent ferociously, circulated freely, people wrote books called it.

But hotel bars weren't about that, they were about something older and more nebulous. I think what they really were about, those thick-carpeted havens, with their hovering expectant hush, their marble bathrooms and their dim lighting, their knowing barmen and deferential waiters, was make-believe, some glimpse of a lost age. It was Scott and Zelda in the Plaza, Dorothy Parker and Robert Benchley in the Algonquin. Whatever else had changed, the great hotel bars still spoke to you of broken promises and unfulfilled dreams, yearning hearts and bouquets of roses, illicit meetings and charmed lives. There wasn't time for fanciful any more: people frowned on it and called it fey. This was the era of the cynic: this was the Age of Irony. No one was romantic any more, there was no call for it, not in the age of the free market, no sir. But if you had any leanings for those lost things, you could find echoes of them in the bars of the grand hotels, just as you could still find stirrings and remnants of Bohemia in the close, fragrant drinking-clubs of dirty old Soho on a Friday afternoon. It depended on what you were looking for.

Just then, because of our youth, and because we didn't care for the eighties and the money cult (did anyone care for it? Really?), we were searching for pretty much everything. So that was why we stayed in a rock-and-roll suicide hotel and walked sixty-eight blocks to drink a ten-dollar cocktail in an East Side mansion with figured carpets three inches thick and gold taps shaped like swans in the bathrooms.

In this uptown shack, we made friends with a friendly fat Texan in a pale blue pinstripe suit and a watch that must have cost six months' rent. It turned out he was in town to buy some art. That was how we found out about the sales.

'Can we come and look?' said Stella. 'My friend here is queer for art.'

I ducked my head. Stella always said that. It was a compliment from her; she was drawn to the obsessive. She liked the fact that Paco knew every song Frank Sinatra ever recorded, could date them, tell you who wrote them, arranged them, and who played the trumpet solo. She liked the fact that I was queer for art.

It was an accident of fate: my mother had no use for pictures on a wall, she was too busy in the real world, saving it. But when we lived in that house in Kensington, there was an Italian called Vito who lived downstairs and babysat me sometimes in the afternoons. He had inherited money when his parents died in a skiing accident and he didn't bother with a job, but his father had been an art-dealer in Rome, and Vito had inherited his love for pictures. So instead of taking me to the cinema or the zoo, he took me to art galleries, and somewhere along the line some chord in me was struck, and it never stopped reverberating. He took me to the South Bank and the galleries along Cork

Street, and he never told me what to think or how to look: he used to stand me in front of something he liked and see what I made of it. He was passionate about Edgar Dime, and whenever there was an exhibition of his work, or an auction where one of his pictures came up for sale, Vito took me along, and by the time I was ten years old and Vito packed up his bags and went back to Italy, Edgar Dime was my passion too.

6 ſ

The Texan told us his name was Joe Goldstein. This tickled Stella mightily.

'I just never thought of Jews in Texas, that's all,' she said.

I knew what she meant. We had only fiction to draw on then: we knew Neil Simon and Woody Allen and Saul Bellow, where American Jewishness was an edgy urban coastal thing. We found it hard to equate ten-gallon hats and cattle herds and barrels of oil and country-and-western songs with a man named Joe Goldstein.

Joe's great-grandfather Louis, he told us, had started life in Warsaw, the son of a tailor who made bespoke suiting for the hearty Polish burghers, the emerging middle class, the traders and merchants, the expansive shop-keepers and the prosperous factory owners. Louis had seen a picture book of the Wild West, the pioneers with their covered wagons and mule trains, and he got a dream of new land in his head.

'He got to dreaming of the prairies,' Joe said, as he bought us another round of bullshots, 'and he couldn't shake it.'

Louis settled first in Dallas in 1889. There were a hundred other Jewish families and they all knew each other; the Temple down near Santa Fé station was already thirteen years old. Louis opened a store and worked at it for ten years, and when there was enough money in the bank, he bundled his family into a truck and drove into the west and settled them on a parcel of land.

'So,' said Joe, 'that's how I ended up a rancher.'

He laughed, putting his head back and laying his hands on his belly. He was enjoying himself vastly, I could see.

'How many cows have you got?' said Stella. 'If you don't mind my asking.'

Joe grinned from ear to ear. He had a sweet, childish smile, at odds with his flashy pinstripe.

'I got enough to get me some art,' he said. 'I want to get a look at that van Gogh at Christie's.' (He pronounced it van Go, in the American way, with extra emphasis, as if it were a command rather than a name.)

'Well, come on,' said Stella. 'You've got to take us. This we have to see.'

So the next day we ended up having lunch in one of those swell self-conscious Upper East Side restaurants where everyone knows who everyone is; us, our motley band, with a Jewish rancher from outside Dallas, Texas.

The restaurant was small and packed. At the end of it was a doorway leading to a smaller room; Joe told us with genial authority that that room was where the nobodies and out-of-towners got sat.

'Bring your sables for that room,' Joe said. 'That's colder'n Siberia in there, that's for sure.'

He was nakedly gleeful at this thought, as we were sat at a prominent table in the right room.

The *maître d'* had given a discernible blink when we arrived. You didn't have to be an anthropologist to figure that we weren't what he had in mind for his tony establishment.

It was one of those bogus places which have bare-wood floors and check tablecloths and white paper napkins, but still the ladies who lunch are wearing Chanel from top to toe, and a hamburger with relish will set you back the best part of twenty dollars.

We were clearly not ladies who lunched. Stella was in a post-punk-rock-chick look just then; she was wearing purple PVC drainpipes, a tight Sex Pistols T-shirt, and green suede stiletto-heeled boots. Personally I thought it was a fabulous look, and when I look back on what most people were wearing in the late eighties, I still think it. Also, if you're Stella, and you're six foot tall and narrow as a whip, you can wear that kind of thing and make like you're the Queen of Sheba.

I was in a black existential phase, and Paco was wearing a suit. Paco has never deviated in his style of dress all the years I've known him: black single-breasted suit, coloured shirts, fat kipper ties. If it's hot or he can't be bothered, he leaves off the jacket and the tie, but he looks the same, even so. You would think this was unexceptional, but in those days he only had two suits, bought at the Portobello Record and Tape Exchange, and the one he was wearing that day had the elbows almost worn through, and his shirt wasn't ironed, because where were you going to find an iron in a flophouse hotel on 4th Street costing under thirty bucks a night? So it was clear that we weren't the widow of John D. Rockefeller, and the *maître d'* gave us a subtle, honed look to make sure we knew it.

I looked nervously over at Stella, because this was the kind of thing that could cause her to make a scene, but she was smiling at Joe. I could see she had a big love thing going with him, that she had decided in her mercurial way that he was one of the good guys; it was his gig, his glee about being on the top table, and she wouldn't do anything to spoil that.

We ate soft-shell crabs and ignored the ambivalent looks from the stick women in their thousand-dollar rags.

'They can't altogether despise you,' said Stella, 'on account of you having so many cows, but, my, how they want to.'

'I'm fat and vulgar and Jewish and Texan,' said Joe, counting them off on his fingers. 'I laugh too loud and drink too much and I don't know the right way to hold a cocktail napkin. But if you got money like I do they can't help asking you to their parties. They send the invite to your bank account, and then you show up with your big mouth and your loud suit and they look at you as if to say, We know this person?'

'What about Mrs Goldstein?' said Stella. I could see that she was worried about him, hoping that he had some nice calming woman to love him just because of the loud voice and the pinstripe suits and the social innocence.

Joe smiled happily.

'She doesn't care for the city,' he said. 'She doesn't have the hide that I do, to bounce the looks off.'

We went to view the pictures in the afternoon. They gave us the same kind of *maître d'* looks, as if to say: What could anyone like you know or care about Art?

I wasn't a fan of van Gogh, not then. He wasn't my boy; he didn't send me in the way that Matisse did, or Dime, or Modigliani. I had only seen the postcards and the posters, the cheap imitations on a thousand student bedsit walls. So although Stella was right when she told Joe I was queer for art, it wasn't Dr Gachet that I was thrilled about seeing.

The pictures were arranged in two long plush galleries. Leading us like a zoological expedition, Joe, determined in his snakeskin boots, strode past lines of pictures in the ten to twelve-million-dollar range. The carpets were soft and thick and smelt of new banknotes; the lighting was bright and warm; locals from the *belle-époque* mansions that lined Park Avenue murmured clipped remarks and watched each other from behind smoked glasses. You could feel the dry hot wind of Texas blowing as Joe walked past.

Right at the end of the second gallery, the Gachet sat, alone on one wall, apart from the rest.

'There,' said Joe, planting himself in front of it like he belonged there.

I thought at first that they had lit it differently, given it extra wattage, pulled out all the stops. It was the pedigree mutt in the show after all; it was the one everyone had come for. There were some serious contenders lining the walls to either side, but somehow they looked second-rate by comparison. It must be the lighting, I thought, some conjuror's trick. But when I got closer I got it, I finally got the point. There was some kind of inner light coming out of the picture, from the paint itself. It wasn't anything to do with those cunning Christie's boys, it was because it was the genuine article.

Most art doesn't reproduce: reproductions flatten it, lose the texture and life of the painting. Good pictures have something animate in them; if you stand up close you can see the ridges and gouges where the artist has used the brush or palette knife; you can picture the specific act of creation; you can imagine something of how it was made. You don't get that from a postcard: you are left with something clichéd and iconic at the same time; it's not the painting of the Mona Lisa that counts any more, only the secret behind that famous smile.

Stella had a very strong opinion about that. We went to the Louvre together a couple of years after that trip to New York, and when we got to the Mona Lisa in her bullet-proof glass box, surrounded by polite busloads of Japanese, Stella stood in front of it, ignoring the crowds jostling around her, and said in a loud, clear voice, 'Is that it?'

I took her arm and steered her away to look at Marie Antoinette's *nécessaire*, which excited her enough to take her mind off it ('All those bottles,' she said. 'She must have had a habit, for sure. They can't all have been for salad dressing') but when we got outside and walked through the Tuileries, her mind reverted.

'I want my money back,' she said. 'That was the Mona Lisa? The most famous painting in the world? It's the most boring thing I ever saw.'

Two young Frenchmen walked by in suits that were slightly too tight for them. Rising shamelessly to their national stereotype, they gave Stella blatant *cinq-à-sept* looks.

'I know what it was, though,' she said thoughtfully. 'That sphinx smile. It's obvious, isn't it, once you've seen her?'

'What's obvious?' I said.

'The secret behind that smile, that corny I've-got-something-to-hide grin,' said Stella. 'Come on, Iris, it's like the hand in front of your face.'

'What is?' I said.

'She clearly,' said Stella, 'was a man. That Mona Lisa was a trannie, that's her secret. That babe was a drag act, for sure.'

This was different, this first exposure to van Gogh. Dr Gachet was not one the postcard manufacturers got hot for, and the picture was absolutely unknown to me then, in that bright New York afternoon; but as I saw it I understood, without having to be told, why there was so much anticipation on the Manhattan streets, why Joe was standing in front of it with a light burning in his nut brown eyes, thinking of how many cattle he would have to sell to take it home with him

Stella came up beside Joe and put her arm through his.

'I think you should buy the fucker,' she said conversationally. 'I'd like to think of him in Texas.'

*   *   *

The sale was wrought to a polite pitch of hysteria from the start. As the limousines and town cars pulled up outside the auction house, blue police barriers and cops on horses were used to keep the crowds and the photographers back.

'Rock and roll,' said Stella, waving at the crowd.

Once we got inside, it was clear how important Joe was, with his bulging wallet and his reputation for high rolling. The normal saps, the gawkers and social commentators, stood in the margins of the room, penned by velvet ropes. Some journalists had been allowed in at the back; I saw the debauched basset-hound face of an English hack who was famous for being drunk all the time and falling under the table at uptown clambakes and getting himself written into the latest state-of-the-nation great American novel. He couldn't even make it into the cheap seats at this gig; standing room only for him.

There was room for maybe two hundred people to sit down, and you just knew that they had the right stuff. There were many expensively dressed women in shiny cocktail dresses and sharp evening suits; real jewels glinted off their ears and fingers.

'Look at those rocks,' said Stella. 'Do they wear those just so you can't get close enough to see the lines on their faces?'

There was a pack of immaculate Europeans, talking broken English at each other. There was one row of Japanese men, all dressed the same in blunt black suits that absorbed the light. They wore Clark Kent spectacles and looked as if they were enjoying a secret joke. The English dealers came in late, wearing three-piece pinstripes, not so far away from Joe's look, except for a certain discretion in the tailoring that marked them as more Savile Row than the Lone Star State, even though there was a definite wide-boy look just then, even to the smartest of the Mayfair boys, and there still is, something a bit raffish and near the knuckle about them, despite their connections and plum accents.

There was a crack of expectation and electricity in the air; over the smack and coo of air-kiss greeting and cocktail-hour exclamation, there was something tense and fraught in the atmosphere. It was the rise and fall of money; the knowledge that someone was going to spend millions tonight was drawn as tight as a violin string over the veneer of social niceties.

Prices exceeded expectations right from the start; reserves were reached and smashed in moments. The dealers looked smug over their surprise, thinking of their percentages. In the press pen, the scribblers were getting restive; they had seen millions spent by people who had millions more in the hold; this wasn't news, this was *hors d'oeuvres*.

Then they wheeled out Dr Gachet. The room shifted and sighed. The auctioneer cleared his throat. The nice girls with clean faces and velvet hairbands manning the telephones frowned and pressed the receivers closer to their pink ears; bids would be coming in from Rio, Geneva, London, Tokyo, voices travelling over thousands of miles faster than silver bullets, loaded with cash offers.

Joe sat up straight in his chair, the good humour drained out of him, every atom of energy focused on the picture twenty yards in front of him. The room was silent: pin-drop clichés ran through my mind like tickertape. Stella and Paco and I looked at each other. I didn't know what we were doing there, in the expensive seats, surrounded by this serious money. It felt as if we were in the middle of some secret cabalistic ritual, one of those rites performed by dying tribes, the kind that are hardly ever observed by outside eyes.

With a snap, the bidding started. The estimate on the picture had been around thirty million; it reached that in thirty seconds. When it passed forty there was an audible gasp in the room. The press had woken up and were leaning and straining to see who was bidding. The telephone girls looked anxious and suspicious, as if they were missing something. At fifty million, people in the front turned round to see who was buying. At sixty, Joe gave a sudden sigh, as if he was in pain, and dropped out. At seventy million, something snapped in the room, as if the normal rules didn't apply any more. The noise level rose as people nakedly asked each other who was bidding. The money was coming from somewhere in the middle of the room, very near to where we were sitting.

'They're looking at me,' said Stella, out of the corner of her mouth. She looked straight ahead, like a soldier on sentry duty. 'I don't dare move,' she muttered, 'or I'll have spent seventy million dollars.'

I suddenly saw who it was: the youngest of the Japanese on the row right in front of us was lifting his hand for seventy-five million. No one else in the room was bidding. One of the pale good girls was still working her telephone; the others had hung up. It was the room against the phone. Murmurs slid round the walls like Chinese whispers: was it Niarchos, Agnelli, Onassis? The Japanese raised his hand one more time, for eighty million.

People were standing on their seats now. The auctioneer had to peer over the crowd to see his punter. Eighty million dollars were on the table. The auctioneer looked at the girl on the telephone. She hardly moved her head. 'Eighty-one million,' said the auctioneer.

Every eye in the room was on the Japanese. He didn't hesitate. It was as if he had all the money in the world, as if he would get home to find a diamond as big as the Ritz waiting for him. He nodded minutely at the auctioneer. The crowd was slack-jawed and breathless.

There was a minuscule pause. The blonde girl on the phone shook her head and put down the receiver. The auctioneer gave the palest suggestion of a smile at the Japanese, said, 'Yours at eighty-two million dollars,' and smacked his gavel down. The room erupted into applause. I swear to God, there, in that Upper East Side temple of taste, women in Dior frocks and cabochon rubies, men in thousand-dollar hand-stitched suits, stood on their chairs, cheering like a baseball crowd.

That was how Dr Gachet got sold. But the art game, for that time, was over. The bubble, swollen to grotesque proportions, burst violently soon afterwards, and for a long time you couldn't flog a post-Impressionist if your life depended on it.

But now, in the last couple of years, prices had been creeping up again. The market was reinvigorated by the new breed of conceptual artists and the shameless confidence of the Damien Hirst generation. Advertising moguls and anonymous private collectors were shelling out; the recession was receding; the stock markets were bullish. People were giving parties again, and they all said the same thing. It's not the eighties, they said. Remember Dr Gachet? We'll never see that again, we won't make that mistake again, not us. It's different this time, they all said, and I think they believed it.

'So what is this party?' said Stella. 'I've been away so long I don't know how anything works any more. Will I have a good time? Will there be a hot band and men I can flirt with?'

Paco looked up from the sofa and smiled, and I saw it and thought how long we had been together, how many evenings we had spent, just like this one, the three of us.

'There are always men you can flirt with,' he said. 'Nothing changes that much.'

'I'm going to take that the right way,' said Stella.

'It'll be a good party,' I said, feeling my heart sink in me. 'It will be a fine party.'

The art parties just then followed three main trends. There were the post-industrial hard-core parties, where the glitterati and literati (book writers now following the art crowd like seagulls after a loaded trawler on its way home from Dogger Bank) trekked off to some distant corner of London, to a redundant warehouse with diesel oil and sawdust on the floor for authenticity. There was no attempt at any kind of creature comfort: no loos, no heating, damp slime on the walls, and only the really inventive could find anywhere to do a line of coke, which along with Art, had raced back into fashion (there were those who said it had never been away). No one could hear what anyone was saying over the junglist DJ, who was so cool that he wore his sunglasses all night and never spoke, because talking was last year's way to express yourself.

The second kind came from the trend for characters to set up art galleries in their own front rooms (or even bedrooms, which could lead to confusion: at one *soirée*, a myopic collector had tried to buy the unmade bed, thinking it was an installation). These parties were very select – a hundred hand-picked guests, Tony Bennett's golden greats on the stereo, and continual moments of smoking panic, because no one could get near an ashtray and they were so used to putting their butts out on warehouse floors that they didn't know what to do when faced with white shag pile.

I quite enjoyed these parties, but after half an hour they became like some pastiche of a sixties Peter Sellers film, where people set fire to backcombed hair with cigarettes jammed into foot long holders and the only way to get through the crowd was to crawl through people's legs.

The third kind was the real old-fashioned comfort party, given by the big collectors, where you could guarantee real champagne and frozen vodka, a band playing salsa, which had suddenly become the only true syncopation, flowers flown in from Ecuador, and a hot breakfast at three in the morning.

This kind of party hadn't been given for a few years: there hadn't been enough visible money, and they had fallen into disrepute. But suddenly they came roaring back into favour, taken up fervently by the fashion and the art worlds, which seemed, just then, to be working in tandem (models and artists were the dearest of friends, although it was anyone's guess what they actually talked about).

The party we were going to was of the third type. It was being given by Pete Street, a determined collector of contemporary art, and a self-made man who had started out with the distinct disadvantage of being born into money. His father was old-school county, with many green acres belonging to him, and pronounced views on the immigration problem. Pete, growing up in draughty halls, longed only for deprivation and hunger to succeed. He grew his hair long and cultivated a carefully classless accent, dropped out of school at fifteen (Not a qualification to my name, was his proud boast) and went to work for a sugar importer on the Commercial Road.

By the nineties, Pete Street was the sugar king, with nothing left to prove; he had five large factories, a turnover in many millions, and notoriously good industrial relations. He also, famously, had no taste, so he hired a stylist called Aurelia Strike who told him what to wear, which theatres to attend, which restaurants to visit, which books to read. Once he had got all that mastered, he decided it was time to buy art.

His stylist went into close consultation with the queen of future trends, Faith Popcorn (this, apparently, was her real name) and advised him to go long on the new conceptual-ists. Charles Saatchi was to do this a year or so later, and Pete Street got a real kick out of reminding everyone who got there first.

Because buying installations of reinvigorated scrap metal and dead sharks in formaldehyde was a bulky business, Pete Street turned over one of his old factories, out on the Commercial Road, to the task. It was the exact same time that the east was starting to become colonised by artists who couldn't afford central London prices. They moved out, to Hackney in the north, Smithfield, Clerkenwell and Hoxton in the east; and miraculously, Pete Street was right there in the centre of it, with his post-industrial space and his large wallet. So everything was merry as a marriage bell.

I knew Pete Street well. Fred's gallery dealt in the kind of art he bought, the front line, the edgy dare-anything artists. My job was (had been) looking after what Fred had called the people side of things. He chose the art, and I found the people. It was my job to look after the artists and to keep the clients happy. Sometimes, carefully, I brought the two together.

I was good at this job and I liked it. Although it was in fashion, I found cynicism a stretch; I had a tendency to see the best in people. This gave me, according to Fred, people skills. What it really meant was that other people sneered and curled their lip at Pete Street, for his vulgarity, his blatant lack of book learning and his love of West End musicals, but he made me laugh.

I liked Pete because he didn't come into the gallery and start talking about texture and urgency and spatial dialectics; he would just walk in and put his cheque book on the table and say, 'Which one should I buy this week?'

What I really liked about Pete Street was that he didn't care about all his money and he didn't care about his name and he didn't give a flying fuck for posterity. His factory was just called 101 Commercial and it was open all hours and there was no charge.

The received wisdom about art is that it is an élite thing. The average Joe, the wisdom goes, the men in the street, have no interest in art. They have no *use* for it. This is the reason that the people who comment on art have strangled voices and use long words that they themselves hardly understand. It's an élite thing, so why not obfuscate it so much that it starts eating itself? None of these sages and commentators ever stopped to think about the logistics. Take away the long words, the grand notions, the snob reviewers, the invisible but tangible no-plebs-allowed signs: what are you left with? Galleries that open nine to five, when most working stiffs are working; galleries that are in the high-rent districts, where the ladies who lunch lunch and the women who shop shop, and the men who loaf wander around drinking double espresso and thinking about when their first drink will be.

In Pete Street's gallery, it took a while for the word to get around. People wondered what was happening to the old sugar factory. The whisper got out that walls were being knocked down, that an indoor garden was being constructed, with a fountain and a skylight and miniature Kew subtropical effect going on. The rumours spread that the whole place was being painted white and the floors covered in basalt.

Commercial Road was still on the fringes of what would later become some kind of new Bohemia: it was a district of work and want. It wasn't a neighbourhood of fiscal frivolity or idle luxuries; the art critics with their precise diction and meaningless jargon wouldn't be seen dead there. There were sweatshops in that district, child labour and packs of illegal immigrants working twenty-hour days for a pound an hour. There was no room for art.

But Pete Street held fast to his idea, as dogged as if he really had started life in a tenement in E2 instead of a Queen Anne mansion north of Oxford. Pete did two unprecedented things with his space. He put in seats, for a starter, proper benches and window-seats and box seats and comfortable chairs, so you could walk in and settle yourself down and you could do what you should be able to do in a gallery: you could lose yourself. (If art is for anything, if it serves any actual *purpose*, perhaps it is for that.)

Outside, you might know that the world was earnest and real, you might know that the rain was falling and you owed money to the bank, you might know that your husband smacked you around when he came home drunk from the pub, or that your wife was taking Prozac with her tea at eleven o'clock; you might wonder if they would ever do anything about the Northern Line or the National Health waiting lists. You might feel despair or disillusion, apathy or fury. But once you were inside that space, once you had the smooth obsidian floor under your feet, so clean and gleaming, so dark and promising, once you had the white walls round you and the light coming in from the glass sunk into the roof at crazy angles, once you had the *art* to look at, to contemplate from the comfort of a good seat, it was taking you away, somewhere away from that worrying nagging quotidian world, where your dreams never quite came true the way you wanted.

Pete Street, for all the sneering of the *haute bourgeoisie*, understood something of this when he built his gallery in Commercial Road and put chairs in it.

Pete Street, for all his failings of taste, understood something even more fundamental, when he decided that his space would be open twenty-four hours.

At first only junkies and vagrants came in during the night hours; the security guards were kept busy stopping drunks pissing on the exhibits (although, as Pete said to me, it was perfectly post-modern: he was learning fast as houses, Pete Street, whatever the starlings said).

I had always wondered why Pete made quite so much money. Business was not a world I understood, but I started to understand a little more about the reason that Pete Street was the runaway success that he was when he developed his art space.

He was determined on twenty-four hours from the start: he liked the idea of open-all-hours. Everyone got to spitting and snarling when they heard that: It's not a roadside petrol station darling, they said, it's not 7-11. Just like Pete Street, they said, to overegg the pudding. They would have understood a bequest to one of the big galleries, with a name on a plaque and a lot of here's-to-the-future bombast. Scoffed, of course, because people like Pete Street couldn't expect to get away with their affluence and their lack of refinement scot-free, but they would have understood it.

But the East End dead-end location, the factory building (this before the vogue for urban realism and warehouse parties, well before that) the free entry, the twenty-four-hour access: this was eccentricity beyond the bounds of reason. So when they heard about the hobos stumbling in and the drinkers pissing on the art, they were discreetly and definitely delighted.

Anyone else but Pete Street might have given up then, but it was at this moment that I realised why Pete was the businessman he was, why his five vast factories rode out financial vicissitudes and adverse currency shifts, and why his workforce loved him, all thirty thousand of them.

He didn't shut down the gallery, he didn't call the police, he didn't change his mind. He revised his staffing plan. He kept the same security guards for the daytime (you need big serious guards for art galleries: it's the nutters' charter to slash canvases or throw acid on them, often in the name of some obsolete political organisation) but he changed the night shift.

He called up someone he knew who worked at the *Big Issue* and he got a detail of five large determined men, all of whom had been homeless themselves. The new guards managed to get the chancers and dossers to move on without hurting their feelings, the art stopped getting pissed on or knocked over, and the other patrons could get back to contemplation.

The scoffers came up with a new hitch: now the lowlifes were dealt with, there would be no clientele at all, not twenty-four-hour, not in the Commercial Road. Of course, went the wisdom, you would never get anyone in to look at art after hours, because in that neighbourhood they would all be at home watching *EastEnders*.

Pete Street stuck to his guns and, sure enough, the people came. Once they understood that they really didn't have to pay, that there was a quiet space where they could sit and rest and contemplate, that there was no rule or regulation or dress code, they started coming. Pete put in a coffee stall next to the central courtyard, where there was a fountain and a skylight and a tropical tangle of plants, so the whole space smelt of foliage and coffee beans. Between twelve and six, coffee and doughnuts were free (Oh! the sneeries said, every free loader in the borough will be in there, every caffeine hound, every something for nothing fanatic).

It was the night people that Pete Street was proudest of. The seamstresses, the night shift, the insomniacs; they all came in, for five minutes or half an hour, to sit on the chairs and drink a milky cup of coffee and listen to the fountain play. They came to look at art that, according to the experts and the Ph.D.s, they couldn't possibly know the meaning of; they sat in front of it and liked it or not. But they were, for all their lack of formal qualification, curious and discerning. As the collection changed and shifted, it got definite and discrete reactions. When Pete bought a couple of Herons, the late shift swelled significantly. The night owls loved those crazy singing colours that Heron used: for whatever reason, it brought them in in droves.

'Here,' said Pete Street to me, at the time, 'is an interesting thing. Most of the people in this neighbourhood don't know or give a damn who Patrick Heron is, whether he is alive or dead, gay or straight, at the cutting edge or hopelessly outdated. They've never heard his name, don't recognise his work. But they want to come and see him. Entry is up twenty-five per cent. How do you explain that?'

Pete had always given parties, right through the lean times. He liked getting out and meeting people; he was friendly and gregarious at heart. He knew that the social starlings curled their lips at him behind his back (although it never stopped them taking his hospitality). He asked them along anyway, because it wasn't in him to hold grudges.

Pete's parties were always good; there was plenty to drink and a mixed crowd and a hot band. Pete had friends in the jazz world, he had been going to Ronnie Scott's long before he became a tycoon.

Normally I would look forward to a party like this, but tonight I felt as if my feet were dipped in cement. My stomach was cold and hollow, empty and heavy at the same time. With Stella and Paco in the flat I had almost managed to forget what had happened. There were moments when I thought that this wasn't really the end, that Fred would call up and say he was coming round, back to say that he hadn't meant any of it. I had drifted into a fantasy where we weren't broken up, he was away for a while, like the times when he went off on scouting trips, to look for new artists. He would hear about someone in Barcelona or Portland, Milan or Havana, and he would set off with a small carry-on bag with nothing more than a couple of changes of underwear, a razor and a paperback, carrying some lingering Hemingway idea of the lone male abroad.

He liked to go alone; he liked to travel light. I sometimes wondered whether he saw women on those trips, whether he met glossy married sirens in Milan or credit-card hookers in the night streets of Panama City. But I never wondered too much. I didn't think he would do a thing like that and not tell me; I didn't think he would cheat and dissemble.

But tonight I would have to see him at this party, and I would have to face the fact that he didn't belong to me any more, and I wanted to run away.

7 ∫

We got to the party late because Stella insisted we stop for drinks at the Dorchester on the way.

'I saw Joe Goldstein in New York,' she said, looking round the bar.

I remembered the first time we had met Joe, in a bar like this one. I remembered his good smile and his pale blue suit.

'He lost all his money,' she said. 'His wife left him for a younger man and he'd signed some insane pre-nuptial thing without reading the small print, so he had to sell the cows and the pictures and she got the lot and now he lives in a two-room apartment downtown and works sewing suits in the garment district. The strange thing is,' she said, drinking her martini, 'that he seems just the same as when we knew him and he had more cows than he could count.'

I felt sad, hearing her say that. I thought of Joe, sitting in his apartment, without even a picture on his wall to look at.

'How does that happen?' said Paco. 'I never know how that happens.'

'Marriage,' said Stella, with a sunny smile. 'It's a dark and dangerous thing.'

After that, we got lost and found ourselves outside the Jesuit church in Farm Street, which wasn't the right address at all.

'We should go in and light a candle for our lost souls,' said Stella. Then she ducked an apologetic look at Paco, who had, after all, been raised in the Roman Church.

'Don't mind me,' he said. 'It's not my hocus-pocus.'

For a moment, I wished I did believe in something like that. It must be so reassuring to believe in God and the saints and heaven and hell, and that all your troubles can be resolved by a quick trip to the confessional box and three Hail Marys. I could hardly imagine what it must be like to know what to believe and not waver from it. Did people like that, the true believers, feel different from the rest of us? Did they have some space in them to which they could retreat because they knew that even the most cruel, the most deranged and pointless, the most meaningless events could be put down to God's grand plan? Did they never have to worry in the same way as the heathens did? Because their God made the world and He was omniscient and He was good and who were we to reason why. Did their hearts ache less because whatever happened they knew it was for the greater good, because their God was in the driving seat and He knew best?

Stella took a look at my face, and linked her arm through mine, and pulled me away gently down the darkening street.

'Come along,' she said to Paco. 'Let's get the hell out of here. Iris is having existential thoughts about why anyone bothered to think up the whole shooting match in the first place.'

'How did you know that?' I said.

'I know,' said Stella. She tugged on my arm and put her shoulder close against mine. 'I haven't been away that long. Most things don't change that much, after all.'

I laughed in the back of my throat. I was glad to have her back, because that hadn't changed at all, and I thought maybe it never would.

'Some things change,' said Paco, and I knew he was thinking of Fred. 'It's not always,' he said, after a pause, 'a bad thing.'

I knew change wasn't a bad thing. I knew that without change we would wither and die, like plants that didn't get enough water. I worked in a business which had change as its pulse and lifeblood; it was something I was schooled in. I wasn't conservative by nature, I hadn't been raised that way; I understood that the world must go forward and not back; I knew that a spurious nostalgia for a golden age when things were so much better was phoney and pointless.

But just then, in the still empty back-streets of Mayfair, with its solid black brick and its clean pavements, its blind windows and its air of secrets and money, I wished, more than I'd ever wished anything, that things hadn't changed.

Stella held on to my arm tight and hard. Paco was walking close on the other side; I could feel the warmth coming off his solid body. I felt like a shadow between them.

There are moments in life, seconds in your daily existence, when time seems to stop and roll back and go into slow motion, and you feel as if you are looking in on yourself, as if you have become some kind of fish-eye lens, distorting your own human frailty.

I had that feeling, just then, walking with these two old friends, these people I had known for so long, through the still suspended streets of Mayfair, and I thought, This isn't happening, none of this is happening, none of this is real. I thought: This happened to some other woman, this didn't happen to me.

I thought: Why is it that we always think the bad things only happen to other people?

I suddenly had a moment of panic. I couldn't remember what Fred looked like. I had heard people say this, about dead loved ones: you saw it in cheesy Yankee films, where the implausibly cute kid says, Daddy, how come I can't remember what Mommy looks like? and Dad, who is one of those Everyman types like the boy next door except for the fact that he earns $20 million a picture, says something like, Why don't you think of her singing and you'll hear her voice? I'd always thought that it was a device, some piece of Hollywood corn, this forgetting-the-face shuffle. But now, in the flat dusk of the city, I couldn't see this face, the one I was missing so much, the one I had spent the last nine years with.

'Stop,' said Stella. She held on faster to my arm. 'We're nearly there, and you look beautiful, and fuck him because he's only a man and odds are you'll be better off without him. You will go on to have a full and rich and varied life, and you will have sex with many strange men, and you will sell many mysterious artworks to rich people who don't need them and you will make many impoverished artists very happy, so just stop, would you please, because it's making me nervous.'

Paco smiled to himself and smoked his cigarette and blew out a thin blue line of smoke at the pewter sky.

'She always could talk,' he said. 'She always could.'

'I'm falling apart,' I said. 'Gravity just stopped keeping me together.'

'You know that's not true,' said Stella.

She stopped walking and turned to face me, and there was an urgency in her, as if she minded more than I did. I brought my eyes into focus and I saw her translucent angular face right in front of me, and I thought that in all the years she had been away, I had never forgotten what she looked like.

'Come on,' she said.

I could see, now she was up close, under the thin evening light, that there were new things about her: some faint marks on her face, traced lines on her forehead, a small crease between her eyebrows as if she had been frowning at something and the skin hadn't sprung back from the effort. I wondered whether it was suffering or just time. Time, I thought, in this hazy loop that my mind was spinning, is the thing that heals all wounds.

'You're going to be fine, Iris,' she said. 'This is the hardest part. You've got to see him now and then it won't be so hard after. The time will pass and one day you'll wake up and you'll have an unfamiliar feeling and you'll be happy again and that's all.'

'She's right,' said Paco.

I looked from one of them to the other. A street-lamp stuttered into life overhead, so their faces were suddenly cast with an orange tint.

'It will be fine,' said Paco. The worst is now, and then it will get better.'

I knew they were right. I knew that I would go to the party, and even though I felt like I was falling apart, I wouldn't. I knew that I would behave with decorum and delicacy. But what I wondered, as I heard myself say, Yes of course, as I watched their faces relax from tension and concern into their normal expressions, as we started walking again – what I really wondered, almost like an irrelevance, was why they accepted so absolutely that it was over, that there was no mistake, no going back.

I just wondered, that's all.

When I first met Fred, in the early urgent days, we used to go to galleries together. That was what we did, for dates.

Whenever I think of those early days, the way you look back into the snapshots of your mind for those moments you remember and treasure and carry with you because you don't want to lose them, because they are part of the fabric and heft of who you are, they are your past and they thread right into what may become your future – when I think back, to the beginning, I remember white walls and single pictures and seeing Fred from the back, across a room, still and distant.

We had an agreement that we wouldn't look at pictures together, because although it's a public act, looking at art – you are on display as much as the picture, in that big communal space, your reactions are as visible as the object on the wall or the floor or the ceiling; and now, in these post-modern times, sometimes you, the observer, become part of the show – it's also a profoundly private thing.

So we went together but we looked separately; we went at different paces; we looked at different things. I remember looking across the room, with that pull and thrill you get in the early days, when it is all new and fresh and hardly believable, and seeing his back turned to me, and wanting to sing because I felt so happy.

That must have been love, surely? Wasn't that what they all wrote about, in the books and the songs and the sonnets? Wasn't it that exact feeling – wanting to burst into song in a public space?

I knew him so well. I knew his history and his attitudes and his postures. I knew the food he wouldn't eat and the books he liked to read and the colours he preferred. I knew the smell of his skin and the feel of it and the look on his face when he was thinking about something else. I knew the feeling I had when I thought I would never love anyone the way I loved him. I remembered the early loss of reality, when I felt like swinging from lamp-posts and telling strangers in the street. I remembered thinking this was more than a human frame could take. I remembered the fearlessness and arrogance of youthful love; I remembered the terror and humility.

I remembered thinking that whatever happens, however

old and grey and wizened and dried up I get, at least I will have had this.

Stella and Paco were talking about something, bickering about some old argument they'd been having ever since I'd known them. I was struck suddenly with this remembering, and I wondered how I could have ever said to Paco I didn't know what love was. Something happens when you are with someone for a length of time; we are all told it and none of us believes it but when you get there it's true. You lose the urgency and the intensity of the early days, that is what everyone says, that is old news. But other things happen too. You stop talking about it – that surging love thing that got you there in the first place – as if you are embarrassed by it, by that heedless flight into a future which holds only the two of you in it. There is room for other people and other things, and sometimes a distance grows between you, which you never thought would happen, and you don't know how to talk about it, so you look the other way and you think it's right and natural and anyway, you're not eighteen any more, and you can't live in people's pockets your whole life.

I thought then, in this Mayfair walk, that perhaps Fred and I had gone through the motions too well. We never stopped talking or having sex; we never reduced ourselves to internecine hostility and point-scoring. But perhaps there had been cracks, and we had covered them over too expertly. Perhaps it would have been better if we had seen them.

I wondered why, when it was so clear to me now that it absolutely was love I felt, that love hadn't been enough.

8 ʃ

The first person I saw when I walked into the party was Jane Doe. For some reason, I had it in my head that the first person I would see would be Fred; I thought, At least I'll get it out of the way at the beginning, I'll have done it.

It didn't happen like that.

There was a hallway paved in black and white tiles, and a mahogany staircase which went up a flight and brought us right into a wide double cube room, without hindrance, so the whole party opened like a picture book. I could see everyone I had ever known in my life, but I couldn't see Fred.

Jane, who was standing at the front of the crowd and visible as an exclamation mark, on account of being dressed head to foot in vermilion slipper satin, smiled widely when she saw us and turned away from the person she was talking to.

'Hello, girls,' she said. She kissed me first and then Stella.

'I heard you were back, Stella,' she said. 'Now you're so famous, maybe I even *read* you were back.'

She laughed and patted Paco on the cheek, and put her arm round my shoulder, and I felt a little better, because you couldn't help it with Jane, that was one of her talents. Once she was smiling her blazing smile at you, you couldn't help but feel your bruised spirits raise up a notch, as if by sheer contagion. It seemed as if somewhere along the line she had cracked the secret of the universe, and she carried it about with her like a fur coat that kept her warm.

'He's not here yet,' she said to me. 'I looked. I should tell you that people are talking, and you'll have to get used to that, because this town is too small for anything else.'

I hadn't thought about it. I hated the idea of people talking, but then, unlike Jane and Stella, I had never had a pressing desire to live a scrutinised life. Me and Paco both, we liked hugging the sidelines and walking in the shadows, where we could be left to our own devices. We let other people go out of doors and make a noise and get noticed.

'Oh,' I said. 'I suppose it's all over town, then.'

'What did you expect?' said Jane. 'The dead art of conversation. People have to have something to talk about. You notice,' she added, 'my discretion in not pestering you for details before. I heard on the Wednesday *before* last, but since you never call and you never write I assumed you wanted to be left awhile. So that's why I didn't ring, in case you were wondering.'

I hadn't wondered. I hadn't been thinking about much beyond my four walls. The world had shrunk to the size of my room. It was easier to stay in one finite place, because at least then I could feel some sense of actuality. Out here, in the world, everything seemed to be shifting, and there were too many people.

'It's OK,' I said. 'I wasn't thinking much at all.'

Stella and Jane looked at each other over my head. I knew that look, I'd seen it before.

'It's all right, really,' I said. 'It's not the worst thing that could have happened. He just left, was all. It's not like he lied or cheated or beat me on a Saturday night when he had nothing better to do. He just left.'

'I'm sorry,' said Jane. 'Nine years is a long time, and

rejection is rejection, whatever fancy name you dress it up in, and none of us is good at that, however much we say our personal affirmations in the morning, so I'm sorry because it's a bloody thing to happen.'

I wondered suddenly what Jane knew about rejection, when she said it in that familiar manner, as if it were something she knew from old. She was so beautiful; that was one of the obvious things about Jane. She was curved and voluptuous, and she carried her curves and her beauty with unaffected panache, as if she had never felt shy or self-conscious or different, which she patently was, not the same as other people; any room you walked into, Jane was the person you noticed first.

I always thought she had something of Marilyn Monroe about her, although without the peroxide and the doomy vulnerability. I mean that she had an irresistible abundance to her, the way she offered all her generous, curving flesh, as if there was plenty more at home. She had eyes set far apart in her face, open a little too wide, so there seemed an air of surprise about her, as if everything she encountered was new and unexpected. She dyed her hair black and wore her lips red, and she was famous for never going in the sun, so her skin was china white, the way they used to wear it in the twenties, before sunbathing became the rage, and she had a nostalgic theatrical look to her, which I sometimes thought she exploited just a little, because the paradox of that and her character, which was sharp and modern and without illusion, pleased her. She liked to wrong-foot people, she liked to watch their faces as they revised their first jumped-to conclusions.

Jane went back with us almost to the beginning. She was famous now for three things: that she was a successful figurative artist in a time that had gone overboard for conceptualism, that everyone who met her wanted to go to bed with her, and that she was a lesbian. When we met her, she wasn't famous for anything. We had heard that there was a new show at a small gallery we knew round the corner from the building where Stella and I lived, and we decided to go. There weren't many people there, which was lucky, because the room was up three flights of stairs and cramped at the best of times.

Paco, Stella and I went together, because we went everywhere together just then.

There wasn't anyone we knew there, but Arturo Sandoval, the great Cuban trumpet player, had come into town for his annual visit, and pretty much everyone had gone down to Ronnie Scott's to see the show. There was a dark girl who looked like something from a forties B-movie standing in the corner not talking to anyone, so we picked her up.

Afterwards, we all had a different version. Stella said it was her green nail varnish that had done it. Paco said that she had reminded him of something out of *La Dolce Vita*, a dark version of Anita Ekberg (Paco was deep in his art-house phase just then; he wouldn't go to a film unless it had no plot and plentiful subtitles, usually white on a white background, so you missed most of them, and only had a half-light fractured sense of what was going on). For myself, I'm not sure what it was. I think I liked the fact that she could stand in a corner of the room, with her black hair and her red mouth, and not look as if she was waiting for anyone to come along and talk to her. She looked as if she didn't care, and later I knew that she didn't.

We went for pizza and drank some cheap red wine and caught the second set at Ronnie Scott's and then we were friends. She told us a week later that she was the artist from the show we had been to see, and then as if it were an irrelevance. She told us that a man in a grey suit that sagged in the wrong places, and I remembered thinking looked like a pervert or an accountant, had turned out to be a software tycoon, and had bought the whole show.

I was young then; it was before Pete Street. I had never heard of anyone buying a whole show before. It smacked of older, headier days, days of profligacy and foolhardiness. I couldn't equate software and ugly grey suits with such *folie de grandeur*. But for all that it was true, and it started a sequence of events that led to Jane Doe becoming taken up and celebrated, shown in New York, Paris and Berlin, seen on television and in the most reputable review sections, and even, on one heady occasion, as a cameo part in an art house film with no plot and subtitles (Paco was beside himself with delight).

I was pleased to see Jane now, not just because pleasure was so intimately associated with her but because when your world is rocked it's nice to find some anchors that won't float away on a high tide.

'Come on,' said Stella, looking round the room. 'I've been out of town too long. Tell us the news.'

Jane always knew the news. She knew the news because it actually interested her. I sometimes thought this tremendous vitality she carried around, this sense of being lit up, of having some mysterious electric current emanating from her, came from the vast capacity she had for enjoyment and curiosity and interest. She was interested in everything, the more twisted and crazed the better.

Jane never took anything for granted; she said that life was fleeting and unreliable so you might as well live it. She got around and she watched and she listened and she asked questions, which is less usual than you might expect, as we race towards the new millennium, steeped in self-absorption. So that was how she always knew the news.

'Your ex is here,' she said to Stella, 'with his boyfriend.'

Stella rolled her eyes and shrugged her shoulders. Before she left for America she had had a short and uncharacteristic affair with Dick Part, the novelist. Dick Part was so obsessed with post-modernism that we were surprised he could do sex at all.

'With state of the art boys like that,' said Jane, at the time, 'you just expect them to sit around and deconstruct sex with irony rather than actually get their hair messed up.'

Dick Part was plastic handsome and highly visible, always at every fashionable party and opening, and when he wasn't out and about, he was on Channel Four, after the watershed. He wrote angry, disaffected books thick with pornography and psychopathy and imminent global meltdown, and when he wasn't being angry and disaffected he liked dressing up in a white tuxedo and drinking martinis with two olives in them. Stella always said she didn't know what came over her.

'Is he gay now?' she said. 'Perhaps it was me that turned him.'

'Don't flatter yourself,' said Jane, smiling.

When she smiled, her mouth stretched open right across her face, and curved up into her cheeks. It was a real smile, not a social convention. It was like the sun coming out on a dark day.

'It's fashion, that's all,' she said. 'It's so outmoded to be straight that he closed his eyes and thought of God Save the Queen.'

'Poor Dick,' said Stella. 'He was quite nice when he forgot who he was.'

'And,' said Jane, finishing her glass and looking round for more, 'the art babies have a new look: their little tottery feet are too sore from last season's three-inch heels, so they've reinvented flip-flops. They say that thongs ain't what they used to be.'

Paco smiled and shook his head. He had a soft spot for the art babies, which was what Jane called the clueless girls who sat front-of-house in the bigger galleries. In the fifties, you got débutantes who did an undemanding job in London until they got married and settled in the country with a double-barrel husband and a yawning Labrador dog and two children dressed head to foot in flower-print Viyella. In the nineties, you got the art babies.

They were thin as sticks because they had no clue how to cook, they had long hippie hair which they skewered up on top of their heads with chopsticks or old Biros, they had sweet smiles and eyes like vacant lots. They were notorious for knowing nothing about art while retaining with steel-trap clarity the most sordid detail of the private lives of every living artist in Britain, and quite a few in New York and Paris as well. They did nothing all day except talk to each other on the telephone and cut off clients when they rang up to speak to their dealers. They wore flimsy sixties skirts and tiny beaded cardigans and mules with vertiginous heels, so they were always teetering everywhere, as if they had had a little too much to drink. The dealers used them because they were cheap and they never complained and they were too daffy to form a union, so they worked for no money and no pension and, aside from the rank inefficiency, they looked very pretty and that kept the punters happy.

Jane loved the art babies, not only because she quite wanted to go to bed with them.

'It's not just sex,' she always said. 'They're all straight anyway, those poor deluded girls. It's the breathless old-fashioned thing of it, as if everything that has happened in the world in the last thirty years passed them entirely by. Did they know there was once a Cold War? Did they know they were born under the threat of nuclear annihilation? Have they heard that the Berlin Wall came down? Did they know that there was one?'

Jane admired extremes; the blatant other-worldliness of the art babies enchanted her. 'They're so pretty and ignorant,' she said.

Stella said that they were encouraging people to live in a time warp. She said they should be punished by being sentenced to a lifetime of giving Tupperware parties.

'All that lisping and giggling and tottering about on those shoes,' she said. 'Why don't they just get their feet bound and be done with it?'

Jane said that they were silly and decorative enough to be forgiven everything.

'And,' she said now, 'they've been very cast down lately because someone told them Picasso was dead. They all wore black cardigans for a week.'

'A nice mark of respect,' said Stella. 'Those clever girls.'

'And,' said Jane, 'Walter Delaware became very excited last Thursday because he heard there was a puma loose in Potters Bar.'

'Walter Delaware never went to Potters Bar in his life,' said Stella.

'I know,' said Jane, 'but it's the kind of thing he gets excited about.'

I was thinking about Walter, the most famously pompous of the art critics (although some people said it was a close run thing with Treve Pettit). I was watching Paco, who was not listening, smiling to himself at one of his own internal jokes, and I turned my head just a half-turn, and Fred came in the door and took a couple of steps into the room and stood in front of me, and blinked and looked surprised and said, 'I didn't think you would come.'

Not hello-how-are-you-is-your-heart-in-pieces-on-the-floor-where-I-left-it? Not sorry-I-didn't-call-to-explain-but-I- never-had-the-nerve-for-it. Just that: I didn't think you would come.

The projector snapped back into focus and the party, which had stopped for a moment, took to life again with a small, polite roar.

'Pete Street is my friend,' I said, talking very slowly and

carefully so as not to let the words fly into a high register where I couldn't account for them any more.

'Of course I came,' I said. 'I can't stay indoors for the rest of my life just because you don't want to fuck me any more.'

I was surprised when I heard myself say that. It wasn't the kind of thing I normally said. It sounded like someone else had written the lines.

I was pleased I'd said it.

It gave Fred a small shock, I could see it flicker in his eyes and slide down the back of his black suit.

He looked down at his feet and then up again and around the room. I felt as if the crowd had lined up behind me to watch the show. I didn't dare look back in case I lost my nerve.

'We had to see each other sooner or later,' I said. 'What did you think? I'd get north of the park and you'd stay east of Piccadilly Circus and that way we'd never have to endure embarrassment?'

He shifted his feet some more and muttered something I couldn't hear.

Suddenly I didn't feel weak and frightened any more. I felt resigned and tired. His face was sliding into patterns and shapes that I didn't recognise. I could see him slipping away from the past in front of my eyes.

'Well,' I said.

I was going to say something about Have a good time, or Have a good night, or See you next year, but I never got to that part, because just then a girl came in the door behind Fred, and walked right up to him and put her arm through his and pulled a small piece of lint from his lapel and kissed him on the corner of the mouth all in one sinuous proprietary movement and I was so astonished that whatever I had been going to say dried right there in my mouth before it got anywhere.

The girl looked up and saw me.

'Oh,' she said. 'Shit.'

Fred cleared his throat.

'This is,' he said, to no one in particular. 'This is.'

I walked away before he could say her name. I knew her face: she was a restorer who cleaned up lost pictures for the Bond Street boys, the old-master specialists who liked to go down to country sales and find a blackened Gainsborough for half a grand and sell it at Christie's, Park Ave. the next month for half a million. She took the black off in a small room over a fire escape behind Bruton Street.

I had no idea why she was draped over Fred, who until two weeks ago had been with me.

I knew that if I stayed I would do something foolish, so I left. It wasn't a grand gesture or a theatrical exit. I had to get out because I could feel sweat starting up on my forehead and it seemed as if the windows were all closed and the walls were slanting in on me, and I could hear a rushing sound in my ears like running water, and I didn't want to make more of a fool of myself than I had already.

Outside, the night was black and still and cool.

I walked down the road and stopped and leant against a building. I could feel the white stone smooth and solid against my back.

I felt an amorphous panic rising in me. I walked forward and back; I turned round and put the palms of my hands against the wall and took a breath and tried to get a hold on myself.

I gave something between a cough and a laugh and then I started crying; loud ugly crying, not movie-star misty melancholic tears, but raw red ones that make a noise and make a mess and come right up from inside of you so that you don't know where to put them.

A car drove past slowly; the driver looked at me with

curiosity but no concern. Perhaps there were too many people crying in the city for it to be anything to remark on.

I felt entirely alone and abandoned and all I could do was stand in that darkened street and cry like a child.

Then Stella and Jane and Paco came out and took me gently and put me in a cab and drove me home.

I lay back on the sofa and drank the brandy Stella had given me.

'He's with someone else,' I said. I heard the words come out loud and actual into the room; I saw Natalie Hedge in my head, with her hands on Fred.

'What is this?' I said. 'How did this happen?'

Jane looked at the ground.

'I heard last week,' she said. 'I saw Michael. He told me.'

'Does everyone fucking know this except me?' I said.

I was angry suddenly. I was spitting roasting furious and I wanted to kill someone.

Paco and Stella were looking at Jane. She looked back at them and shrugged up her shoulders.

'I don't know,' she said. 'I never heard anything. I was as shocked as you are.'

There was a silence. No one wanted to speak first.

'Come on,' I said. 'How much worse can it get? I've just been humiliated in front of four hundred swinging Londoners. My boyfriend's left and he's sleeping with someone else and everyone knew but me. If Michael knows, everyone knows. He never could keep a secret. So how much lower can you go?'

'I didn't think you were humiliated,' said Paco, his voice coming strong into the room. 'I thought you walked out of that party like you had a vocation.'

'I was going to vomit,' I said.

There was a silence again and they were looking uncomfortable. A lonely thought wandered through my head: perhaps, I thought, one day, a long time from now, I'll look back and think this was funny. Or perhaps not.

'How long?' I said.

'Two years,' said Jane.

'Two *years?*' I said.

I felt my mouth slide open in cartoonish disbelief.

'That's what Michael said,' said Jane. 'I don't know.'

'No,' I said. 'That's not right. I would have known. You know things like that. That's the whole point. There are signs, and you read them, and you know. It can't be, it can't, it wasn't two . . .'

I heard my voice peter out and I put out my hands in a supplicating gesture, as if they could tell me it was all a terrible mistake and we could go back to the beginning and start again, this time with the right story and the right people.

They talked some more. I sat and pretended it wasn't happening to me, that it wasn't true.

But it was true, whatever I wished. Fred had been sleeping with Natalie Hedge for two years and everyone knew but me.

9

The weeks dragged slowly past. Stella and Paco moved out. Stella's old flat from our Soho days had come up for rent again, and even though the rates were sky high, on account of Soho having been ponced up enough for it to be a most desirable quartier these days, filled with media hot-shots and les boys, swinging their beautiful legs around with a new blatancy, Stella could afford it.

Her first book had been bought by Hollywood and was locked in development hell in a white-walled office in Burbank, but the money was in the bank, so she didn't care. They were sure to butcher it, whichever way it came out, so she said she'd rather have the money and the film never get to celluloid. That way, she could afford the rent and eat out when she wanted. (Stella hated cooking; the blast of heat that came out of ovens and off stove tops made her sweat and blush, she became flustered and distracted. Let someone else do that, she said, it was worth the money.)

The flat had been opened out and knocked into the one upstairs, where Frank Mitchell used to live, 'Before they carried him out feet first,' said Stella, with macabre relish.

Frank's abused heart had finally stopped three years ago; he lay in his bed clutching a bottle of Irish whiskey to his chest for two days before anyone thought to look for him. The mortician, it was reported up and down Old

Compton Street, had been surprised that the body didn't smell worse. Pickled in alcohol, said the pundits, preserved in Bushmills; Frank had drunk so much in his lifetime that he didn't rot. The lushes who still climbed the afternoon staircases to rooms famous in the fifties found tremendous consolation in this, and drank to Frank's memory with renewed vigour.

The owner of the building, relieved to get rid of Frank with his sixty-a-day Embassy habit and his erratic financial arrangements, knocked down a couple of walls, bunged the local councillor to get round planning restrictions, painted everything white, put in a modern zinc kitchen, and called it, somewhat ambitiously, a duplex.

'Oh, please,' said Stella, when Paco told her this. 'I came three thousand miles to get away from things called duplexes.'

Despite this and the stratospheric rent, she took it 'for old times' sake, if nothing else', and Paco moved into the second bedroom, and they said it would do for the time being.

They were loath to leave me. They were worried, I could see. They weren't sure what I might do, left to myself.

I encouraged them to go. I felt tired; I wanted to be left alone. They were too vital, too full of energy and life. I sat, devoid of ideas or propulsion, as if someone had inserted a needle into a strategic part of my body and drained out all the vital fluids. I said it was all right, that I would be all right, that they should go.

'I need,' I said, 'to be by myself for a while.'

'This is what happens,' said Stella. 'You don't go out and you sit and think, and you sit and worry at it like an old scab, and you think of the old times and the good times, and you fall into a decline, and you stop eating, and you sit up all night when everyone in the world is asleep except for you, reading terrible old novels and writing long and winding entries in your diary, and you sleep in the day, and you walk around feeling like you've got jet-lag, and you get dislocated and disassociated and you feel as if the rest of the world has got nothing to do with you, and before you know it, you've dug yourself into a black pit and you can't climb out, and there you are.'

'Is that what happens?' said Paco. 'All that happens?'

'It was a long time ago. It was after my mother,' said Stella. 'I tried to be brave but it didn't work very well.'

'You were young then,' I said. I put on a calm, level voice and made my face look straight and not too fucked up. 'This isn't death. It's a thing that happens. I'll be fine. Maybe I'll even go and see someone.'

'Grief counselling,' said Stella, taking on an encouraging everything-will-be-fine voice. 'That's what you need. Go and find some nice couch to sit on and talk all about it.'

'It's only a man,' I said, joining in the spirit of the thing. 'I don't know if love is meant to last for ever anyway. Who started that big idea? Who spread that rumour?'

'I don't know,' said Stella. 'I don't see it working so very well. The biologists say that polygamy is the most natural state, but guess who gets to have the multiple partners? Not the woman, that's for sure.'

'Oh,' said Paco, looking stricken. 'More than one at a time? It's bad enough having to deal with one.'

'You're such a cynic about love,' said Stella. 'You just walk around convinced it's going to end in tears so you never even try.'

There was a small pause. Paco looked away and screwed up his face.

'Not surprising,' he said.

Stella realised what she had said and didn't know where to look or what to say.

'It's all right,' said Paco. 'You know. It is.'

'I'm sorry,' said Stella. 'I'm sorry, I am. That wasn't sensitive.'

Paco's mother used to get beaten by his father; every week she had purple swellings round her eye, blue and yellow bruises over her cheek. She had always walked into a door, or fallen down the stairs, that was the official verdict. Paco didn't question it, but he and his sister heard the heavy sounds of dispute coming up through the floorboards of their bedroom when they were supposed to be asleep. They heard the shouting and the stumbling and the horrible dead sound that knuckles make when they connect with flesh. His father left when Paco was ten; he walked out to go to the pub and was never seen again. People said he might be dead in a brawl, on account of his pugnacious nature. There was talk of another woman, living somewhere in Chalk Farm. Paco still wondered if one day he would run into a familiar face on the Underground or in the street and find it was his father.

But that wasn't the worst of it. The beating was bad, but domestic violence is such a commonplace that Paco and his family saw no reason to make a big number out of it. They got on as best they could; money was tight, but there was a taut sense of relief in the house because there wasn't someone coming back with a bellyful of beer and swinging fists on a Saturday night, although no one ever talked about it. It was what happened. (Stella was once asked on a radio phone-in on feminism why in this enlightened age the figures for domestic violence were rising, why men still hit women so routinely. 'I'm not a psychologist,' Stella said, 'but I should imagine it's because they can.')

Paco and his sister grew up good as gold, not wanting to worry their mother. They worked hard at school, kept their clothes clean, were polite and amenable to suggestion. They ate their greens and went to bed when they were told.

Paco's sister, Jeanie, was a year older than he, and

when she was nineteen she got pregnant and married her boyfriend in a rushed but happy ceremony at Westminster register office.

Six months later, Jeanie's husband threw her down a flight of steps and she and the baby died.

Stella and I weren't prepared for that. We were used to sitting with Paco in cafés in Soho arguing about pop music and selling out and other teen subjects: suddenly we had to deal with death. We went with him to the funeral, and to the wake afterwards, which didn't last long because it seemed obscene to be talking and drinking tea and acting normal after what had happened. Later we went back to Soho and Paco sat in Stella's flat and drank at a bottle of brandy we'd bought him.

'Brandy for shock,' said Stella, young and human and helpless. 'That's all I know.'

We talked for a while. Then we ran out of things to say and Paco sat on the bed and cried all night long.

After that, he never spoke about it. He went to his mother's house and cleared out all his stuff, went back to his one room in Beak Street and never saw her again. I think he blamed her in some way; for not throwing his father out earlier, for letting Jeanie repeat the same pattern. After a couple of years, we heard that she had moved to Spain to be with her mother and, as far as I know, she's there still.

I thought of that time, after Stella and Paco moved out. It wasn't something we talked about now; if you hadn't known that Paco once had a sister, a mother, you would never guess. Sometimes I watched American TV shows late at night on the commercial channels, and everyone was always talking on them, determined to keep their secrets out in the open, sanitised with talking. I wondered why we didn't do that. I couldn't tell whether it was because we weren't American, or because we weren't on TV.

I wondered if I was failing Paco, whether I should ask him about Jeanie, whether he still thought of her, whether he was haunted by the vision of her bent and broken body at the bottom of the staircase. Although he could talk when the mood was in him, he would go for days without saying much. He watched and listened, and he had a whole internal deal going on, some antic inner life that sometimes took him off guard and made him laugh. His face would change and you knew that he wasn't with you any more, and he would smile or laugh out loud and you got used to the fact that there was never any point asking him the joke because it was between himself and this inner thing and you had to be there.

As I sat alone, in the nights after he and Stella moved out, I thought about this. I remembered the funeral of his sister; I remembered the clean crematorium and the stilted readings and the blank disbelieving faces and the coffin sliding irrevocably through a black gap in the wall. I remembered thinking, This isn't right, this isn't real. I was very young and I didn't believe in death.

Now I thought, This is exactly what happens. Life is a series of losses; it's inevitable, there's no fighting it. You lose your parents, your grandparents, along the way some friends, maybe a cousin or a sister. You think these things won't happen to you, but they do because death is random and sure at the same time. There's always the chance it will get you first; you have to factor that into the equation. You might have a sudden tumour or a speeding motor, there might be something as mundane as a careless trip on a concrete step, or as exotic as a disease they don't have a name for yet.

You lose other things, as well. You lose innocence; you

lose illusions and perhaps vanity too; you learn that life happens to all of us, pretty much the same.

There was a knock at the door. I started. It seemed to me as if I was sitting on the same chair, in the same clothes, in the same frame of mind as I had since Stella and Paco left. I had a moment of confusion. I didn't know how long I'd been sitting there. (Days? Weeks?) I had turned the telephone off and locked the door and now I didn't know how much time had passed or where it had gone.

This, I thought, is how it starts. I'd always wondered, about the mad sad women, the ones with the bright starting eyes and the grey skin and the fanatical gleam in their faces as they stalked the city streets, because they knew about the end of the world and the imminent alien invasion and the numberless government conspiracies; they *knew*. I wondered how it was they got that way; they must once have had lives and jobs and families and hopes. I wondered what happened for them to let all that slide away.

I suddenly saw. It didn't take much. It didn't take death or destitution; it didn't take something big and screenworthy. It could just be unhappiness, because unhappiness gets like a habit and there's no reason to pull yourself out of it and one day you wake up and you're sixty and your hair is uncombed and your face is the colour of old teeth and you go to the shops and tell anyone who will listen that it wasn't a lone gunman, it was J. Edgar Hoover in a frock.

My landlord was standing at the door.

I hadn't seen him for a while; he had been travelling. He had never done that when he was young, he was too busy being a baby tycoon, but now he could walk down London streets and look up at stone walls and figured cornicing and say, That's my building, just like he always wanted, he was making up for all the trips he never made. The last three weeks, he had been in Alaska. He said he'd always wanted to go to Alaska, on account of his mother playing a song when he was young that went 'I'm going no-o-orth to Alaska, I'm going north, the rush is on.'

I was fond of Jem and usually I was pleased to see him. But now all I thought was here was someone who didn't know the whole story and I would have to tell it to him.

He kissed my cheek and said hello, and I stood back from the door and let him in. He looked around and I wondered what he thought about the mess and the air of neglect that hung over the apartment, as if someone didn't really live here any more. It smelt stale and flat. I went to open a window, but they were already open. It wasn't stuffiness, that smell, it was lack of life.

Jem smiled at me; he had a wide genuine smile which always made me wonder why he had become a business-man. It was the smile of a violin player; it was open and uncomplicated and uncontrived. It didn't belong to a shark and a speculator.

'I want you to find an Edgar Dime for me,' he said.

This wasn't the conversation I had been expecting. He was supposed to say why was the rent late and what was I doing here at home on a work day and why did I look like shit.

'Fred and I broke up,' I said, trying to get things back on track.

'I know that,' said Jem.

He took a ball of builder's putty out of his pocket and started rolling it in his fingers. He did that sometimes, when he was bored or in need of reassurance. He was improbably tall and his arms and legs seemed to fold over themselves in an attempt to find a place to fit, but he had small neat precise hands. I watched them now, tugging at the putty, pulling it as far as it would go without breaking.

'Is it published somewhere?' I said.

I was angry, but in a distant second-hand way, as if it was coming at me through a layer of felt.

'Does everyone know?' I said.

I could hear a singsong plaintive note in my voice, unlike me.

'Is it on the Net?' I said, still in that alien tone of voice.

'I saw Paco,' said Jem. 'He told me. I thought maybe you wouldn't want to talk about it.'

There we went again, not talking about it. It was voguish, just then, to say that we were living in the confessional age, the therapy age, but I wondered sometimes. I thought we were making a category error. We saw American films and American television shows and *Jerry Springer* and *Oprah*; we ate McDonald's and called it food; we read Bellow and Roth and Stephen King; we listened to Madonna and the soundtrack of *Grease*; we sometimes thought we *were* American.

Then you go to America and you see the real thing and you wonder how on earth you could have made that mistake.

We thought we were baring our souls and sharing with the group, but really we were doing what we had always done, in true British tradition, which was sitting at home and not talking about it.

'You're right,' I said. 'I don't want to talk about it. One day everything is fine and expected, and then Fred says he's leaving and I find out that he's fucking someone else and that he's been fucking someone else for two fucking years and everyone in this whole stinking town knew about it except me. So,' I said, staring at Jem belligerently, like it was his fault, which in some ways, just at this very moment, it was, because he was a man, and there are times when you think they are all the same, fucking and cheating and lying and bashing, because they *can*, 'what's there to talk about?'

Jem wasn't the kind who would come over and hug you to him and tell you to let it out because otherwise you might go mad with it all held tight and hard in your chest. He had been brought up by a mother who told him that touching was sissy, along with crying, complaining, demanding and, most of all, talking about it.

'There's this Dime,' he said.

I told him I didn't want to do it. I told him the whole bloody art world could go and take a running jump. I said I hoped they all contracted some tropical disease and died slowly with their skin flaking off and the blood vessels in their eyes bursting so that they cried tears of blood.

'You don't mean that,' said Jem, mildly. When he wasn't ruthlessly sharking his way round the property pool, he was a mild and reasonable man.

'You don't know I don't mean it,' I said. 'I'm lost and betrayed and don't tell me to grow up and be a big girl because I don't want to.'

'I wouldn't tell you that,' said Jem. 'I want to find this Dime and I know that you can do it and I can't, because I don't have that kind of talent and that kind of knowledge and you do.'

'Are you doing this out of pity?' I said. 'Is that what this is?'

'I'm interested in the painting, that's all,' said Jem. 'And I heard you'd quit your job.'

'You can stop being so fucking rational,' I said. 'You can stop sitting there and acting like it all makes sense.'

'You'll feel better soon,' said Jem. 'The first two months are the worst, and you think there's no point to anything and you might as well sit by the railway tracks and watch the trains go by. Then it gets better.'

'You don't know that,' I said. 'You're just saying that.'

'I know,' said Jem. 'I was the man standing at the altar while Dustin Hoffman came and started yelling and Katherine Ross picked up her skirts and ran down the aisle the way she came.'

I stared in sudden shocked fascination. This, I realised, was as close as Jem got to talking about it.

'You were jilted at the altar?' I said. 'When did that happen?'

'Fifteen years ago,' said Jem. 'Last Wednesday, actually. It wasn't the altar, exactly. It was a registry office. It was Caxton Hall.'

'So what happened?' I said.

Jem gave a brief smile.

'I thought my life was over, and then I thought, Fuck them if they can't take a joke, and I did my first big deal and I made a shed load of money and then I'd done it and I'd shown everyone I could do it, even though I was officially too young for that kind of game. It was better after that.'

'I don't have a head for business,' I said.

'But you can find me that Dime,' said Jem.

Jem sat and looked at me like it was a sane and usual request. He lay his long body back against my warped green sofa and let the silence build.

I found myself looking at him, suddenly, shockingly, as a sexual entity. I thought I would never imagine going to bed with anyone ever again; now, abruptly, I found myself wondering if I could go to bed with Jem. People say only men do that, and I think in some ways it's true, men do it more automatically, it's their calling card, their handshake, their first seven seconds: Could I go to bed with you?

Men say, men I know, that the answer almost always is Yes.

I think it's different for girls. But then I think almost everything is different for girls.

I looked at Jem, in that unexpected, unasked-for moment, and I wondered. And the answer, just in case you're curious, was No.

10 $\int$

Jem left after a while. I sat and thought after he had gone; I wondered if he had been sent, whether Jane or Stella had got a hold of him and told him to amble along and give me a project, something to keep my flat mind off my empty aching heart.

Here is something else I wondered, in those drab weeks: *why* does it hurt in the heart? It hurt first in the stomach, and there was a numb aching in the head, the feeling of having your skull caught in a vice; but as the days passed and the initial shock subsided into knowledge of this fact, this unarguable *thing*, that Fred was gone and belonging to someone else, my heart started to ache, with a dull persistent yearning pain.

I did biology at school; I know that the heart is nothing more than a pump, a reliable and clever piece of mechanics that keeps everything else on track. I've seen pictures of the heart, so red and compact, with its auricles and ventricles, its membranous sac and its sprouting arteries (those same arteries that get silted up with fat and high living and cause it to seize up and stop without warning). It doesn't suggest anything romantic or spiritual or metaphysical. Those pictures, of that small bag, no more than the size of your fist, don't make you think of Keats or Donne or Shakespeare. But all the same, those old poets, they knew that the heart was where it happened.

It's so busy pumping and beating, what time does it have for breaking and aching and yearning, what does it know about sorrow and loss? But that's where you feel it, a pulling ache in the left side of your chest, until you want to hit yourself there, just to make it stop, until you think you can't stand it any more.

Maybe, I thought, Jem did want to find the Dime. I wondered if it was to do with love or money. Edgar Dime was dead and gone but his pictures sold every year, they were where money was, and where money was, Jem was sure to shark his way, sooner or later. Money gets like a habit, like that, like a needle in the vein: people don't want it any more for what it can get them, they just need the hit of the next million.

Jem might have been a mild and a reasonable man when he was out of the office, but he had the scent of money too far in his nostrils now ever to lose it. There was a whiff of ruthlessness that hung about him like cigar smoke. He walked like us and talked like us, but he was different all the same. It was easy to forget, because he seemed ordinary and personable on the surface, he could be shy and gauche on occasion, he had perfect manners and remembered people's birthdays. But to make a lot of money you have to really love it. I don't mean Stella kind of money, I don't mean a quarter of a million green dollars for a film deal: I mean serious money, the kind of money you can't spend, the kind that makes things happen.

To get that you have to love it, you have to want it, you have to believe in it. To me it was dead and inexplicable pieces of paper; it had no mystique or allure. But to Jem it was a living thing. I sometimes thought he had an almost sexual relationship with it; he spoke of finishing a deal as a man might talk about seducing a difficult woman. He loved money, and he wanted money, and however much he got, it was never quite enough. I thought he would still be cutting deals when he was eighty, crippled arthritic fingers clutching at the telephone receiver, reedy old voice giving instructions to buy it all.

That was the difference between Jem and me. Sometimes I liked it, I thought it a touch of the exotic, like a hothouse plant from some foreign jungle; other times I found it disturbing and sinister. But then, I don't think I had ever forgiven money for that sale in New York, for the absolute degrading of Dr Gachet, when the society witches in their Chanel suits and their Harry Winston rocks stood on their seats and clapped wildly as the hammer went down on eighty-two million dollars and change.

I wasn't sure that I could find the Dime, and I didn't know if I wanted to try. I didn't know if I wanted Jem to get his hard, fiscal hands on it, to get it and punt on it and sell it on to the highest bidder. I didn't know where it was, if it still existed, whether it was stolen and sitting in a vault in the holiday mansion of some Swiss banker, only seen in the crepuscular light of a windowless basement room. I wondered if it might not be best left where it was. I thought sometimes things were best left alone.

I knew that most of this was justification. Right now, I didn't want to do anything, because my bloody heart was aching too hard in my chest, and I didn't see any point in anything, not even finding a lost Dime.

So I put it out of my mind, and went back to lying on my sofa and gazing at the ceiling and listening to Billie Holiday records, which seemed to be my routine just now. Sometimes I broke for lunch and ate a cheese sandwich.

The only thing I did believe, just then, was that time would heal. I couldn't believe that I could go on feeling like this for a great length of time: my body wouldn't sustain it, this aching and emptiness. I thought time would heal because it had to; I thought if I sat still, one day things would seem all right again. I felt like I was in a closed twilight zone of my own. I had a nostalgic and distant memory of normality; I thought, if I was quiet and patient, that would come back to me. That was my plan.

The more I thought about it, the more I thought it was a good plan. I could turn off my telephone and close out the world and wait for the storm to pass.

Two weeks into my plan, there was a knocking at the door. (All these knockings at the door; I had a sudden absurd memory of a play I'd seen once, some confused tangle between Ibsen and high farce, walking a thin line between tragedy and bathos and comedy, everyone always knocking at the door with portent and urgent news and the wrong man's wife.) This was unexpected and unwelcome; also inexplicable. I had called those who might interrupt – Stella, Jane, Paco, Jem – and told a white lie. I said I was going away, to get a rest from the city and gather my resources. I said I was going to the Scottish mountains, to the Highlands, to look at the heather.

I was expecting opposition, from Jane in particular, who always said that she came out in hives if she had to go further into the country than Essex. I was expecting them to make suggestions of their own, to offer to come with me, keep me company. Company was the last thing I wanted. Company wasn't in the plan. But the mere mention of mountains seemed to work some kind of magic, like a secret password. Oh, yes, they said, that's a fine idea. Perhaps they felt a small shameful relief that I was doing something, going away for a moment, so they could return to their own lives and take a week off from worrying about me. However much you love someone, there are limits to compassion. Compassion fatigue, they used to call it, in the eighties, when greed was good.

I told my lie. By the fourth time I entirely believed that I was about to pack up and take the fast train to Inverness. I had a vivid picture in my mind of driving to Wick and taking the ferry for Stromness or Scrabster. I had always dreamt of Orkney and Shetland. They were the most distant points on the weather map; they seemed in some magical way like the end of the world, the last point before you fell off the edge. I had heard stories, I knew that the light was different there, that the accent was more Nordic than Scottish, that everything stopped flat on Sundays.

After I put the telephone down on Paco, the last one I called with this story, I started to the door, as if I had really packed a bag and planned a route, consulted maps and charts, timetables and hotel guides. Then the fantasy stopped abruptly, and I realised with rank satisfaction that now I could get back to my real plan, which was being left alone and waiting for time to do its thing.

So when the knock came at the door, I felt surprise and resentment and also a brief access of fear. I had been watching late-night television, which seemed to consist entirely of stalkers and crazies and waiters at the gates, preying on a series of hapless women. Women in those films are always blonde and slightly weathered, as if they went out in the sun too much, without a hat. They are the kind of women you might think would be tough and resourceful, but always turn out to be clueless and borderline alcoholic. The stalkers and rapists and psychotics are cold and clinical and utterly efficient, until the last reel, when they lose their medication and unravel just in time for poor Blondie to get rescued by a burly and modest police detective.

The vision of the stranger at the door was fast followed by a picture of Fred, penitent and begging for restitution.

I wondered when my plan was going to start working.

I opened the door. My cousin Pansy stood on the doorstep, accompanied by a very elegant man dressed in an emerald green suit. I was so surprised that I stood there for a moment blinking at them.

Pansy had never been the kind of girl who let a silence lie for long. Pansy was always moving, and when she wasn't moving, she was talking. I remembered this instantly from our childhood, from our teen years in north London.

She put her arms round me and said Hello here I am and walked into my room and looked around and held out her hand towards the man in the green suit and said this was her friend William and they had just that minute got in from San Francisco and wasn't this the damnedest thing and when was it we had last seen each other.

'Pansy,' I said, in astonishment. I started laughing, it all seemed so absurd and unexpected.

'Is it the suit?' said William, gazing with despair at one lapel. He looked over at Pansy. 'I said it was too pale. Didn't I say it was too pale? Didn't I say that, with my colouring?'

'Oh, stop,' said Pansy, twisting round on one heel. 'You know green and black work perfectly. You know that. You're jet-lagged is all. Anyway, she's not laughing at you, she wouldn't do that, not my cousin Iris I haven't seen since I can't remember when, not since we were young and foolish and still believing in happy endings. Iris wouldn't do that, would you, Iris?'

I brought my eyes back into focus. I felt as if I were at the theatre, at a fringe show somewhere, where they did this kind of thing.

'No,' I said seriously to William. 'I wasn't laughing at you.'

He gave me a doubtful smile and looked down again at his suit. I wondered how it was that he could have survived a trans-atlantic flight to emerge so pressed and polished. It seemed as if he had a faint sheen over him; he stood there, epicene and brilliant, lighting up my neglected room.

'She's laughing because she wasn't expecting to see me,' said Pansy.

She looked from one of us to the other, and then she stretched her neck back, as if it was aching a little. I remembered that gesture as if it were yesterday: she always used to plant herself somewhere and stretch her neck, slowly and gracefully, as if she were some kind of wild animal. Pansy made you think of an animal, although you were never sure what species; the kind of animal they hadn't invented yet. There was something lawless and feral about her, for all the talking and the Lower East Side haircut and the three rings in each ear, for all that she was clearly a product of some sophisticated metropolitan centre. There was nothing fey or wistful about Pansy, she was a street girl to her fingertips.

I always thought you could put her on any block in any city in the world and within a half hour she would have a clique of bosom buddies and know where to get the best Thai food for under ten dollars. But despite her clearly artificial nature, despite the fact that she was absolutely her own invention, I thought whenever I was watching a nature programme that something like Pansy would prowl across the screen one time and take me by surprise.

'Say something, Iris,' she said, dropping her bag on the floor and taking out a pack of cigarettes and lighting one up and blowing the smoke out in a long dun-coloured stream. 'Say Welcome to England.'

'Welcome to England,' I said.

I suddenly realised I meant it. I was happy to see her because she was my cousin and my friend and when you were with her you knew that none of the usual rules applied.

There's a horrible cliché people use: a breath of fresh air, they say, but that's truly what she was like. When she walked into a room, she brought something with her;

not fresh air, exactly, but *different* air, something new and exciting, something suggestive and evocative. So how could I not be pleased to see her, with her beautiful and immaculately dressed friend?

'Welcome,' I said, 'to bloody England.'

They sat themselves down and William got out a bottle of dark rum, which he had bought duty-free.

'I don't normally drink rum,' he said, with a hint of apology. 'I'm not really that kind of boy. But I suddenly had a yearning for it, good dark rum, all the way from the Caribbean.'

He pronounced it Carr-*i*-byan. He had a lilting West Indian accent, mixed in with some American, and sudden unexpected bursts of English.

'William comes from Grenada,' said Pansy.

The Spice Island, I thought hazily. If things had been different, we might have been related.

'Half Grenadian, half Irish,' said William, pouring out his rum, the American in his accent incongruously strong. 'You do the math.'

We clinked our glasses and drank the rum down and subsided into our chairs, as if some arcane ritual had been performed, and now we could relax and get on with the main action.

'So,' said Pansy, 'tell me about your life.'

'You first,' I said. I shook my head. 'What were you doing in San Francisco?'

Last time I heard from her, a hundred years ago, she was in New York, taking a postgraduate course in ecology at NYU. She had enough of her hippie mother in her to want to save the planet, although she had flirted with the idea of rebellion in her teens. Problem was, rebelling against a libertarian, dope-smoking, free-speech-protesting, political-prisoner-writing, consciousness-raising mother meant becoming a rabid old reactionary, and Pansy said she just didn't have it in her.

'I did think,' she said to me, down a clear transatlantic line, in the days when we were still keeping in touch, 'of wearing blue serge and voting Republican and supporting nuclear power and becoming pro-life and marrying a nice chauvinist who would call me his little wife and expect me to cook three courses to impress his clients, but I knew I couldn't do it.'

So Pansy never got to rebel, she just grew up and went her own way, which was exactly what my aunt Ursula had wanted. Pansy said she felt in some obscure way that she had missed out on something.

'When your mum has gone naked at Woodstock and experimented with every drug known to man and embraced free love,' she always said, 'there's not much competition. Anything I would call rebellion, she would call yester-day's news.'

For all that, Pansy and Ursula got on fine. They had some-thing I didn't see too often with mothers and daughters: they *admired* each other. (Sometimes I felt envy at that; I sometimes wondered what would have happened if my mother had stayed. I wondered whether my whole life would have been different, whether I would have grown into a different woman. It was pointless, this wondering, because I would never know. I just thought about it some-times, that's all.)

'I went to San Francisco,' said Pansy, 'because New York was cold.'

'Too hot in summer,' said William. 'And humid, I'm telling you.'

'And humid,' said Pansy, nodding. 'I had a bad love affair, and I was sad and bruised and wanted a change, and someone had sent me a postcard of the bay and it looked so blue and open and inviting and I thought, It won't snow in the winter there, I won't trek out on my stoop and find the neighbourhood bum has frozen to death on the sidewalk, so they had to scrape him off the asphalt when they came to take him away. It looked like the land of milk and honey to me, so I packed a bag and went.'

'That's when she met me,' said William. He looked around. 'Do you have a cracker?' he said.

'William is always hungry,' said Pansy.

'In the cupboard,' I said. 'There's something. Help yourself. There's cheese in the fridge.'

'I like *cheese*,' said William.

'So I got myself to San Francisco and I found a place in North Beach, and I got a job, and I stayed, until now, when I left,' said Pansy.

I remembered this too; she would make complicated and tortuous events sound simple and compacted, as if travelling clean across a continent to a new city, finding an apartment, getting a job and settling were as simple as going down to the shop and buying a pint of milk and going home and making tea with it.

I knew also that she would elaborate later and in her own time, so I let it go. I wondered that I knew all this about her, despite not having seen her for thirteen years, but I did know, and I found that I was glad.

'Time for a change,' said William. 'It happens to the best of us, especially in that town.'

'It was too many funerals, in the end,' said Pansy. 'I think that was what it was.'

'Too many funerals?' I said.

I had a violent vision of her living in a blasted neighbourhood, an urban wasteland, where the kids got mown down in drive-by shootings on their way to school. I thought I really had been watching too much late night television.

'Aids,' said Pansy. She shrugged her shoulders and put her head on one side and gave me a what-can-you-do?

kind of smile. I felt young and sentimental, watching her, remembering all that past that we had together.

'That was my area,' she said. She laughed a little, some ironic noise in the back of her throat. 'What else are you going to work in, if you move to San Francisco and you were brought up by a mother who was determined to change the world? It was worst at the beginning. It wasn't so long after they had closed down the bath-houses and people were dying like flies. It got so that I was going to a funeral every week. I saw every kind of interment you would ever need to know about, in one lifetime. I went to drag funerals and theme funerals and funerals where everyone had to dress as Elvis, even the girls.'

'*Especially* the girls,' said William, who had found himself a piece of cheese and was eating it.

'I went to funerals where everyone came as their favourite movie star,' said Pansy, 'and funerals where trapeze artists performed over the open grave. I've been to funerals where they played show tunes throughout the service and funerals where the minister was dressed as Judy Garland. I've been to *Rocky Horror Picture Show* funerals and *Hello Dolly* funerals. I just went to too many funerals, that's all.'

'It wasn't so bad lately,' said William. 'The drugs are getting better, people are more careful and more scared. It's not like lemmings any more.'

'When they stopped,' said Pansy, 'the weekly funerals, when it started becoming one a month or less, we suddenly realised people weren't dying any more, not like they used to, and everyone started walking around with a cautious hopeful look, as if they were holding their breath, as if it were a cease-fire in a war zone.'

'But we had funeral fatigue by then,' said William. 'It was too late for us. We'd just been to too many funerals.'

'The strangest thing,' said Pansy, 'is when you see death all around you, you start to forget what it is. You forget

131 •

that it's the end of everything. It becomes something that happens to practically everyone you know, same as people changing their hair or moving to another city. Oh, we used to say, she's moved to Seattle, and he's died of complications from a sudden pneumonia. Same inflection, same idea.'

'In the East,' said William, 'the Far East I mean, not the coast, they'd probably think that was a good idea. Life and death as one indissoluble whole.'

'It just freaked me out,' said Pansy, shaking her head. 'I thought maybe I was losing sensation, like when doctors run sticks up your feet to check if you're paralysed after an accident and look at you and ask, Can you feel this? I couldn't feel this, so I thought it was time to leave town.'

'She's very decisive,' said William, in admiration. 'So I came with her.'

11

William left at seven o'clock. He stood up gracefully from his sofa, shook my hand with grave formality, thanked me for my hospitality, as if I were a society hostess at a diplomatic dinner, said he had to be at his aunt's house in Kensal Rise by seven thirty and where would he get a cab?

'In Piccadilly,' I said. 'Turn right out of the door and walk down to the first cross street. There'll be taxis there.'

'I can't believe I've never been to London,' he said. He started to smile, like someone whose number has just come up. 'I shall be walking down Piccadilly,' he said.

'Don't get picked up,' said Pansy. 'Down the Dilly is famous for all sorts of bad boys.'

William gave her a sorrowful look.

'I have family *business*,' he said.

Pansy kissed him on the cheek, smoothed his lapel, saw him out of the door and said she'd call him tomorrow. Then she turned back to me and gestured at the sofa.

'Can I stay?' she said. 'Just for a couple of nights?'

It wasn't in the plan at all. I didn't want company and intrusion; I didn't want suggestions and sisterhood, not just then. I wanted to be let alone to suffer until it was finished.

'Of course stay,' I said. 'Stay as long as you want. *Mi casa es tu casa.*'

Pansy nodded and gave me a second look, sat down and said, 'I will stay, even though I know that you'd rather be alone.'

'How did you know that?' I said.

'Because you never speak Spanish,' she said.

I knew I couldn't fool Pansy, and I felt comforted by that. There was no point trying to get things by her because they just didn't fly. She had an acute sense of the not-quite-right; she saw straight through any attempt at flannel or smokescreen.

'I wanted to be alone,' I said. 'The man I was with left after nine years, just up one day and walked out into the night without a word of explanation, and it turns out he had been seeing someone else for the last two years, and I got sick of people being concerned, and I got ashamed that I was so sad, and I thought I'd hide away until the worst of it had passed. I thought I'd come back into the world a new woman and start again.'

I sat back in my seat and looked at the ceiling. I wondered why something so simple as telling the truth made you feel so much better; I wondered why it was so hard to do.

Pansy lit up a cigarette and stubbed it out after one puff.

'Fuck it,' she said. 'I'm trying to give up. I don't want to die old and dusty and withered with half a lung and tumours on my tongue.'

She got up, poured herself a glass of water, sat herself back down and looked at me. She put the glass on the table.

'Thirteen years is too long,' she said. 'We shouldn't stay apart that long again. You're the only cousin I have and look what happened.'

'It happens,' I said. I made a sweeping gesture with my hand. 'All this happens. You grow up and you get your heart broken and your plans don't turn out the way you wanted and you marry the wrong person and people die of diseases and get run over by trucks and everyone loses someone they love, one way or another. It's just life, that's all.'

'Oh, I see,' said Pansy. 'So that means you don't have any right to complain about it? Is that what this is about?'

'What this?' I said.

'Hiding and hoping it will all go away and not wanting to bother anyone with it.'

Pansy gave me a look I remembered from when we were younger. You couldn't run or hide from that look. I used to think it was to do with her being so tall. Now I thought that height didn't really have much to do with it.

'I don't know,' I said. 'I feel like a piece of dog turd that someone scraped off their shoe, and what's the point of talking about it and discussing it and trying to get over it? Why not just let time do its thing and not bother with all the amateur psychology and the agonising and the comparing notes?'

'Iris,' said Pansy, 'you are a stoic, aren't you? You're a Puritan. This is very English, this stiff upper lip thing, I'd forgotten about this, they don't do this on the west coast, not in my neighbourhood anyway.'

I felt grumpy. I hated being told what I was, I always had.

'You don't have to reduce me to a cultural stereotype,' I said. 'I expect you'll tell me it's a chick thing too.'

'But it is,' said Pansy, in delight. She swung her legs over the sofa arm, as if she was settling in for the duration. 'Of course it is. We're all raised not to make a fuss, not to make a noise. We're taught to compromise and take the blows and not bother with the fussing and fighting, because that's not ladylike, that's not called for.'

I felt crosser than ever.

'Our mothers never taught us that,' I said. 'Who is doing all this teaching?'

'Everyone else,' said Pansy. 'Newspapers and magazines

and films and television and general particles of information floating randomly in the air. The women who complain are called nags and scolds and ballbusters. Stay silent and be loved, that's the message.'

'You've been reading too much Germaine Greer,' I said.

'Don't say a word against Germaine,' said Pansy, starting to laugh. 'She's got enough to deal with.'

'Just now, I'd like to drive everyone in the world into the sea and watch them forget how to swim,' I said. 'The sick and twisted side of me wants everyone else to suffer, even if it is in silence.'

'But all of this is *normal*,' said Pansy. 'You loved someone and they left you and betrayed you and you are hurt and lonely and humiliated so how did you expect to feel? This isn't a Fourth of July parade, this is heartbreak and it hurts like hell. You should be comfort-eating and drinking bourbon, you should be on the telephone to your girlfriends ranting about how all men are bastards and you're going to join a commune. Couldn't you be a little bit more hysterical about it? Couldn't you be a bit more theatrical? It's going to hurt whatever you do, so you might as well milk it.'

I started to laugh. I couldn't help it. I'd forgotten that Pansy had a slightly skewed view of the world. Not so very strange or eccentric, not so much as to mark her out as a social misfit or outcast, just enough so that she would suddenly come at things from an unexpected angle, a little off kilter. I wished she had been here before. I wished she hadn't been away for thirteen years, going to funerals.

'You know what you need?' she said, the next day at breakfast. We were eating cheese with our coffee, on account of my having nothing else in the fridge. ('It's a Swedish breakfast,' said Pansy, with studied nonchalance. 'I understand that Nordic trends are going to be very big this season.')

'No,' I said.

'That's all right,' said Pansy equably. 'I'll tell you. You need a project.'

'Oh, please,' I said. 'I can't do with positive thinking this early in the morning.'

'It's true,' said Pansy. 'You've had to jack your job, which was one of the loves of your life. You've not only lost one love, you've lost two. You're in double bereavement.'

'Don't tell me to get a puppy,' I said, giving her a tough look from under my eyebrows. She waved it away like someone swatting a fly.

'Not a dog,' she said, with a nice degree of contempt. 'You don't want to clutter up your life with another dumb mutt that follows you round drooling.'

'I think it's too soon for you to start referring to Fred as a dumb mutt,' I said.

She looked at me for a moment, contemplating.

'All right,' she said. 'I'll be forgiving now. Then maybe in a couple of weeks' time I'll get really offensive. That's a good timetable. But you still need a project.'

'I'm not in the fifth form,' I said. 'I don't need a *project*.'

'What else are you going to do?' said Pansy. She was so bloody reasonable, I wanted to give her a slap. 'You can't sit around here for the next six months using up your savings and watching daytime television. You start believing the whole world is made up of pastel sofas and fat women who sleep with their brothers, you get to walking the streets in your night-clothes, and next thing you know, you're on a soap box at Speaker's Corner telling people that the government is nothing more than a puppet for a cynical multi-national corporation dedicated to global warming and dumping nuclear waste in sacred burial grounds.'

'But everyone knows that's true,' I said.

'Yes, yes,' said Pansy. 'You need direction. For nine years you've had the same job and the same boyfriend and now you're cast adrift on a wide sea and if we don't do something you'll just flail around until you drown.'

'Cheer me up, why don't you?' I said.

Later, we got a sandwich from a booth round the corner and went up to Leicester Square to catch an afternoon movie. It was Pansy's idea. She said there was no point not working unless you went to the cinema in the daytime.

'Come on,' she said. 'Make nice. I've got jet-lag and I'm disorientated and I'm back in a town I haven't seen since I was nineteen and I don't know anyone except you and I want to see a movie. I want popcorn and hot dogs and a double feature. Come on, admit you want to.'

I didn't want to, but I went anyway.

We headed up to one of the giant multi-screens in Leicester Square, which showed eight different features all day long and sold popcorn in buckets.

'This is good,' said Pansy, looking around in satisfaction. 'This is right.'

The square was full of its usual population: wandering visitors, doing the slow tourist shuffle (I sometimes wondered how they ever got anywhere, they meandered so slowly; I sometimes wondered if they spent their whole two weeks in this rainy northern town just getting from Piccadilly Circus to Seven Dials), students and winos, mingling together on the benches under the tall canopy of plane trees, a trail of earnest theatregoers waiting patiently at the half-price ticket stall, and the passing stream of media girls and boys, distinct from the rest by dint of being dressed entirely in black and being in a hurry, walking with purpose – they didn't want to be in this square, not like the rest of these patsies, they were on their *way* somewhere.

At the Piccadilly end, within striking distance of the chiming Tyrolean clock at the Swiss Centre, a small crowd gathered around the hucksters offering to draw your picture in charcoal for a bargain-basement twenty-five pounds. These street artists always surprised me; there was another small enclave at the south end of Shaftesbury Avenue, and further afield than that – you saw their brothers (they were always men, for some reason) at Montmartre and the Piazza Navona in Rome; and the astonishing thing about them was that they all drew in the exact same style. I could never figure out why that was. Was there some secret academy for pavement Picassos that the rest of us never heard about? Was there some painting-by-numbers correspondence course? To advertise themselves they put out pictures of famous film stars, thick clouded charcoals of Brad Pitt and Madonna, wistful studies of the teen-throb *du jour*. They looked barely anything like their subjects (is that Leonardo or Keanu? Sandra or Kate?) and they all had the same misty moody chocolate-box bogusness.

'Oh, come on,' said Pansy. 'Kitsch is back. Let's buy one. Let's start a trend.

'How strange it is,' she said, looking round the square, with its forty-foot hoardings and genteel neon and counterfeit air, 'that it really hasn't changed at all. I mean, they've tidied it up some, and the Odeon's had some work on it, and the Capital building is new, but it hasn't really changed. It's just the same as it was when we were sixteen.'

'Maybe nothing really changes, that much,' I said gloomily.

'Oh, come along,' said Pansy, taking my arm, 'humbug and humbug, my heart is broken, my life is over and I'm going into the garden to eat worms.'

I looked at her, and then, in the middle of Leicester Square on a perfectly unremarkable Thursday afternoon, I started to cry and once I started I couldn't stop.

'I'm sorry,' I said helplessly, 'I'm sorry. I'm sorry.'

'It's all right,' said Pansy. 'It's fine.'

She led me over to one of the benches and sat me down.

Later, I realised that I hadn't cried, not since the night at Pete Street's party, I realised that for the last few weeks I had been building up a small sea wall, a sandbag defence, putting one block on top of another, in a dogged stubborn way, so that I wouldn't have to feel like I did now. Because it *hurts*, that's why we all try to avoid it, that's why we distract ourselves with drink and fags and drugs and food and television, because if we put it off long enough and ignore it hard enough maybe it will just go away and we won't have to feel this hurt which isn't aching in the heart or pounding in the head but like someone has put something sharp in your gut and is twisting.

It's the feeling you get when you think that you have been entirely abandoned. It's the worst feeling in the world and it hurts so much that there's a part of you that thinks, I'm not built for this, they didn't do this test when they ran the prototype, I shall shatter and burst and break. I knew this, because I'd felt it once before, on a day not much different from this one, when the sun was shining in an inoffensive way and everyone was going about their business, the way they did in cities, and I came home to find my mother packed and waiting for the taxi that was going to take her to the airport.

She had to tell me twice before I realised that it was a one-way ticket, that this was the end, that there was no more mother, because she had done her best, and now she was leaving.

She said she thought it was better this way, better that I didn't have time to think about it. She said she thought a *fait accompli* was the best thing for both of us.

I remember her face from that day. It was pale and flat and without expression. It was the face she used for me. Other people, the causes she espoused or the battered wives she counselled, they got expression. They got smiles and eyebrows arching with surprise and deep-line frowns of concern. The flat face was reserved for me. That day it was flatter and blanker than ever, like an empty thing waiting to be written on.

I suddenly knew that she had been waiting for this moment for the last fifteen years, that she had been counting the days until she could set herself free.

She told me that my aunt Ursula would be expecting me later that evening, so I had time to pack up my things. We were living in a women's shelter in Brondesbury Park at the time, where my mother gave advice and comfort to cowed and beaten women, on the run from violent husbands. We only had a couple of rooms and there wasn't much stuff. My mother had two suitcases with her, to take away to her new life. There was a song she liked which had a line in it about an old girl who carried her world in two carrier-bags. My mother's world was in two blue suitcases; they sat by the door, malevolent and sinister; I couldn't stop staring at them, those two bags.

I felt something swelling and rising inside me, in my stomach and up into my throat, like some kind of alien being, like something you saw in a horror flick. I could have let it go, shouted and made a scene, but I didn't, I'm still not sure why. It was pride or fury or something; I would have rather died than show her how much she was hurting me. So I held on to it, tight as I could. I nodded and answered in monosyllables, as if I'd always known this day would come, as if this was a perfectly normal thing to happen when you were fifteen, that your mother turned round to you and said Your time is up.

I think maybe the real reason I didn't shout and storm was that I knew she wouldn't get it. The way she saw it, she had done her best for this thing she'd never wanted; she'd fed me and clothed me and given me Kate Millett to read. She'd taught me about self-sufficiency and independence and not living in thrall to the patriarchal society. She'd taught me everything that her good liberal mind knew, and now she was finished, and she was leaving.

I nodded my head and said Yes oh oh yes, and then the taxi arrived and the driver came round and hefted my mother's two bags into the boot, and she stood for a moment, for the first time a little awkward, at this actual moment of parting, for the first time not knowing quite what to say with her calm, wide face.

We stood there for a beat, looking at each other – I thought wildly, This is your mother, look at her, this is your last chance, look hard at her, so you remember what she looks like – and then she leaned forward and put one hand on my shoulder (I felt the weight and heat of it there like a brand for days afterwards) and she said 'Well, goodbye then,' and a crazed voice in my head was breaking into show tunes and singing Thanks for the memories, and I nodded and said 'Have a good trip', and then she got into the minicab, which was a maroon Ford Sierra with a dent in the passenger door, so she had to slam it twice to get it shut, and it drove off and I was left with the empty street, and it felt for one streaming moment as if the whole city had emptied, as if some apocalypse had arrived, so that all that was left was not people and trees and cars and buses and dogs and buildings, but a grotesque vacuum, and I was the only person left standing in it.

It was then that it hit, the complete and utter abandonment, the end of the world feeling, the one that gives you the sensation of being hit and pulled at the same time, as if you've been whacked round the head with a flat metal object, as if something is digging and clawing right down deep in your stomach, and you think you are going to be sick and you think you are going to cry (then you realise you are crying already) and you have a moment of abject and uncontrolled panic because this hurts too much, no one can feel this way and survive. I felt it then as I watched the Ford turn away at the end of the road, because I was too young to protect myself from it. It hit me like a train rushing down the track, and I remember standing, dazed, in the middle of the street, staring like a fool into the distance. I remember coming to, and looking down at my arms and legs because I was convinced that they must have been broken.

And now, fifteen years later, in the middle of Leicester Square, which hadn't really changed all that much, I was getting the second act of that feeling. It was happening again, and I'd sworn, after I'd picked myself up and got myself together and walked down to the Underground station with my bags to catch the train that would take me to my aunt Ursula's, I had sworn that I would never, ever feel like that again, not as long as I lived.

12

We didn't go to the film in the end. We sat until I stopped crying and I was left, tired and winded, as if I had run into something. Pansy sat by my side, holding my hand until I was finished.

'It's all right,' she said. 'It's all right, really. We'll just go home. We'll go home.'

We went back to my place and lay down, one on each of the two sofas. They were such old and comfortable pieces of furniture; the springs on one were starting to come through in the seat, so you could feel them nudging against you through the velvet. One green and one purple, I remember buying them from a dingy auction room down near the river. I liked the colours and no one else seemed to want them. The delivery boys got a shock when they arrived in Bond Street and saw that they were going to have to walk up five flights. They must have thought from the address that they were going to some swank gallery or swell clothing store, that they were going to dress up some ground-floor showroom in shabby chic. When they saw it was residential use and five floors up without a lift they weren't pleased ('Not too clever,' they said, without irony) and I had to bribe them with chocolate cake and money or they would have left them sitting on the pavement, for the smart women to trip over on their way into the Chanel boutique next door.

Pansy got us a beer each, and put some Ornette Coleman on the record-player and lay back on the green sofa.

We lay in silence for a while; I think I must have slept. Suddenly it was dark. Ornette Coleman was on repeat; he paused and started up again, from the beginning.

'Did I sleep?' I said. 'I think I was asleep.'

Pansy rolled over on her side and put up one hand to shade her eyes, even though the room was in half-light now, the sky a deepening blue outside the window and the yellow and purple shadows of street-lamps starting to gleam in the evening light.

'You should sleep,' she said. 'You need a rest.'

I lay back and looked up at the ceiling.

'I don't know,' I said. 'I don't know what I need.'

'This will pass,' said Pansy. 'This part will get better.'

Paco said that, I thought. Did Paco say that?

'That's what everyone says,' I said. 'That's what they all say. I want to shrug it off, literally. I want to shrug my shoulders and feel it fall off my back and then I'll be normal again, I'll be able to think and eat and walk and laugh and live my life.'

'Everyone has to do this,' said Pansy. 'You can't escape this unless you live in a box your whole life and never go out.'

'There's always medication,' I said.

'There,' said Pansy. She sat up and looked at me. 'That's a joke. You still have your sense of humour. You're not dead yet.'

We sat there the whole night, listening to the record play over and over, and drinking more beer. Pansy said we might as well drink a bit because sometimes it helped.

'Do you think about your father ever?' she said.

'Sometimes,' I said. 'I wonder if it would have made a difference if I knew who he was. Sometimes,' I said slowly,

'I think about it in abstract terms. You know, why do we need to know, what does it mean about identity, why do we think blood is thicker than water. Do you think about yours?' I said.

Pansy's father was another of those sixties love affairs: fleeting and remembered through a cloud of patchouli and cigarette smoke. He was an American actor in London with some experimental theatre group and he slept with my aunt Ursula for one summer and then went back to New Jersey. He's rather famous now; known for supporting the Democrats and saving the whales and giving interviews to magazines about his solid family life and his artistic integrity.

'We have lunch once a year,' said Pansy. 'I think he writes it off against tax. He has a neat little nose job and a mistress in Beekman Place.'

'Blood and water,' I said.

'Do you think it is thicker?' said Pansy, sitting up and taking out a cigarette. 'Blood, I mean.'

'I don't know,' I said. 'Somewhere out there is a man who is my father, who is my DNA, my blood and bone. Somewhere in the world there is a man who walks like me or uses the same inflections in his voice or has the same shaped head. And it means nothing, because he doesn't know I exist or what I look like or what I dream of at night. So that's not thicker, is it? But with Paco and Stella there is no blood and we know everything about each other.'

'Stella and Paco,' said Pansy. 'My God. I remember them. What was it, just before I went to New York, when you moved to Soho? You still have them?'

'Yes,' I said. 'They aren't my blood, but I still have them.'

'But,' said Pansy, 'I feel blood is thick with you and me. I think that means something.'

'Yes,' I said. 'But what if we didn't like each other? It's

only luck, that's all. So we can be friends and say, Well, there we are, we're cousins too, we are bound tight by that blood tie, and that means something. That means that we can not see each other for thirteen years and pick up right where we left off. But if you were the kind of person who collected beer mats for a hobby and I liked trainspotting and stuffed animals I don't know if we'd feel the same at all.'

'You know what I think?' said Pansy.

She was in the early stages of drunkenness now; you would hardly tell, unless you knew her very well. It was just that everything she said was very precise and she asked many questions (You know what I think? Shall I tell you something? Did you ever notice?).

'Tell me what you think,' I said.

'I'll tell you what I think,' said Pansy. She grinned slyly at me. 'You think I'm drunk, don't you?'

'I am too,' I said. 'That's the whole point.'

'You haven't seen nothing yet,' said Pansy. 'You haven't seen *anything* yet.'

'What do you think?' I said.

'What?' said Pansy.

'You said, "Shall I tell you what I think?"'

'Shall I tell you?' said Pansy.

'Tell me,' I said.

'I think,' said Pansy, sitting up very straight, 'that you deal too much in hypotheticals.'

I admired Pansy. I always had. You try saying hypotheticals without a pause after six bottles of Spanish beer.

The next morning we went walking for our hangovers in Hyde Park. There was a bitter and persistent wind coming from the east, and the park was empty, apart from a few old men in heavy overcoats, out for their daily constitutional, and optimistic pairs of lovers, walking arm in arm, eyes shining with novelty.

'Was it like that for you, in the beginning?' said Pansy, stopping to look at one of the loving couples blow past in a haze of new emotion.

'Yes,' I said. 'It was. It seems a long time ago.'

'It was a long time,' said Pansy. 'The curious thing is that I never got beyond that stage. I was always meeting people and falling in love and then it would all collapse like a house of cards. I don't know what that day-to-day thing is like. I don't know what it's like to go to the supermarket together. I just got the white-heat part and then bust.'

(I thought, Isn't that what Stella said?)

'Luck of the draw,' I said. I don't know if I really thought that, but I said it anyway.

'Did you ever get bored?' she said. 'Did you ever think, This is all routine, I want someone who will come along and thrill me like those early days, all over again?'

'Sometimes,' I said. 'More exasperation than boredom, I think.'

I thought back. Nine years seemed to have gone by so fast; now there were only memories and snapshots and small fractured pieces of the past.

'That's why we never moved in together,' I said. 'I didn't want to get to the boredom part, when you run out of conversation and you do the same three positions once a month and you have no curiosity any more.'

'So that plan worked,' said Pansy, nodding her head.

'It did,' I said. 'It was good. It was a good relationship. It was. It was something.'

I suddenly felt something burst in my chest, an explosion of absolute fury. 'So why,' I said, my voice rising, 'did he have to go and fuck it up?'

'I think you need closure,' said Pansy.

'I never know what that means,' I said.

'You are angry and you are hurt and you are confused,

and you need to lay the ghost and get on to your life,' said Pansy. 'You know what they say in California? They say, He's just taking up space in your head.'

'So I need closure,' I said. 'How do I get that?'

Pansy looked at me with her grey eyes, which, strangely, were also my eyes, because we both got our eyes from our mothers, so sometimes it was like looking in a mirror. We looked more alike than sisters, except she was taller and she got small flat ears and wide leaning cheekbones from her father.

'I think,' she said, starting to smile, 'that you need *revenge.*'

I said it was a terrible idea. I said that I had got through tough times before and I would again. I grew bullish and said it wasn't so bad and I had my health and who needed men anyway?

Pansy just smiled and smiled to herself, and said that I should think about it.

I didn't want revenge, but I wanted something. I wanted to know why. I wanted to know what had gone so wrong; I wanted to know what it was I hadn't seen.

The next day I told Pansy that I was going to the dentist. She gave me a look, but she let it go. I suppose I could have been going to the dentist, but we both knew I wasn't.

I walked up to the gallery and when I got there I didn't stop or pause, I walked straight in just like nothing had changed. I thought it was strange that I had walked in at that door five days a week for the last eight years, that I knew every brick of that place as if it were my own and now it had nothing to do with me. There was a piece I didn't recognise in the window, and as I walked in I had an imperceptible feeling that I had crossed over some invisible barrier, that I was on the other side of the green baize door.

There was a new girl on the desk, an art baby for sure, the pretty empty face and long twisting hair proclaiming her status like a neon light, but not one I knew. Perhaps she had just arrived from the provinces, from hill country somewhere, where she had been used to riding horses all day and walking barefoot in the summer.

She looked up at me with a sweet and vacant look, and said, taking care to get the words in the right order, like someone for whom English isn't their first language, 'Can I help you at all?'

I smiled politely and asked if Fred was in.

'He's in the back,' she said. 'Shall I say who's calling?'

She gave me the benign inquiring look again, her finger poised over the intercom button.

'I'm an old friend,' I said. 'It's a surprise. Let's surprise him.'

I felt like a fraud, pulling her into this small deception. I had never held anything against the art babies. For all their tiny skirts and blinking eyes, they weren't the one fucking my boyfriend.

'I'll just go on in,' I said. 'I know the way.'

The back room was divided from the rest by an opaque glass wall. The door was big and heavy; you had to put your shoulder and your side against it and lean with the weight of your body to get it swinging. After the first move, it would shift fast under its own momentum. People who didn't know the secret sometimes kept pushing too hard and came tumbling into the room; it was one of the things that used to make Fred laugh.

I pushed just enough and the door swung open without making a noise and I was in the room before Fred realised it.

He wasn't alone. I had thought he would be at his desk – it was just before lunch, he was always on his own at this time. I thought I would ask him why, that's all. I wanted to know why he didn't want me any more and what went wrong and what made him change his mind. I wanted to know why he hadn't said anything, why everything had unravelled silently, why he had felt the need to deceive me so successfully. I hated not understanding things; I hated not *getting* it. I didn't know why he couldn't just have said something, before it all got so twisted.

But when I arrived and the door swung open, slow and silent, and I stood in front of Fred's desk, with a civilised smile starting on my face, he wasn't alone, he was sitting on the sofa against the left wall, and he was kissing Natalie Hedge, and her shirt was open so that I could see she was wearing a red bra with broderie anglaise straps and she had a ring pierced into her belly button, and the muscles along her stomach were tightening and clenching because Fred had one finger in her mouth and one in her vagina, and her head was thrown back so that the soft flesh at the base of her neck was pulled taut and she was making a noise between a laugh and a sigh.

13 ∫

I walked home very smooth and controlled, as if I were one speed up from slow motion. I felt as if I were on camera and I had to remember where my mark was and how it had gone in rehearsal.

When I got back I walked in and sat down on my green sofa. I thought vaguely that I should cry out or collapse on the floor in some melodramatic way; I had visions in my head of Vivien Leigh (as whom? Scarlett, Blanche, one of those fucked-up women she played so well) lying on a bed and pounding her fists against the pillow, twisting and turning so that she messed up the counterpane.

This isn't right, I thought. It was supposed to be rational and ordered and explicable; it wasn't supposed to degenerate into porn and soap opera.

I sat there for hours, with the light dying around me, and then Pansy came home and took one look at me and picked up the telephone and she called Stella and she called Jane, so by ten o'clock the four of us were sitting there like some kind of witches coven.

'Tell me again, from the beginning,' said Stella. 'I don't want to sound like a cornball, but I don't believe this. You must be making it up, just to make us gasp and stretch our eyes.'

I felt curiously detached.

'I went in,' I said in a slow rational voice, like it all made sense, 'and he and Natalie Hedge were on that big leather chesterfield that he keeps against the wall, and he had his finger . . . and it was making her sigh and sing out loud.'

'Oh dear,' said Jane, starting to laugh. 'Couldn't he just go home and do it on a bed like a normal person?'

We all looked at her.

'What?' she said. 'I don't have to be consistent.'

Pansy was mixing up something she said was a *caiparena* made with pure Brazilian sugar cane spirit. No one drank any more in California, so coming back to Blighty was like the end of Prohibition for her.

'I once had a boyfriend,' she said, 'and it was all going fine and I went round to his apartment one night an hour earlier than I said I would and found him doing it with the pool attendant.'

She paused and smiled her wide good smile at us.

'Who was a seventeen-year-old boy,' she said.

'Oh, yes,' said Stella.

'That was when I was visiting Los Angeles on the week-ends,' said Pansy. 'It's a terrible town for swimming-pools. All those brawny out-of-work actors with too much stifled ambition and time on their hands.'

Stella said, 'I was never with anyone long enough for them to cheat on me. Or at least,' she said, 'if they did, I never found out about it. So I don't know about this.'

Pansy handed out the glasses. The drink was opaque and pale green and frosted, like absinthe or alchemy. It smelt of salt and turpentine.

'It would be easier if Natalie Hedge was a bimbo,' said Stella, 'because then we could hate her, but she's perfectly intelligent.'

'I wish,' I said, 'they would all fall off a cliff and I wouldn't have to think about it any more. It's not like I lost my sight or was told I only had six months to live. It's just a relationship. It was just a thing.'

'No, no,' said Jane, shaking her head. 'It's your hopes and dreams and your notions of yourself. It's never just about the other person, it's much more complicated than that. And anyway, misery isn't relative.'

'I can go and see someone,' I said. 'I can go and see Stella's shrink and get my head sorted. It might be my great life change. Natalie Hedge might have done me a favour.'

'Tell me truly,' said Stella, sitting up straight and looking me right in the eye. 'Isn't there a primeval part of you that just wants to kill Fred, nice and slow, to watch him beg and plead and *suffer*?'

I thought about it for a moment.

'All right,' I said. 'I want to hurt him and humiliate him and watch him creep and crawl. I want to make him suffer the way he's made me suffer, but that kind of thinking won't get me anywhere except back in the Stone Age.'

'Ha,' said Stella. 'But you do want it, in your forbidden self.'

'She's a woman,' said Pansy. 'Of course she wants it. We've been ignored and abused for the last five thousand years, so there's a part of all of us that would quite like to have a bit of our own back, thank you very much for asking.'

'Oh, no,' I said. 'This is not going to be a feminist thing.'

'It's not a feminist thing,' said Pansy. 'It's a life thing. And I mean that in a real human way.'

'The personal is political,' said Stella. 'You know that's true.'

'I'm not doing this,' I said. 'It's not going to achieve anything.'

'But you know you want to,' said Pansy.

She and Stella gave each other a real conspiratorial look, and I saw at once that they were made for each other, cut from the same cloth. I wondered if the reason I had become friends with Stella was that I was looking for another version of Pansy, for someone to take that place in my life, right after she had got on an aeroplane and gone away, all those years ago.

'You know you want to,' said Stella.

'Come on,' said Jane. 'This kind of opportunity may never come our way again, not while we're young and strong and brave and we have our looks.'

I looked round at the three of them, at their clever open faces, flushed slightly with the Brazilian sugar spirit, and I knew then that there was no going back.

'OK,' I said. 'Fuck it. Let's do it.'

There was a banging on the door and I jumped, half expecting it was the thought police, come to arrest us for conspiracy.

Stella got up and opened the door, and it was Paco, breathless from running up five flights.

'What? he said. 'What did I miss?'

Most times, when you look back on your life, you realise that so much of what happens is just contingency or happenstance, that changes come on you as unexpected and casual as if you just ordered in pepperoni pizza instead of ham and mushroom. I mean, no one actually plans their lives, do they? Do they?

I knew I didn't want to be famous, I didn't want to be rich, I didn't want furs and yachts and castles in Spain. But after Fred went I realised how much I'd assumed. I thought assumptions are a kind of hubris, a bet that you can beat the odds, that you can live for ever, that it will never happen to you. In the closed dark of the night hours, I had to admit that I'd thought Fred and I would grow old and grey together, look back on our youthful follies and laugh about them, tell our children what it was like, living in the last decade of the twentieth century.

And there it is, the real cherry; I thought we would have children to tell all this to. And now I was tipped over thirty, and there was just a blank space.

Once we had agreed that revenge was the next step, I felt fatalistic and light in the head, as if some decision had been taken from me. I wasn't sure if revenge was the thing I really wanted or whether I was just going along with the crowd. Sure as hell, everyone else wanted it for me, and I didn't feel strong enough to say no.

Stella always said I liked the quiet life. She said because of not having a father and a mother who left so precipitately that I was afraid of asking too much of life, because I knew that it wouldn't deliver. So it was best to be quiescent and accepting, because that way it was less likely that you would suffer disappointment.

I wondered about that. I thought it wasn't such a bad way to live your life. Maybe it wasn't wild and quixotic and crazy. But it was harmless; I was never going to damage and wound and wreck things. I wasn't self-destructive or cruel, I never wanted to take it out on the world that I hadn't got some of the things I might have liked.

I once asked Stella what she knew about herself, if she knew so much about me.

'Oh,' she said, 'that's easy. It's just that I have to be every single thing except what I saw when I was growing up.'

Stella, who came from a textbook dysfunctional family – alcoholic father, depressive mother – said that she realised when she was nineteen that she could either go that way, take too many drugs, drink a bottle a day, hook up with some handsome man who would bully her in private, seek rehab and ask everyone who would listen what choice did she have, with her background, or decide that the buck stops here.

'It wasn't so easy at the time,' she said, when she told me all this, one late night, when it was just the two of us, drinking a bottle of something and letting the light die around us. 'Looking back it seems obvious, that if I hadn't figured it all out I would be a dolt, someone who didn't deserve a break. But the fact is I got lucky, and I got angry.'

'It was as if I was given a choice,' Stella said, that long night when all this came out. 'I could pretend none of it ever happened and go on hopping on one foot and calling it living, or I could make an informed choice that I was not going to turn into my mother.'

There was a bitter poignancy to this: Stella's mother never got the point. Stella had just turned fifteen when her mother took that whole pot of pills in one go. Only ten people had come to the funeral, which was held in a small bleak building in Golders Green, where they cremated ten bodies a day with conveyor-belt efficiency. Sometimes, in the early days, when Stella and Paco and I went everywhere together and didn't seem to need anyone else, I wondered whether it was that this history of death and desertion held us together stronger than any ties of blood could. (When Jane came along, not so long after, and we drew her inexorably into our small contained axis, it was felt as strange but never mentioned that she had two perfectly nice normal parents who lived in Merton, a civilised middle-class suburb.)

So Stella got lucky and got mad and got even.

'That was all I wanted,' she said. 'Not to turn into my parents. I'd always heard that predestined stuff, and then the Darwinians got in on the act, and started telling us that it didn't matter how many shrinks we saw because women were genetically programmed from the Dark Ages, so all this fuss and fighting was for nothing. I didn't think it worked like that. So I went another way, that's all.'

After they left that night, and Pansy and I were alone in my dim fifth-floor room, I thought that maybe this was some kind of chance, an offering of something different. It was the first coherent and optimistic thought that I had had since the whole sorry mess had started and I clung onto it with a mulish determination.

I thought maybe it was time for me to start kicking over some traces and breaking some patterns and asking a bit more from life. I thought, suddenly, shockingly, that perhaps those years with Fred had been a kind of surfing. It's so easy when you are in a couple, a socially recognised unit. No one asks you questions or looks at you as if you are some kind of radical. It's the single girls that get all the shit, and they go and write apologetic books saying they don't mean it, not really, they go to bed dreaming of the redemptive love of a good man. They didn't want to scare the horses by not doing the usual thing. Men got reassured: these free women couldn't take over the world because they were too busy staying home watching reruns of old sitcoms and fretting about their cellulite. They were too busy drinking nasty white wine and smoking low-tar cigarettes to think about revolution. So the old order went spinning on and no one mentioned the spiralling domestic violence figures because anyway, what was a little smack now and then, in the privacy of your own front room?

Yes, I thought, *yes*; this is it at last. I am angry after all.

14

It was Stella who came up with the idea. We sat around and thought about all those hackneyed revenge ideas that you read about in the red-top papers. Paco said there was a revenge site on the Internet, but when we tried to access it it turned out you had to hand over your MasterCard number and a deposit, and we didn't think that was any kind of idea.

There was talk of letters from clap clinics and bogus Jehovah's Witnesses and stalk mail over the Internet (*We know who you are*). Pansy said she knew a boy in New York who spread a rumour about town that his ex had genital warts and a habit of calling for his mother at the point of orgasm, but that the strategy had backfired because some people decided that was an advantage in a man.

We had revenge lunches and revenge dinners. Stella got us to dress up nice and took us to the American Bar at the Savoy, where we ate all the free potato crisps and asked for sherry in our Bloody Marys.

I was carried along on this: this sense of action, of purpose, seemed to stop the worst of the aching and the introspection. I had somewhere to go and something to do. It wouldn't have been the same if we were just hanging out together, slagging off Natalie Hedge and wasting time. That would have felt futile and juvenile, a throwback to our teen years, when we could spend three hours over a cup of coffee in some streetside café, looking at the music papers and playing the Space Invaders machine. But this, this felt like a mission.

And then, one morning, Stella called and said I should get over to her flat, and when I got there and admired what she had done with the place (unpacked three crates of books), she said we were going to perform a seamless and perfectly orchestrated art fraud, and Fred would fall for it, and we would expose him, and his credibility would be in the dirt, and that would be the sweetest revenge of all.

'We're going to make some phoney art, and we're going to sell it to him, and he's going to rise to it like a trout to a fly, and then we'll see who's sorry,' said Stella. 'Never say that I don't have an idea in my head.'

If I had thought that we would get away with it, I don't know if I would have said yes. I was angry and raw and shaken up, but I didn't know that I wanted to destroy his entire life.

To tell the truth, I never thought we would get away with it. And like this whole trip so far, it seemed to be out of my hands. It was almost as if this idea, this plan, took on a life of its own, and I felt that it hardly had anything to do with me.

I watched it with a slightly detached interest, because I never ever for one moment thought that it would work.

The art world in London at that time had blown wide apart. Everyone was scrabbling for meaning. The artists went their own sweet way and did whatever they wanted, and then someone came along, some marketing man or style guru, some media sage or social commentator, and gave it a name of its very own and, before you knew it, a label was born. There were the neurotic realists and the post-industrialists, the latent existentialists and the retro-ironists; in Shoreditch, a small splinter group reproducing Marxist tracts in lurid colours and 3D were called the neo-polemicists.

There was an air of unreality about it all: since the fifties, the British had become resigned to a genteel decline. They sat aside and watched politely as America took over the world, with its fast food and dramatic politics and abstract expressionism. America was the new world: it was where the refugees wanted to go, and so many of the great artists were refugees, of one kind or another.

In the sixties, London shook itself for a moment, threw out the Beatles and the Stones and Mary Quant and David Hockney ('I never really saw the *point* of all those swimming-pools,' Stella said once, 'but then I know fuck all about art') and settled back into quiet nihilism and loud punk rock.

But now it was the nineties and there was swinging London all over again and journalists got it into their heads that this renaissance had to be given names, and the big collectors started inventing their own labels for disparate groups of artists, which the sceptical called one big marketing exercise, but then half of it was about spin and hype, and wasn't that fitting after all, in this post-modern age? Irony, that great British invention, was worth top dollar; you could do anything, just then, if you did it with irony.

There was a small nucleus of good work going on, because it always had and always would, and some of it was taken up and lionised because it fitted in with the prevailing wind and there was a rash of Artist as celebrity (Artist starving in garret was suddenly very last season) and some of it went unnoticed, because it wasn't considered fashionable by the breathless hypesters and trend-spotters. There was a detritus of junk and flimsy, which got talked up because no one wanted to be wrong; no one wanted to be so bourgeois that they didn't *get* it.

Some critics stuck their noses in the air and hated all of the new stuff on principle, and some were more discerning and saw through the worst of the hype, and some embraced anything novel with an ardent fervour; and some developed a bitter hatred of the fanfare and the circus and stayed at home writing furious articles about the hucksters and shysters who were pretending to make art when all it was was dog food taken out of tins, and rolled-up pieces of Blu-tack, and bubble-gum straight from the artist's mouth, and garbage scattered over the floor, and video footage of a man sitting in a prison cell.

If ever there was a time when you could pull the wool over the punters' eyes, it was now, because Is It Art? had been declared a redundant question and everyone was an artist and what the artist said was Art was, so unless you got down to playground slanging and he-said-she-said, how were you going to prove the difference?

Working in the midst of it all, I hadn't taken much notice of the indignant column inches and the salon chat. I liked the work we dealt in, mostly. Some of it I thought was good and some was ephemeral and some of it made me laugh; I thought if rich time-passers with money and no sense wanted to drive up prices on objects that had no more than fifteen minutes of fame in them, then they were welcome to it.

It wasn't as if any of this was new. In the seventies Newton Harrison practically got lynched at the Hayward for showing a piece that involved the ritual electrocution of live catfish. There were protestors on the South Bank and a famous comedian picketed for Rights for Fish (some people said this act was more conceptually interesting than the exhibit itself; the post-modern groupies were beside themselves with delight).

In the seventies there were performance artists who stuck steel tacks into their arms and others who stood in an empty space and lit one match. There were artists who made blow-job machines out of holographs and sculptures of strait-jackets with bulbous genitalia hanging down like an invitation. And by the end of the century no one remembered their names.

This had all been done before, and everyone had got furious then, and lines were drawn, but the fatuous get forgotten, most times, except for a footnote in some hagiography of the scene (eye-witness, written in basic grammar by someone who had spent the last ten years in rehab), and the good stuff got remembered, and it seemed to me that was rough justice, so song and dance now wasn't worth the trouble. Let them all be artists if they wanted; let them can their own shit.

There were those who saw irony in all this, that the Freeze generation now commanded such huge prices that they had turned from rebellious outsiders to art establishment in one quick jump; there were those who said the joke was that it was the traditionalists who were now the anti-establishment figures, that figurative painting in oils was as shocking as self-immolation. So those who got that gag went around laughing quietly to themselves and not bothering anyone much.

I wondered if I should have cared more. Everyone was out there desperately *minding;* they really cared whether it was art or not; they minded intensely about charlatans and impostors. And I sat back and thought, Let them get away with it if they want to. If someone went to all that trouble, to adopt the persona and flaunt their imperfections, why not let them have their moment in the sun?

But now I thought perhaps it was all part of the same piece, that I didn't ask much from life because I was afraid there wasn't going to be much to get, so I took the easy route, the safe option.

I was suddenly taken with a spasm of disgust. Perhaps this was why Fred left, perhaps that was why he was half sitting half lying on a beaten leather sofa with his fingers in Natalie Hedge. Perhaps Natalie Hedge was a passionate apostle, a fearless polemicist; perhaps people said, Say what you like about Natalie, but she knows what she thinks.

Perhaps, I thought, in the silence of my lonely room, Fred had grown tired that I didn't have half an essay to say on the state of the art and had gone to find someone who kept half a dozen gimcrack arguments up their sleeve, for daily use. Perhaps I should have made more of a noise, after all.

'Perhaps it's not him,' I said to Pansy. 'Perhaps it's me. Perhaps I only have myself to blame. Perhaps this idea of getting my own back is entirely spurious.'

'That's a good word,' said Pansy. She was eating tortilla chips with HP sauce on them. Looking at her, I realised that what I envied in her was her absolute and inviolable sense of self; she knew what she thought and she knew what she wanted and she knew who she was, and I felt like I was still fishing in the dark.

'I don't know anything,' I said.

'That's natural,' said Pansy placidly. 'You're floating through the void, so you're not exactly going to be feeling *confident*.'

She smiled at me, as if that was all right. Then she frowned, a thought striking her.

'Aren't you used to it?' she said. 'Things not being settled? It's not as if we were ever bred to that, you especially.'

'I got settled,' I said. 'I got a regular man and a regular job and a regular life. I learnt to do things by routine. You know, Tuesday night I ate fish, that kind of thing. On Fridays in summer we would go and listen to jazz and in the winter we went to the pictures.'

'Oh, I see,' said Pansy. 'So that was a defence, that was a reaction. OK, I get it.'

'Perhaps that was why he left,' I said. 'Perhaps I had become staid and unimaginative.'

Pansy laughed. 'I don't *think* so,' she said, with a West Coast irony. I had heard that before, on the television.

'Why don't you?' I said. I was curious. I wanted her to tell me something true, but I wasn't sure if I'd recognise it if I heard it.

'Because,' she said patiently, 'we go all the way back and you are my blood, whatever you think about it not being thick enough, and because no one changes that much, even in thirteen years.'

'People change,' I said. 'People do it all the time.'

'There,' said Pansy. She sat up abruptly and pointed her finger at the air. 'That's something,' she said. 'That's something you know. You should give yourself more credit.'

'I'm all out of credit,' I said. 'I'm all out.'

'I think I went and became a creature of habit,' I said to Jane, the next day.

We were drinking coffee with milk in a small Italian café near Shepherd's Market. It was cramped and there was brown linoleum on the floor and tables with dappled plastic tops and wooden chairs with rush seats that creaked with complaint when you sat down.

There were photographs and postcards taped to the walls, end to end. I wondered whether regular clients sent postcards over the years, from package holidays and trekking vacations, business trips and honeymoons. Did they sit in an anonymous hotel room far from home and miss their morning coffee made just the way they liked it? Did they sit down and write a card to bring them closer to the familiar?

I liked this place because it was defiant in the face of the nineties and everything changing. It was just a regular place to come and have coffee and perhaps a piece of cake or some twisted pastry, covered in a fine layer of icing sugar, which they made in the back.

In the middle of the far wall, incongruous among the family snaps and the postcard collection, there was a high counter made of garish speckled maroon marble. On top of it was the coffee machine and a monstrous contraption that would tell your fortune if you put tenpence in the slot. This was managed by the owner's daughter, who was bullishly plain and seemed to have no other interests apart from listening to Talk Radio on a piece in her ear. (This sometimes made it difficult to get her attention.) I always bought my fortune, because tenpence seemed worth it.

Today, when I put my piece of silver in the slot, pulled the stiff ratcheted handle and got my minute rolled-up scroll in return, it said: *Fine living will bring you surprises.* Even allowing for the fact that this device was made in Italy and the translations were sometimes loose, I found this baffling. I showed it to Jane, who looked at it solemnly and said she would use it in her art.

'You see,' I said, once we were settled with cups of coffee and a plate of brittle almond biscuits, 'I think I turned into some kind of repetitive unimaginative person when I wasn't looking. I became like one of those terrible married couples who don't talk any more because they know the answers to all the banal questions. They know it's steak on Monday and bingo on Tuesday and there are no surprises.'

'It's rambling talk,' said Jane, 'but I think I know what you're saying.'

'Come on,' I said, 'this is life and death. This is no time for frivolity.'

'Life and death,' said Jane, serious as the newly converted, 'is when you need frivolity most.'

I thought she sounded like something out of the fortune machine; I wondered whether she had been writing the mottoes herself, in secret, whether it had been her idea all along.

We finished our coffee and paid the bill and went outside and looked up and down the long slope towards Piccadilly and started to walk south. We headed up the straight incline that leads to the cloisters outside the Ritz hotel, that strange, stranded arcade that holds shops which never had any customers; emporia of woollen goods and leather luxuries, entirely empty. Stella always said that they were clearly efficient fronts for international money-laundering operations.

'So,' I said, as we started walking, 'do you think I'm being weak and foolish? Do you think I should stop dwelling on the past and the might-have-been?'

Jane walked a few steps before she fell into a moving rhythm. She walked naturally with a rolling gait, as if she were on board ship in a high wind, as if she knew that however much the deck under her shifted and swelled she had its measure, that she would never get swept overboard by a freak wave.

'I don't think that,' she said, swinging up towards the beckoning glitter of Piccadilly. 'You're the one who thinks that.'

'I don't know what I think any more,' I said to Paco, the next day.

We met in the afternoon at the Museum of Mankind in Burlington Gardens. It's a hidden museum, hardly frequented by the tourist busloads and eager hordes who pour into the Royal Academy just round the corner. It's in a small oxbow lake of Mayfair, the short stretch of street that links Savile Row with Bond Street, only used by gentlemen coming out of their tailors and art dealers on the move.

I liked it. There was a spacious marble atrium and some eccentric and startling exhibits and it was always empty, as if no one else knew it was there.

Paco and I walked around and looked at some intricate jewellery the Celts had made when they weren't out fighting for territory.

'No,' he said. 'That's understandable.'

For a moment I felt a terrible rushing rage that all this should be so explicable, so ordered, so *expected*. Was I really just like everyone else? I wanted to spit.

I stared at a small and astonishingly intricate hair adornment in vulgar shining gold that looked as if it had been made ten days ago. I wondered if the Celts had felt all these exact same feelings, when they hadn't been invading places.

'Yeah,' I said, taking a deep breath and remembering that this was Paco, whom I loved like a brother, and that I was lucky to have friends like this, because not everyone did; the grey crazed women didn't, that was for sure, as they rampaged round the low-rent neighbourhoods telling everyone about the Second Coming.

'Yes yes yes,' I said, like a child. 'I know you're right. You are right. You're all right.'

Paco lifted his head quickly like a bird-dog and looked right at me. I could see that there was a part of him that was surprised, but there was something else as well. It looked, faintly, like relief.

'You're angry now,' he said. 'Is that what this is?'

'What *This*?' I said. 'There is no This. I just don't fucking know anything any more, that's all. It's not chaos theory.'

Paco started to smile and when the smile reached across his whole mouth he shook his head and started to laugh.

The dozing attendant in the corner woke up and rearranged her folded face into lines of acceptable disapproval.

'What?' I said, in a shooting whisper. 'Don't *laugh* at me.'

'Come on,' said Paco, still laughing quietly to himself, his shoulders hopping up and down with it, like a cartoon character.

He took my arm and led me down the wide light marble staircase and into the street and he stopped at a flower barrow and bought a fold of tulips and pressed them into my hand and started walking again, across Burlington Gardens and down Cork Street.

'What?' I said. 'What are these flowers? Where are we going?'

'We're walking,' said Paco, 'so I can look in the windows at the pictures and you can get some of that spleen out of you.'

'Spleen is derogative and nugatory,' I said, spotting a high horse passing by and jumping right on it. 'I don't have *spleen*, I have righteous anger.'

'There,' said Paco. 'That's good. That's good for your liver.'

'What does that have to do with it?' I said, wrong-footed one more time. Say what you like about Paco, he never let you get complacent in your old age.

'Suppressed anger fucks the liver,' he said. 'It's documented.'

I stopped walking and took a deep breath to say something but it never came out. I felt myself taken by surprise, as if someone had bumped into me from the back, and I started to cry.

'That's better,' said Paco.

He hated people crying, he looked away and shuffled his feet and often left the room. He was standing his ground now and even through these sudden flooding tears I could see that he was doing a manful job, because I knew this was really difficult for him. For some reason, this made me cry even harder.

'I am so fucking angry,' I said, pushing the words out between tears, 'that I feel I could *explode.*'

Stella came round that night and made me a dish of spaghetti with parsley, which was the only thing she could cook. Pansy had gone out with William to eat goat curry and rice and peas somewhere north of the Harrow Road.

'That one is going back to his Caribbean roots just now,' she said. 'Don't ask me why. He never ate rice and peas in San Francisco. It was all sashimi and carpaccio with him then. Who's to say what a boy will do?'

I told Stella about crying in the middle of Cork Street.

'Ah,' she said thoughtfully, adding Spanish olive oil to her pasta. 'Did all those beady dealers come out of their galleries and have a look?'

'No,' I said. 'When you cry in London no one takes the blindest bit of notice.'

'The English,' said Stella. 'What car are *they* in?'

She carried over two plates of yellow spaghetti, flecked with green from the parsley, and a dish of tomatoes.

'See,' she said. 'Now I am an Italian mamma, just like that boy Paco. It's official.'

I looked at all that food piled up in front of me and I didn't feel strong enough to eat it. Stella pretended not to notice.

'Do you feel better at all?' she said.

'Nine years,' I said. 'Nine years is just too long, you know? It takes a minute, to get over nine years. Actually,' I said, 'maybe it's not the time at all; maybe it's something else.'

'Maybe it's betrayal and ritual humiliation?' said Stella. 'Normally I find that puts me in a shitty mood.'

'Oh yes,' I said. 'That could be it.'

'It's like the books said,' said Stella, putting on a fatuous moony look and taking my hand. 'You're going to have to learn to trust again.'

'Fuck that,' I said. 'Just fuck that and the horse it rode in on. I think we should do your idea. I think we should take revenge.'

'You do?' said Stella, sitting up straight. 'I wasn't sure if you meant it. I thought you were saying yes to humour us.'

'I was,' I said. 'But now I'm angry and I'm bitter and I don't want to be rational. I want to split him into small pieces and let him see how easy it is to put himself back together again.'

'Oh, good,' said Stella. 'I must tell my shrink. I'm sure she'll regard this as progress.'

15 ∫

At the beginning, we gathered in Stella's flat and ate take-out food and talked. We started ideas and let them languish; we looked at pictures; we read magazines; we talked, hesitantly at first, about art. There was a Tom Tiddler's ground going on, unspoken. There was the residual idea of Art as something untouchable, that it had some sanctity, that to parody and pastiche it would be like dancing in a cathedral.

'Come on,' said Pansy, on the third day. There was a sense of anticlimax and restraint in the room. We didn't seem to know how to start. 'It's not holy ground.' She rifled through one of the art magazines we'd bought at the newsagent in Old Compton Street. 'Listen to this,' she said. 'This is what we're up against. In 1996, Jez Handing installed a homeless man in the Tate as a Living Work of Art.'

'Oh,' said Jane. 'Mark Wallinger did that with a horse. He bought a racehorse and called it *Living Work of Art*.'

'What about this?' said Pansy, picking up another book. 'Can anyone tell me what this means? I'm quoting: Russian mail artist Ivan Ronic is to have a show at the Tate Gallery Liverpool called 'Post Coitum Omne Animal Triste Est'.'

'Catchy title,' said Stella.

'From his home in Volovon on the edge of the Pripet marshes he will post a letter to every resident of the

Toxteth district of Liverpool as a gesture of solidarity from the starving peasants of Siberia to the starving peasants of Merseyside.'

'Do they still have peasants on the Mersey?' said Jane. 'I thought all that went out with the Age of Enlightenment.'

Pansy frowned. 'I think they're being funny,' she said. 'It's hard to tell. Anyway,' she said, continuing to read, 'the letter will invite them to the gallery for a feast of potatoes and vodka, all specially imported from Siberia. After the guests have been carried out from the free supper, the tables will be left untouched in the gallery for the duration of the exhibition. Visitors will be provided with plastic bags and encouraged to take leftovers home. By the end of the show, Ronic expects the installation to be overrun by street rats "as big as cats" for which Liverpool is famous. "Use food to best world and early Christmas for post," observed the earnest Ronic.'

Pansy put the magazine down carefully.

'I think,' she said, 'that's a joke. Surely that must be a joke, no?'

'It's hard to tell,' said Jane. 'To promote the new Tate Bankside, one artist, I can't remember her name, came up with the concept of a wedding taking place in Borough Market.'

'A normal wedding?' said Paco. 'White dresses and confetti and till death us do part?'

'Someone's actual wedding,' said Jane. 'The sceptics got all riled up about it and the Tate put out a press release saying something like The Wedding Project shifts definitions of what is considered public and what is considered private; it is about the aesthetic of public events and formal celebrations and the phenomenon of their documentation.'

'I like that,' said Paco, meditatively. 'The phenomenon of their documentation. That's just another way of saying taking snaps, isn't it?'

'You would think,' said Jane, who despite a keen sense of the absurd liked to keep her mind wide open.

'Oh, this is good,' said Stella, who was looking through a catalogue. 'This is Hayden Bustle.'

There were two critics most known for their impenetrable prose and conviction of superiority. There was Hayden Bustle, a furious American expatriate, who had come to London for the culture in 1973 and been talking about it ever since; and Treve Pettit, who had a voice like a strangled weasel and a face to match.

Hayden loved anything novel, irrespective of any apparent artistic merit; the shock of the new sent a hundred volts through her every time and lit her up like a small town at Christmas. Treve, at the other extreme, thought anything after Monet was mindless tat; he was even equivocal about Picasso, whom he considered over-hyped. Give him a room full of Vermeers and he was happy man, or as near as he ever got to happy. He was on record as saying that art students were intellectual pond-life and that their explanations of their own work were streams of gibberish. He was asked to the best parties and went to them all and drank cups of hot water with a slice of lemon and let off small controlled rants about the success of men who put sharks in tanks.

'Oh, Hayden's always good for a laugh,' said Jane. 'How we love to watch that girl go.'

'OK,' said Stella. 'Catalogue notes. Using the notion of collective memory, Shane Diamond, David Dean and Jeanette Farson each locate their work firmly in fiction through a multi-faceted take on manipulation and funky working processes. David Dean's cartoon images with their revamped Cindy Sherman *à la* fanzine mentality, dispense with subtlety of nuance and use self-consciousness as a tensile strength.'

'Oh, *now* it all makes sense,' said Pansy. 'I see exactly.'

*　　*　　*

As we had these meetings, these lunches and teas, these coffee hours and walks in Green Park, talking about paintings and pictures and installations and readymades and sculptures and trends, about conceptual art and pop art and figurative art and what it all meant, in the back of my mind I was thinking about the missing Dime.

When Jem had called round and sat on my sofa and rolled his piece of builder's putty in his hands and said I want you to find me a Dime, I hadn't been in any frame of mind to evince an interest. My life was officially over, there was nothing I wanted to do except take a slow boat to China and never think about love again.

I suddenly realised that this absurd project, this revenge notion, had brought back some semblance of life to me. I was bruised and furious still; wounded in my heart. I thought that nine years weren't going to be got over just like that. One night when I was lying awake, my eyes dry and open, staring at the ceiling as if there was something damaged in my neck which prevented me from moving my head – staring madly at the ceiling like some rocking inmate of a white-walled institution – I had thought that there was something unfitting and obscene about the idea that whatever happened, you just dusted yourself off and got on to the next trick.

The theory went that life was what you made it (how long did they take to come up with that one?): there was no such thing as being at the mercy of your emotions, your life was in your grasp. You could decide that you were not going to feel despair, envy, terror; you made the call, you controlled your destiny. It was all a question, said the bookstore sages, of perception, which won you a coconut every time except when it came down to the actual execution.

In the first days after Fred left, I thought I should be able to skew my thinking: not bereavement but release, not the end but a new beginning. It was basic enlightened nineties pop psychology, it made beautiful reading. But I couldn't do it. And then I got angry and cussed, and I started to think that to get over it too fast, to have a moment of sad grace then go out for cocktails, held a kind of indecency. There was something improper and obscene about such resilience. What about mourning, I thought, what about a statutory period of black crêpe? Something was destroyed, something was finished; I felt an old-fashioned notion that it was proper to mark its passing.

I was angry and I was sorrowing, because I had been in love and that was all smashed and broken around me, so I was going to carry through this preposterous plan, however baroque it seemed, because I needed to do something, and because, in some intangible way, it had brought back to life some part of me which I had thought was killed stone dead.

It was in the dead zone that Jem had visited and I had told him that I wasn't interested, but now that I was able to get through the day without feeling as if my feet were dipped in tar, I started to wonder about that Dime.

I called Jem up and put on a neutral voice because I didn't want to sound too interested.

'What about that Dime you asked me about?' I said. 'Did you ever do anything about it?'

He didn't sound surprised, although I had made no small talk or introduction.

'I didn't do anything,' he said. 'What might I have done?'

'I mean,' I said, 'did you go to anyone else?'

'No,' said Jem. 'I didn't know anyone but you.'

That was a curious thing about Jem. He could tycoon his way round the property pool, but out of water he was helpless as a goldfish. He could have found out who the acknowledged experts on Dime were with two telephone calls. I knew no more than anyone in my line of work; I had no specialised knowledge; I knew a few people, that was all.

Jem didn't need me, but it made him feel safer that way. He would have been shy and awkward ringing up some strange gallery, having to explain his interest. Although he liked to look at art, and he occasionally bought something, he would never go into a gallery on his own: he would ring me up on a Saturday and ask me to go with him and even then he would sidle uncomfortably round the walls, rolling his ball of putty smaller and smaller, looking as if he was about to be arrested for tax evasion.

'All right,' I said. 'I might be interested. But,' I said sternly, in case he should get the wrong idea, 'I don't know if I will do anything and I don't know if I can do anything and it's almost certainly lost for ever, so don't get your hopes up, that's all.'

'I'll buy you lunch,' said Jem. 'And we'll talk about it.'

Jem's office was west of Soho Square; he liked to eat in a small Greek place on Frith Street. He always ordered the same thing: keftedes and salad and a thin pastry confection heavy with honey and studded with slivers of green pistachio nuts. He had been going there since he was twenty-two and just starting doing deals and even though now he could have bought the whole restaurant with the change in his back pocket they still treated him as if he was an errant schoolboy bunking off class.

'How did you hear about it in the first place?' I said.

I was interested in Jem's life because so much of it was a mystery to me. He was reticent about his personal life; I didn't know what he did in his large house down by the river and I didn't ask.

'Someone was talking,' said Jem. 'I heard it at a dinner I went to. Someone was talking about lost pictures, about farmers walking into Sotheby's in Chester with a grimy old canvas and it turning out to be a Renoir, that kind of thing.'

'It does happen,' I said. 'There are people who make it a life's work, looking for lost pictures. They go round the auction houses and the junk shops in obscure provincial towns, hoping they will find something that has been forgotten in someone's attic for fifty years and turns out to be a Reynolds. Sleepers, they call them. They get sold for nothing, as school of or period of, and then someone gets a bit of a feeling, some hunch or intuition, and they scrape away a little corner of dirt or paint, and suddenly it's a Millais. There are four-hundred-year-old sculptures by Italian masters that get discovered covered in moss and lichen in some old major's garden, used as a bird-bath for the last eighty years, no one looking at it twice.'

'Yes,' said Jem, nodding slowly. 'That's what these people were saying. They were telling stories. And then someone said that there was a Dime that had gone out of circulation and no one knew where it was and I started wondering.'

I knew the picture he meant. Edgar Dime was born at the turn of the century, and unlike many British artists of his era he had never got caught into a school or movement. He wasn't of the St Ives school or numbered among the Vorticists, although there was a famous photograph of him drinking with Wyndham Lewis at the Gargoyle Club. He was born in time to catch Paris when it was still a centre for Bohemians and poets and roving American expatriates and Fulbright scholars; he was around when an artist could afford to rent a loft in SoHo, when it was still an industrial district, years before it became overrun with coffee stalls and designer-clothing outlets. Dime lived for a while in New York, in a loft which now would cost five thousand dollars a month; he worked on a series of dark pictures with the rattle of machinery coming up through the floorboards. Dylan Thomas was drinking in the Village and Kerouac and

Ginsberg were floating around on street corners and the stretched limousine hadn't been invented yet.

Dime was born in time to meet Picasso, to visit Matisse in Nice, to drink with Hemingway on the Left Bank and exchange letters with T.S. Eliot. He was a notoriously eclectic man, which perhaps was why he never belonged to a movement of artists; he was equally at home with poets and musicians. He did a famous and monumental series of paintings of black musicians in the early fifties, in an age when segregation was still regarded as usual and boarding-houses all over London displayed ill-written signs advertising No Irish, No Blacks, No Dogs.

There was a sense, with Dime, in his life and sometimes even in his work, that he was holding something back, that although everyone else might drink themselves into stumbling oblivion and dance on table-tops, that parties might end with people passed out on the floor and going home with the wrong date, Edgar Dime somehow walked away straight and unaided, to his own bed and his own house, and would be painting in his studio the next morning by nine. He once said that the only way to be a good artist was to keep bankers' hours.

The missing Dime was part of a series he had done towards the end of his life. Some artists reach a triumphant peak in their late middle age then descend fast into bombast or whimsy, but Dime didn't decline; quite the opposite. When he was seventy-eight he produced what many people think is his greatest work. It was a series of pictures of women, drawn from history, famous women, iconic women, the Mona Lisa, Madame Recamier, Venus, Odalisque. Dime took the faces of these famous females and instead of painting them as they had always been painted, genteel and still and trapped by the artist's gaze, the perfect picture of docile womanhood, perhaps with a hint of a secret, but no movement, no action, nothing threatening or human, as if they were caught in amber, preserved for ever in a state of non-threat, he took them out and gave them life.

He painted them laughing. He did the heads and shoulders only, and he painted them full of movement and texture, worked with a palette knife or a stick so that the paint came up off the canvas in eddies and eruptions. He had all the technique and painterly eye of Freud without the distance; with Dime, you felt he was right there in the canvas with his sitter. It was never just about flesh and skin tone for Dime. He had painted women before, it was one of the things he was known for. When the art world got reappraised in the light of the second wave of feminism, Dime was one of the few white male artists who didn't get trashed as part of the patriarchal conspiracy.

With this series of laughing heads, people said that Dime had reached his peak. They were vital and beautiful pictures, tactile and full of movement. You wanted to touch them and you wanted to sit and stare at them for hours and you wanted to take them home and if you went back to the gallery and looked at them again there was always something you had missed first time round.

After that, he went back to the abstract work he had done years before. He had started out doing abstractions, tiny canvases and boards filled with colour and texture that gleam and glow at you out of their tight black frames. He refined and refined that work until it was pure and minimalist and then, as if he had pared it down as far as it would go, he broke out into vivid figurative pictures. Here it is, he seemed to be saying, it was here all along; now I shall show it to you.

After the laughing heads, it was as if he had pushed the figurative tide as far as it would go; this was all he had to say on the subject, so he went back to the purity and seamlessness of abstraction. He went right back to the beginning, to the same scale and the same form, but this time with an old man's eye. They were beautiful glowing pictures that came out of the wall at you and made you feel that death and decrepitude were for some other sucker.

He didn't hurry. He painted a picture a year, one perfect gleaming canvas, every year until he died, aged ninety, in his sleep.

The pictures are in museums and private collections now. They are on smooth walls in Switzerland and Maryland, Cape Town and Madrid. You can see them in the Tate and the Guggenheim in Venice, in museums of modern art in Los Angeles and San Francisco and Chicago and New York. They don't come on the market too often, and when they do there is always interest and intense bidding, whatever the state of the economy. Even when people aren't buying, you can always sell a Dime.

And, famously, there is one picture missing. It has been talked about for the last fifteen years; there have been articles run about it in the broadsheets and it has been discussed on Radio Four, all the top experts in the field have bent their minds to it, but it remains lost. And now Jem came along and thought that I might know where it was.

16

By mutual consent, Stella's flat became the studio for the duration. It was central and it was big and it didn't have much stuff in it, and in some way Stella had become the ringleader, so it seemed right to go to her.

I knew that I should start looking for a new job but my mind shied away from it like a spooked horse. I was living on severance pay and I knew that wouldn't last for ever but it would run for a while longer and I thought I shouldn't think too far ahead.

I thought I could follow this revenge scenario, play this sting and see what happened, and then I would wake up and return to real life and get back in the loop. This felt like dreamtime now; everyone else was in their offices and factories and cars and buses, everyone else was doing the expected thing.

At this exact time, I found myself surrounded by this group of friends who didn't have regular jobs with regular hours. Pansy was looking, in a vague way; she was living on savings too, what would have been her pension if she had been that kind of girl; she knew that she would find something soon enough and she was fatalistic enough to allow it to take its time.

'I haven't been in London since I was nineteen,' she said. 'I want to get the feel of the city again before I commit myself to something I can't change.'

Jane was between shows, Stella was between books, her second novel delivered to the publishers; both of them were in that time of recuperation you need after you've completed something.

Only Paco was busy in the world, setting up a new basement club. He was talking with people and looking at sites and getting the money in place. Everyone was pleased he was back after his time in Paris. He had gone there for a change of air and set up a lounge bar in the Marais and just as quickly shut it down when a famous young actor and his girlfriend, an equally celebrated young supermodel, arrived in a limo with bodyguards and entourage and VIP demands. Paco never wanted to run that kind of joint, he was a neighbourhood boy to his fingertips. Once celebrity wanted him, he shut up shop, sold the lease expensively to an eager buyer and came home.

Now he wanted to set up a chess club, because he thought that people were sick of loud music and coke in the lavatories and wanted somewhere to sit down and have a drink and play board games; dominoes and backgammon and low crooning jazz on the stereo and comfortable seating and chicken sandwiches at two in the morning if you wanted them.

'I know,' he said, when he told me this idea, 'it's not rock and roll. I just wanted somewhere where you don't have to network and you don't have to do drugs and you don't have to yell at braindead people over "Smack My Bitch Up" at full volume. It's old age.'

'Not at all,' I said, thinking dreamily of sofas. 'Sitting down is the new rock and roll, everybody knows that.'

So Paco was working, but the rest of us were in a hiatus, in stolen time, and it was that part of it that I liked best. It was for that reason that I really got up and went round to Stella's every morning.

We would go across the road for coffee with milk and

Danish pastries and watch the boys walking past in pairs and the cycle messengers snarling past the pedestrians and the eager early-bird tourists starting to scratch for worms. Each morning as we did this I forgot about Stella being away for so long and I forgot about my world being turned upside down and I got some notion of sense and continuity; we made desultory conversation and felt the forbidden luxury of being able to sit with nowhere to go at nine in the morning, and I thought, This is all right, I can do this, I can sit and drink a cup of coffee and make some conversation without my heart splitting wide open all over the pavement.

I thought: I can fucking *do* this.

'What do you think?' said Stella, looking about her, at the beginnings of the day.

I thought that she was calmer than I had known her before; that the fury she carried round with her like summer lightning seemed to have burnt low; that there was something more forgiving and philosophical about her now. Perhaps it was those years in America. Perhaps it was that she had got what she wanted.

'I don't know,' I said. 'I'm trying not to think too much or too hard, in case something breaks.'

Stella thought about this for a while.

'Yes,' she said. 'I know that one. But it doesn't work that well, because you don't have much control over your cerebellum, however much you like to think you have.'

'In India,' I said, 'there are men who can train their bodies to stay warm in sub-zero temperatures. They sit outside in the frost with only a loincloth on, warm as toast. There are men in Nepal,' I said, 'who can make one hand burn like fire and the other freeze like ice.'

'Oh, yes,' said Stella. 'But women don't have time to go off and be yogis. We have lives to be living. We're too busy to learn to lasso our thought processes. So we get to thinking even when we wish we didn't.'

'Mostly,' I said, knowing she was right, 'I think this plan is the dumbest idea anyone ever thought of. I don't think it will work and I don't think it should work, but what the hell, I'm one rung up from pond life for the first time since I can remember, and you have to do something when your heart gets broken up, otherwise you end up like one of those insane women who people walk blindly past in the street, because they are too crazed to look at safely.'

'There's a philosophy for life,' said Stella. 'I don't see why we have to be sensible all the time, just because we turned thirty. Who made that the law?'

I'm still not really sure how it started. There was a point when I thought all that would happen was that we would meet up and talk, like a study group or a book club. In America they are more advanced than us timorous English, they have women's groups and divorce groups and men getting in touch with their inner hunter groups (they go into the woods in plaid shirts and shout at the moon, or at least that was what Pansy said). It felt like one of those programmes on the television about friends who have improbable amounts of free time and great hair.

We lay about Stella's flat, and people came and went. Paco dropped in on his way to meetings with secret men with cash in briefcases and numbered accounts, Pansy left for the afternoon to see William. Stella and I were there all the time. Jane sometimes had people to see but didn't say who they were. It was like a floating crap game or a musical comedy. It wasn't like life and I liked it that way.

There was a lot of sitting and talking. Stella said, drinking coffee on the pavement one morning, that that was how the artistic process worked with her.

'I sit,' she said, 'and I don't think about technique or

structure or plot or devices. I let my mind go slack and it
I start to dream a little. It's one notch below consciousness
and then something spools out, like it was all tight rolled
up in there, waiting to come out, like someone else had
written it first and you are just catching it as it flies by. Oh,'
she said, stopping herself abruptly and looking round to see
if anyone had heard, 'that was a bit mystical. Of course,'
she said, making her voice firm and businesslike, 'then in
the second draft there is a lot of form and structure and
it's highly professional and businesslike. It's only at the
beginning that it's dreaming.'

'It's all right,' I said, 'I won't tell anyone you said that.'

Stella prided herself on being a clean modern creation; it
wouldn't do for anyone to know that she had a dreaming
side. That wouldn't play with the dyed hair and the purple
nail varnish and the smart talk, which she had decided was
what the public wanted.

So we sat and talked and took our time, and then one day
we started making things.

Stella went out one Tuesday at lunchtime and wasn't seen
for two days and came back with a series of black-and-white
photographs: close, unforgiving shots of naked women, the
kind of women you don't normally think of as beautiful
objects; an obese woman, an old and wrinkled woman, a
woman with a birthmark over one cheek.

We stuck them up against a background of page-three
girls, airbrushed and tititvated. They made a curious contrast
against the garish newsprint.

We called it *Beauty in the Eye of the Beholder.*

'Where did you get these?' said Paco. 'These are good
pictures.'

'They're just people I know,' said Stella. 'That's all.
They're just ordinary people I know.'

After that, there seemed a shift, as if the ball had got

rolling and was moving of its own volition, as if the ground had shifted, as if we were running downhill with a following wind.

Jane went along to her art-shop man and came back with supplies: boards and canvas and everything we needed. And, like children in a kindergarten, we started cutting and pasting and painting and arranging, and we made things.

We did *Junk Male*, a triptych of blown-up photographs of football hooligans from the tabloids, with accompanying headlines – England's Shame, Drunken Brawls, Hooligans on the Rampage.

Jane took on the role of Hayden Bustle: she put on a face of tortured rapture and spoke fluent art speak.

'Of course,' she said, 'this collapses the space between voyeurism and horror, between tabloid reality and collective revulsion.'

'Collapses' was Hayden's favourite word: any artwork that didn't collapse something wasn't any good to her.

There was *Sex Object*, which was a jar of Vaseline in a glass case.

'Collapses the gap between erotic and functional,' said Jane.

There was *The Impossibility of the Functional Independent Female in the Mind of the Traditional Male*, which was a picture, done by Jane, with such flat realism that it looked like a photograph, of a beautiful smiling woman, smartly dressed, carrying a copy of *Ulysses* and a briefcase and a bunch of flowers; she was suspended in a tank of water, tinted green to look like formaldehyde.

'Of course,' said Jane, standing in front of it, poker-faced, 'a self-referential piece that combines the zeitgeist with the traditional and confounds all expectations in the process. Collapses the space between feminism and conceptualism.'

Then there was our favourite of all, *Elvis Has Left the Building*. This was a big canvas, ten by six, painted with eight thick layers of white gloss paint. In the bottom right-hand corner we stuck a polystyrene McDonald's container, with the remains of a half-eaten burger in it, a little bun, some shredded lettuce, a pickle.

'Ah yes,' said Jane, nodding wisely, 'collapses the space between iconography and the mundane. Demonstrates the paradox between the ubiquity and the power of found objects.'

When I went home each night, I sat in my room and thought about the Dime.

I thought that I would never find it, that it was an impossible demand. But there was a hidden, thrilled part of me that wondered, just wondered, like a challenge or a dare, if I could find it where everyone else had failed.

Dime was known for destroying pictures on a whim. The Venus had only been exhibited once; when the show came down and the pictures were sold, that one wasn't on the list. It was assumed that it went back to the studio and for some reason, in his unpredictable old mind, Dime took a sudden hatred to it and burnt it or chopped it up.

People had been present in his studio when the normally mild and calm man (no artistic histrionics for him, no public displays of creative temperament) had an abrupt change of mood, a fleeting fury that led to canvases being slashed and burnt. The stories got told and embellished, but even in the wilder versions these fits of temper never lasted; they were dangerous and intense while they did, and one critic told a famous story of how he lifted a canvas from the wall and held it out of Dime's reach until the destructive mood passed, so saving one of his most famous pictures. I was never sure whether I believed that: there are critics who like to make out that they are more important than they really are, inseparable from this artist or that, shaping the creative direction, supplying some kind of muse. I wondered how many were quietly thwarted painters themselves, their relationship with working artists an inextricable mixture of love and hate, admiration and jealousy, enthusiasm and despair. The I-was-there-when stories were legion, and some of them were true and some of them weren't, but I wondered how much that lily got gilded, out of sheer wishing.

The next day I told Stella I wasn't coming round to her flat and I sat at home and started up my computer and got on the Net and typed in Dime.

I went quickly through the obvious sites; I found potted biographies of Dime and reproductions of his most famous pictures. I looked in archives and found the history of much of his work, who had bought and sold it, who his big collectors were. I found articles and scholarly essays: there were theories about the Venus, that she had been painted over, cut up, given to a friend. There was one strident piece that insisted she had been stolen to order from Dime's studio and now languished in a vault in Queensland.

I didn't believe that was true. I thought the Venus was destroyed. She was in some ways the joker in the pack, painted with a darker and more emphatic style than any of the others. She was the last of the series, and perhaps Dime knew that she would be the last figurative work he ever did, and he gave her life and darkness and some kind of contained fury, as if saying goodbye to this medium was more painful than he let on. (In interviews, he was certain and unmoved by the change: 'It felt like the natural thing to do,' he said, dismissing ideas that he had any grand plan.) I wondered whether he felt that he had given too much away, allowed a forbidden glimpse into what went on behind closed doors. And so she disappeared, seen once for a tantalising glimpse, and then gone.

*   *   *

I rang up my friend Leonard Swift, who was the top Dime man in town. He was an academic, quiet, self-effacing, and when he wasn't writing and teaching and reading about twentieth-century painting, he was indulging in an unexpected passion for mountain-climbing. He was short and thin as a reed and looked faintly consumptive, but he had been to the top of Everest and he never talked about it. I was impressed by that. I always wondered what the world must look like from up there.

'I'm sorry about you and Fred,' he said.

I flinched instinctively and took a breath.

'Well,' I said, 'what can you do? Life must go on. I do nothing now but speak in clichés.'

'Is that what happens,' said Leonard, 'when your heart gets broken? I thought it only happened to me.'

Leonard had a trick like that, of making you feel better about things.

'Perhaps,' I said, 'it happens the same to every single person.'

'Ah,' said Leonard, and I could picture him nodding slowly at the other end of the telephone. He had a long, thoughtful face, with deep lines running down either side of his mouth and dark bruised pouches under his eyes, which gave him a melancholy cast. 'But when it happens to you it feels as if you are the only one, that no one else ever felt this way, and no one else can understand, not really.'

'Yes,' I said. 'I feel as if I'm insulated from the rest of the world, as if there is a thick pane of glass between me and real life, and some days I forget it's there and I smash right into it.'

There was a pause, as if I had said too much. We knew each other, but not intimately.

I cleared my throat and said in a different voice, 'I was calling to ask you about Edgar Dime.'

'Yes, yes,' said Leonard. 'I'm writing something about him

now. They're doing a show of his works on paper in Madrid. I'm writing the catalogue notes.'

'That will be good,' I said. 'At least we'll be able to understand them and there won't be ponderous sentences and many long words and dense passages of obfuscation.'

'That's kind,' said Leonard. There was a laugh breaking in his voice and I wondered again if I'd said too much.

'Someone was talking to me about the Venus,' I said. 'Apparently people are talking again, saying she might still exist.'

'Oh, that,' said Leonard. All at once he had something of the intellectual in his voice, an impatience in his precise mind for the haphazard wool-gathering of amateurs. 'She certainly has held on to all her mystique. Every year someone starts talking, there is another idea, another rumour. Every year someone thinks they have come up with an angle no one else thought of. I don't know why her, particularly. It's not as if she is the best picture he ever made, certainly not in terms of structure or technique. Perhaps it's something to do with it being the last in that series, before he moved back to abstract. I don't know. I never liked her so much myself. Months go by and I don't even give her a thought.'

'So,' I said, 'you don't think there's a chance that she still exists?'

'No I don't,' said Leonard, very definitely. There was no doubt in his voice, no curiosity or prevarication. 'That picture wasn't sold in that show. For whatever reason, it wasn't for sale. He must have taken it back to his studio, and when he died, it wasn't there. I think he burnt it, to tell you the truth. He would do that, on a whim, no one knew why. He was a quiet and personable man, he remembered people's names and suffered bores who wanted to talk to him about art. He was kind to children and gave up his seat on the bus to women and pensioners. He was one of those men about whom the neighbours say, Such a nice quiet gentlemen, always kept himself to himself. But every so often, he had a freakish fit and he destroyed things.'

Leonard paused for a moment and sighed down the telephone.

'I know a great deal about him,' he said, 'but I'm not a psychologist. I have no idea what those moments of fury were about, what demons they represented. But every so often he ripped up a picture and put it on the bonfire, and sometimes he would burn whole piles of sketches and studies. We'll never know how much we've lost because of it.'

'Well, thank goodness for Artie Silver and his dancing feet,' I said, with a small dose of scepticism.

Leonard laughed out loud.

'If Artie Silver saved that picture, I'm the Queen of Sheba,' he said. (For a fleeting moment I had an interesting vision of him decked out in gold lamé and lace, adorned with precious jewels, flowers in his hair.) 'Artie Silver,' he said, with precise disdain, 'would tell you that his grandmother had a venereal disease if he thought it would get him a little attention.'

'So,' I said. 'if someone was thinking of setting out to look for the Venus, you would say they were wasting their time?'

'Yes,' said Leonard. 'I'd tell them to go down to Sotheby's next week and bid for that nice head of Frank Auerbach, if they had some spare cash lying around. That's what I would tell them.'

I told Jem that he was pissing in the dark.

'Oh, well,' he said, philosophical. 'Never mind. If she's gone, she's gone. I liked the sound of her, that's all.'

'There's a good sale at Sotheby's next week,' I said. 'I'll go with you if you want.'

Jem shook his head. 'No,' he said. 'I'll give it a rest for a while. I just wanted that one picture, that's all. I liked the look of that girl.'

I thought of what Leonard had said about her enduring mystique; I wondered what it was.

'You never know,' said Jem, 'in twenty years' time, just when we're least expecting it, we could stumble across her, in the most unlikely place, somewhere you'd never think of looking.'

'Jem,' I said, 'I've looked at the information about Dime; I've spoken to the most eminent authority on him, who told me categorically that picture was destroyed, in his professional opinion. It's not a dusty old Reynolds, it's one of the most famous pictures of the twentieth century. You can't hide a picture like that, eventually someone starts to talk, a leak appears, a hairline crack. The news gets out. It's worth a fortune; if someone had it, it would have come on the market by now, it would come out. And it hasn't. There is no clue, no lead, no hide nor hair of it for twenty years. 'It's gone, that's all.'

Jem shrugged and looked stubborn as a small boy told he can't have any pudding.

'Maybe,' he said.

'Why,' I said, 'do you go on insisting in believing that she still exists?'

Jem's face brightened and he stopped fidgeting and looked right at me.

'That's easy,' he said. 'Because I want to.'

17 ʃ

The next week Paco and Pansy did *Fourteen Dreams*, fourteen
blown-up black-and-white photographs of Pansy, taken on
a motordrive as she was closing her eyes, so the first one
was with the eyes wide open and in the last one the eyes
were shut. They did them close up and highly lit so that the
features were bleached out and all you got was the eyes,
floating in a white space. It reminded you of something,
but you weren't sure what.

'My eyes,' said Pansy. 'I always wanted my eyes to get
the fame they deserved.'

'They're beautiful,' said Paco, straight as a die, 'your
eyes.'

There was something in his voice I hadn't heard before
and I gave him a second look, but his face was still and
giving nothing away.

Jane took the pictures and painted the background in
each one a slightly different shade of indigo and we lined
them up and put them in a box frame, behind glass, so
there was a slight distance between the room and the
photographs.

'Well,' said Jane, putting on her Hayden Bustle voice,
'I should say now that we're veering towards the disarm-
ingly evasive rather than the theoretically correct, wouldn't
you?'

'Here's one,' said Stella, who was lying on the sofa reading magazines. 'An artist in the north-east is exhibiting a shed with holes in it. When asked what it all meant he said, and I'm quoting now, "It deals with the currency of belief by creating a trans-substantive form. It reflects the wonderful human desire for the non-empiric to be empiric, the unprovable to be provable."'

'He got all that from one shed?' said Paco.

'Now I understand,' said Pansy. '*Now* I get it.'

Stella got it into her head that she wanted to do something about statistics.

'Can't we do a nice meaty polemic about how many women get beaten by their husbands?' she said. 'Can't we have an *agenda?*'

William was round that day, sitting elegantly on the sofa in his dark suit with the sloping pockets and the long vent at the back. He seemed to like it there, with all the activity going on, and he was another one who wasn't busy in the day, so he had taken to coming round most afternoons. He was too perfectly dressed to want to join in, but he said he liked to watch. He never said much; sometimes we forgot he was there, as we talked and pasted and painted and read out streams of art gibberish to each other.

'It reminds me of San Francisco,' he said. 'I was a performance artist once, for a day. I sat in a box in a deserted warehouse down near the Presidio. It was for some Save the Whale thing. It was to do with perception and space and the destruction of the planet.'

'There you are,' said Pansy. 'Everyone is an artist, these days. Everything is art, even sitting in a box.'

'Tilda Swinton slept in a box for a week at the Serpentine Gallery,' said Jane. 'It was a runaway success.'

'You see,' said Pansy. 'And Iris thinks we're not going to get away with this.'

'Of course we're going to get away with this,' said Stella. 'You watch. But I want to do something about statistics. I want to make an overt feminist statement.'

'Here she goes,' said Jane.

'Don't you do that in your books?' said William.

Stella gave him the sharp, forgiving look she reserved for people who hadn't read her.

'Statistics don't work in a novel,' she said. 'It doesn't look right. It arrests the eye or something. You can't be running along telling a story and have someone say, Oh, and one in four women suffers domestic violence and women are paid seventy-five per cent of what men are paid and only ten per cent of company directors are women and they've got bruises all over from bumping their pretty little heads on the glass ceiling. You just can't do it, it doesn't work. There are funny rules about things like that.'

'What rules?' I said. 'I thought you always said that no one was going to push you around. I thought that was the whole point.'

Stella looked shifty. She stared at the ground and scuffed her foot, like a child being hauled up in front of the headmistress for talking in class.

'Oh, all right,' she said. 'It's a feminist thing. People think you're writing a feminist novel and you're branded and labelled and everyone thinks you want to kill anything with a penis and it's not good for your profile and only the *Guardian* loves you and that's on a good day and don't tell me I'm selling out because I'm not. It's a certain pragmatism, that's all.'

'I see,' I said. 'What? I get it. It's fine.'

'It's just,' said Stella, 'everyone hates feminists. Even women hate feminists. You can't win. You say that dirty word and everyone instantly assumes that you want to cut men's dicks off and you think all sex is rape and you grow your leg hair and wear dungarees and lecture people about the Taliban and female circumcision and how they drown girl babies in China. It's the most terrible epithet and you can't win, that's all. I mean,' she said, turning and giving me a straight look, 'you wouldn't call yourself a feminist, would you?'

'I don't know,' I said. 'No, I probably wouldn't. Not in so many words.'

'Would you?' said Stella, to Pansy.

'Don't do labels, baby,' said Pansy, falling back into California-speak, which I noticed she sometimes did when challenged. 'People already put me in enough boxes without my adding to the confusion. I think William might.'

'It was the same week I was in the box for the whales,' he said.

'Yeah, yeah,' said Stella, 'very funny. But see, even Jane won't use that dirty word,' she said, looking over at her.

'Well,' said Jane, easily, 'it's enough for people to deal with that I'm a lesbian, without putting a political slant on it. I suppose I don't want anyone to think that I sleep with women because I read Andrea Dworkin at a formative age. I'd like people to think I'm a little more original than that.'

'You see?' said Stella, turning up her palms. 'If it wasn't for feminism, we wouldn't be sitting here because we'd all be at home washing whites whiter and keeping the home fires burning, but none of us will say it.'

'I will,' said Paco, suddenly. 'You didn't ask me. I bloody well am a feminist, and I don't care who knows it.'

Stella didn't do a statistic piece in the end. She did a series called *Objects of Desire*, which were images, some photographed, some painted, pulled together from different sources: a catwalk model, a still from a hard-core porn film ('Paco got it for me,' she said, 'the man in the shop wouldn't give it to me. Probably could tell I was a feminist and having to restrain myself from torching his shop'), a woman with a bruised face and a split lip, an eight-year-old girl like something out of Enid Blyton, a donkey, a rent-boy, a lap-dancer.

She was really pleased with this one.

'See?' she said. 'Object of desire because men want to fuck all these things, but also they make them into objects because all they want to do is fuck them. They don't want to have to talk to them or understand them or anything.'

'When was the last time you tried talking to a donkey?' said Pansy.

'When was the last time you tried talking to a *model*?' said Stella.

'Now now,' said Jane mildly, 'don't let's generalise. Some of those girls read *Finnegans Wake* when they're not thinking about frocks. We don't want to fall victim to cultural stereotyping.'

'But Stella likes that,' said Paco. 'Nothing she likes better than a sweeping generalisation.'

'*Hey,*' said Stella. 'You're supposed to be on my side.'

I left early that evening and walked down Piccadilly to the bookshop, where I bought a biography of Edgar Dime that had recently been published.

I didn't think that there was anything in this Venus thing. I thought Leonard was right. I thought she was gone and that Jem was asking the impossible, but all the same, I felt some interest.

No, that's not right. It wasn't just some interest.

I thought she was still there; I thought she must be. My rational mind said Don't go chasing rainbows. But the Venus had become my pot of gold. I knew that I couldn't make things go back to the way they were before; I knew that Fred was gone and lost to me and I didn't know why and it made me so angry that I felt as if

I was going to take off like a rocket into a dark night sky.

I wanted Fred to come back and beg, I wanted him to say he had made a terrible mistake and that I was the one he loved. I wanted him penitent and humble and telling me that Natalie Hedge was an early mid-life aberration. I didn't fully understand why I couldn't make that happen, although I knew I couldn't.

I thought, If I can find that painting, I can reassert myself against all the forces lined up against me. If I can make that picture exist, I can prove the impossible, and like a totem against the random nature of the world, it would keep me safe. See what I can do. I am still alive.

Oh, fuck, I thought. None of this made any sense. But it was all I had to cling to, in the shifting sands I was treading on. It was my piece of driftwood, my holy ground. Let her exist, I thought. Let her not be gone.

I lay in bed that night and tried not to think about the work we were doing and the elaborate lengths we were going to on my behalf.

Curiously, I liked the stuff we'd produced. It wasn't ground-shaking or startling or anything that hadn't been thought before, but it arrested the eye for a moment and some of it made you look twice and some of it made you smile or ponder and that was more than I could say for some of the stuff that ran around town calling itself art and refusing to acknowledge that Duchamp or Rauschenberg or Joseph Beuys had done it all before and better first time round.

I didn't know if we would get away with it: some nights I felt the weight of a hundred eyes turning on me in accusation, waiting for an explanation that someone had left town with the day before.

*   *   *

There were things I didn't know about Edgar Dime. I didn't know that he had been friends with Frank Mitchell, that they had a short intense friendship in the late fifties when they went everywhere together and played furious and fraught games of two-handed canasta which Dime always won.

I looked at the name on the spine. Patricia Darling; it wasn't a name I knew. I had no face or reference to put to it, there was no information on the dust-jacket, aside from the fact that this was her fourth book and she lived in Sheffield. She seemed to have the inside track on a lot of intimate information I hadn't read before. I never knew that Dime was a card-sharp; I never knew that when he returned to London from New York in 1957 he spent most days with Frank, drinking through the afternoon at the Colony Room.

There was a blurred black-and-white photograph of the two of them together, Dime looking upright and respectable and slightly self-mocking, dressed in a good suit, as if he was ready for a day's work in a firm of chartered accountants, and Frank, already dissipated but surprisingly handsome, his hair combed up into an untidy quiff, an old shapeless mackintosh on, a cigarette clamped in his left hand, smoked down to the stub. He had his arm around Dime and he was leaning into him and smiling a brazen grin at the camera which seemed to say, See? See? I know how to keep company when I have to.

Frank was starting out then, his first play had opened in Shaftesbury Avenue, all the glory and decline were still in front of him. I found it curious, looking at this photograph of his younger self; I found it curious that he didn't know then that he would end up in one room off Dean Street, living in a building with a couple of girls who avoided his groping hands and made resigned jokes about how much whisky he drank. This younger self didn't know about the solitary death, the liver engorged with fatty deposits from years of fierce living, the body that would lie undisturbed for days, because there was no one to claim it. This younger self didn't know about the dismal funeral, the empty pews, the brief embarrassed words from the priest, hurrying on to the next corpse, wanting to be gone.

There was something in the eyes, perhaps, something which knew he would never end up in a nice house in the suburbs with grandchildren and a pipe. Perhaps people know from the beginning; perhaps they get intimations and hauntings; perhaps they catch a glimpse of their fate and decide not to fight it, because what's the point?

I asked Stella the next day whether she knew that Frank and Edgar Dime had been friends.

'Oh yes,' she said. 'It was a long time ago, before Frank was really famous. He met Dime in a bookshop in Cecil Court, that's what he said, and they got to talking and went for a drink and started meeting to play cards. He had a Dime sketch; Dime gave it to him to pay a bet. Frank used to boast about that: "My little Dime," he used to say, "could buy all you fuckers out ten times over." It was worth a fortune but he never sold it.'

'I never knew that,' I said. 'I didn't know all that.'

A Dime sketch, I thought, my mind suddenly racing into implausible possibilities. *He had a Dime.*

'Yeah,' said Stella, not much interested, her mind away on statistics and overt political statements, most likely. 'Well, you didn't see as much of him as I did. You left the building. He was too lonely by the end, the least I could do was listen on the stairs for a half-hour here and there.'

'Did you see his flat, after they took him away?' I said. 'Was the Dime still there?'

'Yes,' said Stella. 'All those years he was strapped for cash and he never sold it. I was surprised it wasn't burgled off him the way he bragged about it all over Soho, and he never locked his windows.'

'There wasn't anything else there?' I said. 'There weren't any other pictures?'

'Oh, no,' said Stella. 'There was nothing there except a chair and a table and a kettle with the bottom burnt out because he left it on the gas one time when he passed out drunk.'

She stopped and frowned at me.

'Why?' she said.

'No reason,' I said. 'I was reading a book on Dime and there was a section about Frank and I hadn't thought about him for years, that's all.'

'It was a long time ago,' said Stella. 'And it didn't do him any good. It didn't do him any good at all, the consoling power of art.'

I walked home shaken with thinking. Frank had a Dime. If he had a sketch that I never knew about, what else might he have had? What if there had been something more between them, these disparate men? What if there had been more to it than card games and gambling debts? What if, since that day in the late seventies when the Venus disappeared, she had been with Frank all the time?

I tried to send my mind back to the times I had been in Frank's flat. I had avoided him mostly, because his yellow teeth and leery eyes had always repelled me. I didn't want him to see it, so I tried not to get caught: he might have been drunk, but he was never stupid.

But there had been times, when I was coming back home after a late night, and I would climb the stairs and Frank's door would be open and he would call me in and I didn't have it in me to say no. Often he had people there, other fifties survivors, women with thick skin and ragged voices, men with curiously dignified tailoring and some remnants of sad grace.

There was one night I always remembered, just before I moved out for good, forsook the dirty old streets of Soho for the ordered calm of my Bond Street eyrie, when it was just him. I had been out with Paco; Stella wasn't with us for once, she was off with some boy who lived in Ladbroke Grove and refused ever to move out of his neighbourhood ('I have to go west,' she said, 'if I want sex, and I suppose I want sex'). My building was dark and silent and it was after one in the morning but I was still humming from tequila and espresso and when Frank called out to me as I was half-way up the stairs I didn't mind so much.

He was sitting alone in his room and he had the radio on to some late-night jazz station and he was smoking a roll-up and drinking from a tumbler half filled with whisky.

He offered me a chair and a drink and I lit up a cigarette and we talked for a while, about nothing much. I never really knew what to say to Frank, something about his decline and defiant drunkenness made me feel shy and inadequate, as if I really were a nice girl who didn't know how to play with the real world.

That night, though, for once, he was calm and lucid. He said that a man had called him up from Latvia about putting one of his plays on.

'Latvia,' he said. 'It's not what you expect. It's not Shaftesbury fucking Avenue. But they have festivals there; they mind about poetry. They read *Beckett*.'

Frank's plays had gone out of fashion: after his star soared in a fleeting arc, he had been relegated to the ranks of the forgotten, the dated, curiosity value only, a museum piece. Stella said that was why he drank so much, although she said he had always drunk that much, even when he was fêted and sought after.

'That's nice,' I said. I wished I hadn't said that. Nice was one of the words that made Frank call the police.

He nodded and let it go. A man had called him up and asked for one of his plays; I could see that this made up for everything, that night.

'You forget,' he said, 'when they don't want you any more, when you can't do it any more. You forget what it was.'

I drank at the whisky he gave me. I felt it burn in me, along with the shots I had drunk earlier. I felt clear-headed and bold.

'Why did you stop writing?' I said. 'What made you stop?'

He narrowed his eyes and for a moment I thought that I had crossed the line; that he would grow angry and bitter and throw me out. But he sat back in his chair and told me.

'You never mean to stop,' he said. 'You never think you will. When you are young and all you are is full of words, you think it will never end. People ask you how you do it, why you do it, as if it's something strange and explicable at the same time. They ask you,' he said, smiling at some inner joke, 'how you have the *discipline*.'

He looked at me, but it was not something I knew about, and I had nothing to tell him.

'What you can't tell them,' he said, and he turned his head and looked out of his open window, as if he were talking to someone else, 'what you can't say when you have your picture in the paper and critics lining up to analyse your work and bouquets raining on you, is that you don't know how you do it. You can't tell them that it's a mystery. You have to talk about form and structure and planning and reason. You can't tell them that it's compulsion, that it's like a drug to you, that if you didn't do it you would have no more point to life. No one wants to hear that. You can't tell them that if you didn't do it you would climb the walls like a junkie without a fix.'

His eyes were lit and animate; his face had something in it of a younger self, before the bottle got him and wrought its devastation. Suddenly I saw what my landlord meant about all those girls, chasing Frank round Soho on Saturday nights.

'It doesn't stop just like that,' he said. 'It's not overnight. You start something that doesn't work, and you can't get it right, and you leave it a while, and you do other things, and there is life, and you think that's all right, because there has to be life, or there would be nothing to write about. But the gaps grow longer, and you get to drinking in the afternoons. And then you wake up one day and you know it's never coming back, and you are just left with life, and it's not enough.'

'What did you write about?' I said. 'When you wrote?'

He brought his eyes back into the room and looked over at me as if he was surprised to find me there. His face fell back into its familiar pattern of cynicism and vice, and it was Frank there again, the neighbourhood drunk, who once was someone.

'I wrote,' he said, with forgotten dignity, 'about love and death. Because what else is there?'

Remembering this now, my head filled with possibility, I tried to cast my mind back to the flat. I had never noticed the Dime sketch, what else might I have missed? Frank's walls were painted dark blue and he only ever had one lamp burning, in the corner of the room; I had a memory of a single pool of light over by the window, lighting up a circle of wooden floor and throwing his face into relief. He had two chairs and a table covered in old periodicals and I had some dim recollection of spilling bookshelves and a guitar in a case.

I couldn't remember anything else. I had only seen his room at night. In the day he slept until lunchtime; at one his door would slam and he would walk down to the pub and spend the afternoon in the Colony Room or some other place where the licensing laws never came into play.

What if, I thought, what if, all the time, the Venus had been hanging on his wall, where the light was too dim for anyone to see her?

By the end of the month, we had enough stuff for an exhibition. By the end of the month, there wasn't any excuse left for hanging round Stella's flat all day long, for mornings spent in coffee-houses and illicit afternoon visits to the cinema. By the end of the month, there wasn't any reason for moving as a pack any more.

For the last few weeks we had entered a still window of time, moved back for a moment to our younger selves, when we did have all the time in the world. There was something potent and evocative about this, as if we were playing ourselves in a film of our lives. But it was destined not to last, and although we never said anything, I think we knew this. There is something tempting and alluring about the power of old friendships, of tight-knit groups; you can say Fuck the world, I'm getting off. When it's just friends, you don't have to worry about the fury and detritus of romantic relationships, you don't have the submerged tensions and responsibilities of family life; you just have each other and it's uncomplicated as glass and you think, If only I could stay like this for ever, nothing would ever matter so much again.

It's an illusion and why not play it for a while? But it's not real life, not when you're past thirty and you know too many of the things that make it not possible to stop the world any more. By the time you get to thirty, you know that the world goes on inexorably and you have to go with it. You know that there is more to reality than a copy of *Sgt. Pepper's Lonely Hearts Club Band* and a Penguin edition of *L'Étranger*; you know that Edith Piaf didn't die for love and that John Lennon probably wasn't shot by the CIA. You know many things that you wish you didn't, and you have a small pulling memory of innocence, which probably never existed but, through the filter of recollection, seems like it was all sunny days and good jokes and toast that landed butter side up.

It was out of my hands now. Stella had taken charge.

'You can't do anything,' she said. 'Fred's not going to take it from you. If we are going to reel him in, it has to look as if it's nothing to do with you.'

So now there was a space again. The fury that had grown in me, replacing the old helpless feeling, was all dressed up with nowhere to go. I felt restless and displaced.

There were too many memories, waiting to besiege me at every turn. Every song on the radio, every inch of my flat, every article of clothing, everything reminded me of Fred. I didn't know what to do with those nine years, which suddenly seemed to count for nothing at all.

But the thought of the Venus was burning in me and I couldn't get it out of my head. I wondered when I was going to learn that lost causes sometimes are lost.

I called up Paco, because he knew everything, and asked him if he knew what happened to Frank Mitchell's stuff after he died.

He didn't ask me why I wanted to know.

'Are you all right?' he said.

'I've been better,' I said.

'Yes,' said Paco. 'You have. There was a cousin,' he said. 'I think she had a sandwich bar somewhere in St James's. She had one of those old-fashioned names, Betty or something. Betsy, that's it. Betsy Mitchell. Frank never had any time for her because she lived a normal life and sold sandwiches and had no ambitions. I think her place was in that arcade that runs off Jermyn Street. She got what there was. It wasn't much, in the end.'

'Thanks,' I said.

I wondered if Betsy was still there, in her sandwich bar. I wondered what she had done with the Dime sketch. I wondered if it turned out Frank did have the Venus, whether I would walk into his cousin's shop and see that picture hanging over the counter, too blatant to be real.

I thought that the only way to find out was to go and see.

I walked down Bond Street and along Piccadilly. The sun was shining and the traffic was snarled up and there were crowds of eager tourists milling around the Royal Academy for the Kandinsky show. I wondered if the Venus was out there in the city, hiding somewhere where no one would ever think of looking for her. I wondered if I was just chasing a mirage.

Sure enough, in the bright-lit arcade, incongruous among the rare book dealers and fine cotton shirt-sellers, there was a small sandwich bar. I walked in; it was very clean and neat, with a glass counter and plates of meat and salads and seven different kinds of bread. The room was empty.

I looked around, not sure what happened next. There were no pictures on the wall, only a long mirror and glass shelves with mysterious bottles of yellow and green spirits.

A woman walked out of the back. She was in late middle age, neat and unremarkable as her shop, with brown hair going grey. She looked incurious and contained.

'Can I help you?' she said.

I wondered if I should buy a sandwich and engage her in conversation, bring her round to talking about Frank in some careless way, as if that wasn't why I was there. I was never any good at subterfuge.

'I hope so,' I said. I felt foolish.

'Is your name Betsy?' I said.

She didn't blink.

'Yes, it is,' she said. 'Is this about Frank?'

I was taken aback.

'How did you know?' I said.

'I don't get passing trade,' she said. 'I have regular customers and I know their faces. Every so often, someone comes along and wants to talk about Frank, for a book they are writing or something. People still remember him.'

There was no fondness or nostalgia in her voice.

'Yes,' I said. 'They do. I knew him when I was younger. I lived in his building.'

She looked straight at me, waiting for the main action.

Does she know? I thought. Is she the one with the secret?

'I wondered,' I said, awkwardly. 'I was wondering . . .'

Betsy Mitchell kept looking at me, without impatience or curiosity or anything at all.

'About the Dime sketch,' I said. 'About that sketch he had.'

'Yes,' said Betsy. 'It was a horrible picture. I sold it to one of my customers. He paid me a good deal of money for it. He wanted to know why I didn't keep it. But I have no use for art.'

'Oh,' I said, wrong-footed. 'I see. I was wondering if, there wasn't, I wondered – I wondered if that was the only picture he had.'

'Yes,' said Betsy, without hesitation. I had no doubt that she was telling the truth.

'That was all he had in the world,' she said.

18 ∫

Six thirty on a Friday evening and I was wondering what I should do that night when there was a tremendous knocking on the door and I went to open it and found Stella standing there, with William just behind her, both of them laughing fit to bust and breathless and not quite steady on their feet.

'Have you been drinking?' I said, letting them in.

'We got the show,' said Stella, speaking rather indistinctly. I heard her well enough but I asked her to repeat it anyway. And then she threw her arms open wide and laughed and laughed until tears came into her eyes.

'We got the fucking show,' she said. 'That's all. We just went and got the show.'

There was some wine in the fridge so I got out two glasses and gave one each to Stella and William and they collapsed over each other on the green sofa.

'So,' I said. 'Do you want to tell me?'

Stella sat up straight and drank her wine and gave me a look over the rim of the glass. Her eyes were lit with wild mischief; she looked as if she had been caught shoplifting in a toy store.

'Go on,' said William, who was calmer. He settled back into his seat, as if to enjoy the spectacle.

'All right,' said Stella. 'I'll tell you. I'll tell you how we got the show. Are you ready for this?' she said, laughing some more.

'Tell me now or I'll kill you,' I said politely.

'Well,' said Stella, 'we had all the stuff just sitting there, and I was getting impatient, so I thought, What the hell, let's take it round to Fred's gallery, and William's cousin has a big yellow van, so . . .'

'You took the stuff round in a van?' I said.

Stella stopped and gave me a dignified look.

'William's cousin has a van,' she said agreeably. 'What? Is there some van law I didn't know about?'

'It's just not how it's normally done, that's all,' I said.

'Normal schmormal,' said Stella, waving her hand at such pedantry. 'Do you want me to tell you or not?'

'Get on,' said William. 'Get to the good part.'

'It's all good part,' said Stella. 'So,' she said, with a hard no-more-interrupting frown at me, 'we went in and Fred was in the main part of the gallery and I said Hello Fred, you may be a dickhead who has been two-timing my dear friend and then dropped her from a great height, but on account of my generous and benign nature I am going to forgive you enough to offer you an exciting new artist.'

'You said that?' I said. I didn't know whether to laugh or leave the country.

'Sure I said that,' said Stella. 'It was a good start, no?'

'That's what she said,' said William. 'Word for word.'

Pansy let herself in with her latch-key and took a look at Stella and William and said 'You got the show, didn't you?' and sat herself down next to me to listen.

'We just started,' said Stella. 'We're at the gallery with the stuff in the back of a van.'

Pansy took this on the chin.

'Then what happened?' she said.

'Fred did a bit of blustering about how he had plenty of

artists and the gallery was booked up till 2002 and a lot of nonsense like that so we had to persuade him,' said Stella.

'How did you do that?' I said. I could feel my mouth starting to gape. I shut it.

'Well,' said Stella, 'I got William and his cousin to start bringing in some of the stuff. We brought in *Fourteen Dreams* and *Beauty in the Eye of the Beholder* and some of the other photographs, they were the easiest to carry.'

'So your cousin was there too?' I said to William.

William nodded.

'My cousin Gilbert from Listoonvarna,' he said. 'He's a hippie. That's why he has a van. He takes it to Glastonbury in the summertime.'

I attempted to picture the three of them in the gallery and couldn't. I tried to focus on something more accessible.

'And then,' said Stella, 'just when I thought I was going to have to strong-arm Fred a bit, threaten his reputation, that kind of thing, we had a stroke of luck.'

'It was timing,' said William.

'What?' said Pansy. 'Get on with it then, I'm irritable with curiosity.'

'Charlie Meldrum came in,' said Stella, a triumphant gleam in her eye. 'He'd been having lunch up the road with his agent or someone and he dropped in to see if there was anything interesting and I still don't know how it happened but he and William got talking and one thing led to another.'

Charlie Meldrum was one of those people who had been around so long you couldn't imagine the world without him. He arrived in London from St Kitts some time in the fifties and he had been playing trumpet at Ronnie Scott's for the month of June ever since anyone could remember. He lived in a top-floor flat in Beak Street and often you would see him setting off to the airport with his trumpet under his arm, a small blue globetrotter in one hand and a copy of the *Sporting Life* in the other, and he would stop off at the betting shop in Wardour Street before getting into a cab, driving out to Heathrow and flying off to Chicago or Amsterdam or Nice or wherever the jazz festival was that month.

When he was at home he wandered about Soho and Mayfair, hanging around the galleries and drinking coffee (unlike his great jazz heroes he never drank; he had some allergic reaction to alcohol, so he took twenty cups of black coffee a day instead). When he wasn't playing trumpet, he moonlighted as an art critic. It was his second great passion after music and he had earned enough over the years to start a small collection. If he was in town, he went to every opening and new show, and often if you went round to an artist's studio you would find Charlie sitting on the couch talking about life and love and the mysteries of women, and smoking roll-ups while the coffee was brewing in the pot.

Charlie was famous for his unremitting good humour, his fatalistic view of the world, and his eclectic taste. The thing he liked doing most, as he got older, was championing the cause of some young artist, some callow unknown, just starting out in a bare room with no heating in the East End, someone the hype and the hucksters had passed by. He'd find a new hopeful, and he'd manage to mention them in every piece he wrote, whether it was about Matisse or Modigliani, the Young British Artists or a de Kooning retrospective.

Everybody loved Charlie Meldrum; he had a laugh like a foghorn coming across a rough sea and a habit of talking rambling streams of nonsense after too much caffeine, and if the light was coming from the right direction he looked a little like Miles Davis and no one I'd ever met had a single bad word to say about him.

'So what led to another?' I said.

'Well,' said Stella, shooting William a naughty testing look from under her black eyebrows, 'I think perhaps it was a brother thing.'

'Was not,' said William, placidly. 'It was a meeting-of-true-minds thing.'

'Yes, yes,' said Stella, laughing to herself. 'That was it. Anyway, he bought one.'

'Charlie Meldrum bought one of our pictures?' I said. I knew this wasn't really happening. I knew that I would wake up tomorrow and find that all the blankets had fallen off the bed after a restless night.

'Is that good?' said Pansy.

'If you're starting out,' I said, 'you want three people most in the world to buy your stuff and Charlie Meldrum is one of them.'

'So come on,' said Stella. 'I knew you'd be pleased.'

I wasn't sure if I was pleased or not. I could hear the distant clanging of steel doors and the slop of prison food. I didn't know what the penalties for fraud were, these days. I hoped I would get a nice open gaol with a tennis court and leisure facilities.

'Which one?' I said.

'*Fourteen Dreams*,' said Stella. 'Pansy should feel flattered. Charlie Meldrum has got her eyes.'

'I suppose at least Jane did part of that,' I said, calculating in my head. 'It's not so bad.'

'Stop panicking,' said Stella. 'It's all going beautifully. So Charlie, being the dearest old cove I ever knew, is doing sincere male bonding with William and I'm talking eighteen to the dozen at Fred, and he's starting to look convinced and then I drop into the conversation that Pete Street has also bought one and . . .'

'Pete Street,' said Pansy, beaming, 'even I've heard of him.'

'Pete Street?' I said. 'My Pete Street?'

'Listen to her,' said Stella. 'Is it a love thing? Do you have designs on the older man?'

'Oh stop,' I said. 'He used to buy through me, that's all.'

'It can be an intimate relationship,' said Stella.

'But you made it up about him buying one?' I said. 'To bait the hook?'

Stella shook her head and smiled blithely, as if everything in the garden was so blindingly lovely that you needed sunglasses just to look at it.

'Oh no,' she said. 'Pete Street did buy, yesterday. I rang up that girl Airedale or whatever she's called, that style bully. I did a little number on her and she came up with the goods.'

'Which one?' I said.

Stella smiled wider than ever.

'*Beauty in the Eye of the Beholder*,' she said. 'It's going to go in his gallery, in the Commercial Road. You must admit.'

'I admit nothing,' I said. 'We're all going to go to gaol. We're going to be locked up for twenty years and it's nothing more than we deserve.'

'Look,' said Stella. 'I think she's pleased.'

With the show in place, everyone went back to their normal lives.

Paco was involved in his club, the money sorted, the builders in. I went to look at the site and admired the bare walls and the concrete floors and the intricate plans for the glass bar. I knew it would be a success because Paco had some golden touch like that, some Pied Piper knack of getting people into a room. It would be full every night and the style papers would write about it and it would become fashionable and the brat-pack actors with their wafer-thin girls would arrive and Paco would sell up and move on to somewhere where people thought that Prada mules were a breed of South American livestock.

Pansy got a job, even though she said she was happy just drifting. Jane introduced her to someone who knew someone who was hiring, and she took a job working in a photographer's gallery near Long Acre.

'It's perfect,' she said. 'It's not high-powered and it's not fast-track to six figures and I shall be surrounded all day by beautiful objects and it has nothing to do with death.'

'Do you think you'll stay, then,' I said, 'in London?'

She put her head on one side and made a twisted grimace with her mouth.

'I don't know,' she said. 'I'm happy here for the time. I miss the bay sometimes, but I like having proper tea and Greater London Radio. I don't know. I still feel like I'm in a strange town even though I lived here for nineteen years of my life.'

'It's all right,' I said. 'I was only asking.'

'I know,' said Pansy. 'I know. We'll see.'

Stella and Jane started working again; William, who was still on sabbatical, visiting his relatives and enjoying a change, went to the pictures alone. Since he was our official artist, it was in our interest that he should be seen to wander the streets and drink at inappropriate times. Mostly he went to the Metro on Rupert Street and watched art-house films, which made Paco envious, because if it weren't for having the builders in that's what he would be doing himself.

I didn't know what to do. Ideally, according to magazine sages, I should be having sex with someone by now. I should be fucking without strings, but I wasn't in the mood.

I felt fragile still; I was conscious of sudden moments of fury burning up in me like smoke and dying away again. I felt as if I were still in some kind of limbo, a metaphysical departure lounge in some monstrous airport complex. I felt as if my flight hadn't been called yet. I felt, in sudden lurching moments of rage, as if I wanted to torch the whole place and watch it burn.

I hated the idea of people who sat around and let their lives disintegrate around them. I thought it wasn't long, what you got, and if you didn't use it you didn't deserve it. Stella said I took a hard line on this.

'You're a paradox,' she said. 'You don't dare ask much of life because you're afraid you'll be refused or let down or disappointed. You're scared that the promises of wine and roses are going to disappear and everyone will be laughing at you for believing in them. But then you get hard-line about people sitting around and feeling sad.'

'Jane doesn't have to be consistent,' I said. 'I don't see why I should.'

'It was just an observation,' said Stella. 'Lajos Egri says that only corpses exist without contradiction. I wasn't expecting you to turn into a physical impossibility.'

'I feel angry,' I said. 'I feel angry at myself. I feel that I should be better than this.'

'You're doing fine,' said Stella. 'I think you're doing very well.'

'Yeah, really,' I said.

'No, but think about it,' said Stella. 'Of all of us, you're the only one who was ever brave enough even to think about a committed relationship. We all make jokes about it, how we don't believe in ties and family values and all that bullshit, but mostly it's fear. Look at Pansy, look at Paco. Look at me, even, with my years on the couch. All of us leaving before it gets too complicated. Even Jane, with her nice family and her confidence, you don't see her making a commitment on a Friday night because she's got nothing better to do. But you did it. And even if it's over now, you know how to give your heart to another person, and no one can take that away from you.'

'It doesn't feel like that,' I said. 'It feels like failure.'

'I know,' said Stella. 'But this will pass. If there's anything I know, it's that this will pass.'

'There are women,' I said, 'who give divorce parties. There are women who burn their old love letters and go to bed with men twenty years younger than them.'

'One swallow doesn't make a summer,' said Stella. 'Although you could go to bed with someone. Meaningless sex can be a great leveller. I heard Dick Part went straight again, maybe you should give him a call.'

'That's very helpful,' I said. 'That truly is a good idea.'

'Don't thank me,' said Stella. 'No really, it's nothing.'

Stella called me the next morning at 8 a.m.

'Did you start your new book?' I said. She kept very early hours when she was writing.

'Oh, yes,' she said. 'It's about love and revenge.'

'Don't ring no bells with me,' I said.

My neck was stiff down the left side. I had a feeling that I was grinding my teeth in my sleep. There was a medical name for this condition but I couldn't remember what it was.

'I called to say that you will feel better when we get to the actual show,' said Stella. 'Once you're standing in that room full of every B-list art groupie in London town and telling them that William never painted anything except his nails, you'll feel better. That's what you're waiting for. You'll see.'

'Maybe,' I said, 'you're right. Maybe that will be an end to it and then I can start staying up late and going to bed with eighteen-year-olds.'

'That's the spirit,' said Stella. She hung up abruptly.

It was all right for her, I thought. She had decided at a young age that art was more reliable than love; it wasn't so much that she wasn't interested in men, it was just that she didn't see why anyone thought they should last for ever. She took them where she found them and mostly she gave them back.

'I don't want to give my heart away to someone,' she always said, 'only to find after five years that I'm sitting at home, lonely and invisible, while they flirt with other women or lose interest in sex or fall into mid-life crises or can't be bothered to talk to you any more. That's not my idea of fun.'

'Did you know,' she said, 'that consistently in surveys the happiest group in society is married men, and the unhappiest group is married women? What does that tell you?'

I wondered if she was right. I didn't believe in marriage, but I did believe in till death us do part. I thought that growing old together was a good idea and I thought I could do it and it shocked me that I was wrong.

19

I spent the rest of the day reading about Dime and racking my brains to think where the missing picture might be and listening to loud music and I was startled when the doorbell went.

I opened the door, wondering if it was a mistake. It wasn't a mistake, it was Pete Street.

'Pete,' I said. 'What are you doing here? It's the middle of the day. Shouldn't you be running the company?'

I felt disconcerted. I had a business relationship with Pete Street: I helped him with his collection and introduced him to artists. I liked him and he made me laugh, but it wasn't personal. He had never been to my flat before. I didn't even know that he had my address. An invisible but tangible line had been crossed without warning; I felt unsure what to say.

Pete didn't seem aware of any incongruity. He was easy-going by nature; he had the kind of sunny disposition that believed it was welcome anywhere, and most times he was right.

He looked around.

'Interesting,' he said. 'I thought there would be more pictures.'

I only had one picture. I couldn't afford the ones I wanted so I went to look at them in galleries and museums; I couldn't bear the idea of covering my walls with cheap, second-rate stuff or phoney reproductions. There was an artist I'd known a few years ago, a quiet slight man who spent evenings drinking in Dean Street. I used to see him around, and then I saw him one night outside Bar Italia, and there was a seat at his table so I asked if I could share it.

It sounds old-fashioned and improbable, but he had a kind face. It was a face that made you smile involuntarily, just looking at it; it had some kind of patent goodness and gentleness shining out of it like starlight.

He told me that his name was Dan Fine and that he was a painter. He was very shy and had a slight stutter, and his reticence infected me, so that first night we smiled at each other and made disconnected remarks about the weather. (It was October and there was unseasonal heat.)

After that we started to have coffee together, and one day he asked me to sit for him, and I took the bus up to his studio in Limehouse, where he had the top floor of an old sewing-machine factory. It was entirely illegal, where he lived, it hadn't been converted for domestic use: there was no kitchen and no bath and only one small lavatory with a basin Dan washed in. I thought it was astonishing that he always seemed so clean. He didn't seem to mind this arrangement. He was pleased that he had somewhere with so much light.

The building had no heat and no electrics; Dan kept warm off a two-bar electric heater and cooked on the kind of Calor Gas ring that campers use, and read at night by an oil-lamp. He had one green corduroy suit and three shirts, which he had bought from Oxfam. He was clever with a needle and turned the collars and cuffs when they became frayed. He spent any money he had on paints and coffee, and he painted big gleaming canvases, full of life and colour.

I went to sit for him and we had to break off every half-hour because even though it was summer it was still cold in his building and I had to stand up and walk around to warm up. It was curious being naked in front of someone other than Fred; at the beginning we were so shy we couldn't look at each other, but then I realised that there was nothing sexual about this, that he was only looking at my body to see the colours of it and the way the light hit it and the shadows on it, and I let out my breath as if I had been holding it, and after that it was like floating it was so easy. At the end of it I felt regret at having to put my clothes back on and cover everything up.

Dan gave me a picture, for sitting for him. I knew that he couldn't afford it, but also I could see that he really wanted to, so I chose one I had been looking at, a small square canvas of a swimmer floating on a blue sea; I liked it because of the colour and because it was what I felt like, as I was sitting for him.

It was still, five years later, the only picture I had on my wall. I kept it over the fireplace and I never got used to it or stopped noticing it; every day I looked at it with pleasure and love. Soon after I sat for Dan he stopped coming to the Bar Italia. I asked about for him, but no one seemed to know where he had gone – even Paco didn't know. One time I went back to his studio, but it was locked and silent and empty.

Every so often, I asked around, among the dealers; I scanned the trade papers, expecting to hear about a show or a picture sold. I couldn't imagine him not succeeding. But I never saw him again, and I never heard of him; there never was a sudden interest in Dan Fine, a flurry of hype and success. He never got taken up by a rich collector, he never got included in one of those fashionable group shows that came around every year since Damien Hirst did *Freeze* in a vacant Port of London Authority building in the far reaches of SE16.

I often looked at my picture and wondered what happened to Dan Fine.

'It's good,' said Pete, looking at it. 'I like it.'

'It's an artist no one ever heard of,' I said. 'He was a friend of mine, but we lost touch.'

I felt protective. This was my private life; I wasn't sure I wanted Pete Street to know about it.

Pete gave me a second look and stepped backward, for the first time looking a little uncertain.

'I'm sorry,' he said. 'Is it a bad time? Should I have called first?'

'It's all right,' I said. 'Sit down. Do you want some coffee?'

I made him strong Italian coffee on the stove and he watched me while I did it. He looked brown and healthy, his skin stretched tight over his bones; he had a keen, athletic look about him.

'I would have come sooner,' he said, 'but I was away.'

I felt a shaft of irrational fury. Why would he have come sooner? I wasn't a charity case.

'You look well,' I said, in a neutral voice.

'I was hiking,' he said. 'In Colorado.'

I took the coffee over and set it down in front of him.

'I came,' he said, 'because I wanted to offer you a job.'

'Oh,' I said, wrong-footed one more time. 'Why?'

'Well,' he said, 'I went into the gallery when I got back from holiday, to see if there was anything new. I saw Fred. He didn't say anything, he acted as if everything was normal. He's representing this new artist I've just bought, William Deakin, do you know about him?'

I nodded. 'I know William very well,' I said.

'Yes,' said Pete. 'Aurelia said he would be a good buy, so I got one, and when I saw Fred he said he was giving

William a show, so that's good. I only heard two days later that you two had broken up and you weren't working at the gallery any more.'

I wasn't sure what this had to do with anything. I was getting used to having Pete Street sitting on my sofa, but only slowly. He was tall and widely built; with his black hair and light blue eyes shining out of his brown face he looked like a wild thing that had just walked off a prairie somewhere. My small room seemed the wrong place for him. Sometimes I thought he should have been a rodeo rider or a ranch hand; he looked like he belonged in an outback or on a range, somewhere where the skies were wider than here, somewhere you could see miles of land, unbroken right to the horizon.

'Well,' I said, 'I thought it would be too awkward to go on working together. It wasn't exactly an amicable break-up. We didn't split the soft furnishings and talk about still being friends.'

I looked at Pete to see what he was making of this. We had only ever discussed art before; we hadn't talked about real life.

He seemed entirely relaxed, as if he came here every day. He leant back on the sofa and stretched out his legs. I wondered what he wanted. I wondered if he was just going to sit here chewing the fat all afternoon in my low white room, while the city went on outside.

I wondered what he knew about getting your heart broken and not being able to find all the pieces again, however much you crawl around on your hands and knees looking for them.

'He was sleeping with Natalie Hedge,' I said. 'She restores pictures. She works in Bruton Street. She's very well thought of.'

Pete's face creased up into concern. I could see that he didn't know. He wasn't interested in gossip; even when people did tell him, he always got the names wrong or couldn't recall the punchline.

'How gruesome,' he said. 'I'm sorry.'

Gruesome, I thought, there was a word. It made me think of guts and gore and cadavers and the walking dead.

'It was gruesome,' I said. 'I didn't know. Everyone knew but me.'

All at once it seemed as if I was sitting on the ceiling, looking down at myself, hearing my voice come distorted and with a slight reverberation. I've said all this before, I thought. I've told this story a million times until it's worn thin with telling.

'Pete,' I said abruptly, 'you know what? Fred was fucking Natalie Hedge for two years and everyone knew but me and then I found out and it was at your party, actually, and I feel like shit, but it's getting a little bit better every day, it's turning from monster movie into imaginably bearable, and would you mind if we talked about something else?'

Pete said he didn't mind not talking about it. He said we could talk about anything I liked. He said did I want to go out for a drive somewhere.

I never thought I would end up going for a drive in the afternoon with Pete Street, but everyone was busy and I didn't know what to do with myself that day.

'Don't you have to be in the office?' I said. 'Don't you have to open another factory somewhere?'

Pete smiled and shook his head.

'No,' he said. 'I don't.'

We got into his car and drove across Trafalgar Square with its lions and fountains and wide light and down Northumberland Avenue to the river. He turned left along the Embankment and we drove out to the east.

'Where are we going?' I said.

The sky was clear and transparent; it seemed very high

and far away. The sun was riding low over the river and no one else was going in this direction.

'To the seaside,' said Pete. 'To eat cockles. That'll cheer you up.'

We drove to Essex, to a short stretch of coast beyond the marshes. The sea lay flat and black in front of us; there was a shingle beach and some peeling boats drawn up in a line. Pete bought two polystyrene pots of fat wet cockles with vinegar from a pub set back from the beach and we took them and sat on a step and looked out over the sea. There was nobody else there.

I stopped feeling strange and decided I might as well run with it. I thought that I worried at things too much and that life didn't always have to be explicable.

Pete Street said that he had always liked the seaside. He said he was taken to Frinton as a child, to look for shells in atrocious Easter weather.

He said things were changing at Commercial Road and his curator was leaving and did I want to run his gallery for him.

I let a pause go by and I looked out at the sea, which was changing colour as the light died on it. The horizon stretched into the distance, empty and clear, and the skies seemed as wide as the ones I imagined Pete would look most at home under.

'You don't mean that,' I said. 'You can't offer me a job like that, out of the blue.'

Pete smiled and looked sideways at me.

'Why not?' he said. 'Who made that rule?'

I didn't know who made the rules, but I knew they got made, and for some reason I was afraid of breaking them.

'I don't know,' I said. 'It feels wrong. I worked in a small commercial gallery. You need someone with more experience, someone who knows about curating. You don't need me.'

'But I want you,' said Pete. He looked at me some more and then he turned away and stared out at the sea where the sun was setting in gaudy glory, like something from a picture postcard.

'This isn't pity,' he said, 'if that's what you take it for. I was thinking this before you and Fred broke up. It seems like a good time now, because you need a job. I don't think it's about rules. I think you should take it.'

It was a great opportunity. I should have been delirious with pleasure.

'Let's go back,' I said.

'All right,' said Pete, standing up. 'But there's something I want to show you first.'

He led the way along a path that ran parallel with the coastline until we came to something that looked like a deserted shack.

'Here,' he said, opening the door.

Inside, astonishingly, everything was tidy and polished and clean; it was an old-fashioned room, furnished with heavy oak tables and benches. The wooden floor was yellow with age and polishing, and there were sepia photographs of groups of serious men on the walls and incongruous pieces of china arranged on plain shelves.

A small Victorian grate sat in the middle of one wall, surrounded with blue Delft tiles, with a fly-blown mirror hanging over it. I saw my reflection, moving, insubstantial, like a ghost, and I looked away.

'What is it?' I said.

'It's a reading room for sailors,' said Pete. 'It's always open. It was founded by some philanthropist with a soft spot for seafaring men. There's one in Suffolk too, I think. I read about it somewhere.'

'It's extraordinary,' I said.

I felt an explosion of pleasure go off in my chest. I had never seen anything like this and I didn't know how Pete knew about it or why he had chosen to bring me here, but something about it made me feel as if I was six years old and I still had the whole world to look forward to.

'But this isn't the best part,' said Pete, and there was the kind of smile on his face that grown-ups wear when children ask whether Father Christmas has come.

'Look in this room,' he said.

He opened a door at the end of the back wall, and led me through into another room, a mirror image of the last, except with more comfortable furniture, a long sofa with the springs showing through, and leather chairs with deep indents from years of being sat in. And on the far wall there was a picture, which was, unmistakably, a Dime.

'No,' I said, and it came out like a laugh and an exclamation, shaken out of me by surprise. For a moment I thought it was my Dime (How had I started thinking like that? Where had that idea come from?). Then I saw that it wasn't one of the laughing heads series at all but a much earlier picture. It was a painting I knew from reproduction and had always had a fondness for; I felt a personal connection with it in some roundabout way, because it was of Monsieur André's sister, Olive Pleat.

It was extraordinary, seeing it now. Whenever I saw it in a book or article, I wondered about Olive; I wondered where she was, what had become of her. I wondered what she would say if she knew that this was where she had ended up, in a bleached hut on an empty stretch of Essex coast.

'I know this picture,' I said. 'How did it get here? All it says in the books is Private Collection.'

'The hut man,' said Pete. 'I can't remember his name. Macintosh, or something. I think he was a Scot. He bought the Dime before he died and hung it here. And the door is always open, and it's probably worth half a million or more, and that's where it stays. Isn't that something?'

I wondered how it was that Pete Street, the sugar king,

who spent his time making money and building factories, who had only ever dealt with me on an entirely professional level, should know that of all the places in the world he could have taken me for a drive, this was the right one.

I found myself smiling all over my face and it was such an unfamiliar feeling that it took a while to realise what I was doing.

'Thank you,' I said, 'for bringing me here. Thank you.'

We drove back. The evening was blue outside and the lights were coming on and people were going home for their supper. We were running against the traffic again.

'I'm sorry,' I said, as we swung through the Limehouse link, 'that I wasn't more enthusiastic about your job offer. It's a great chance, really it is, and don't think I don't appreciate that. It's just, it's, ah, I don't know – I need a moment, I need a little piece of space to get my head straightened out and turn round and get on with the next part.'

Pete kept right on driving.

'I'm sorry,' I said again. 'I can't seem to be much more articulate than that. Does any of it make sense to you?'

'Oh, yes,' said Pete. 'It makes sense.'

Does everyone know about this? I thought. Does everyone know how this works except for me?

Stopped at a traffic light in the Aldwych, Pete turned round in the driving seat and said, 'Do you want to eat something?'

We hadn't spoken for the last half-hour. I was sitting back in the thick leather seat of the car and dreaming about the Dime in the wooden hut. It seemed like something magic. It seemed that if I ever went back there I would never find that beach again, that stretch of coast, that I would drive up and down and find only towns and buildings, concrete and steel and gaudy amusement arcades and cheap roadside stalls. I thought that it was a dream, an illusion, that the hut was gone but I should always remember it, carry it in my head as if it were real.

'How did you know about that place?' I said.

'I found it one day,' Pete said. 'I went out driving and I stopped for something to eat and I went for a walk and I found it.'

'How did you know it would still be there?' I said. 'How did you know that it wouldn't have been bulldozed and razed to the ground and the land developed for flats?'

'I knew it wouldn't,' said Pete. 'I believe in places like that. I believe they last for ever, despite what everyone says.'

I laughed. I felt as if I were on holiday in a strange country where I didn't speak the language and all the road signs were no more to me than symbols.

'What does everyone say?' I said.

'They say that nothing lasts for ever and only stones endure,' said Pete. I thought that I had never heard anyone say that.

'So,' said Pete, 'shall we go and eat?'

We ate in a fish restaurant down an alley between two theatres near St Martin's Lane. It was dark and empty and the waiters all seemed very old. We ate prawns with mayonnaise and Dover sole with green beans and afterwards we drank a small glass of brandy each, and thick black coffee in white china cups.

Then Pete walked me to my door and he didn't seem ready to go home so I asked him in and we listened to some music and talked for a while.

We hadn't talked about Fred because how much is there to say? Something ends and it hurts like hell, and it's all been said before, it's been written about in mystical prose by poets who could make a shopping list sublime, and it's been hackneyed to death in magazine articles by people who shouldn't be allowed out in public.

You don't believe it will ever heal and then one day, somehow, there is a small intimation of pleasure, or life stirring, or something, some shift, some change, and you know, without anyone having to tell you, that you will survive it.

'You are being very kind,' I said to Pete.

He was lying along the green sofa. He had his arms linked behind his head and his legs were crossed over the sofa arm and he looked very relaxed for such a big shot. I had a stereotypical view of big business: I thought it must involve a great deal of standing up to take conference calls.

He turned his head to look at me, and he smiled so that the skin round his eyes fell into deep lines and I suddenly thought that he was twenty years older than me, and I wondered if that made a difference to anything.

'It's not kind,' he said. 'You don't know, this could be self-interest.'

'Is that what they teach you in *How To Make Friends and Influence People*?' I said.

'It could be that I want you to do this job, so I'm buttering you up, making you like me so you'll say yes,' he said.

I didn't think it was that, although I didn't know why.

'Is that it?' I said.

'No,' he said.

Later, he said, 'Did you think that you and Fred would last for ever?'

'Yes,' I said. 'I couldn't imagine the end, so I never thought it would come. I never saw it coming. It hit me like a freight train coming down an empty track.'

'I think,' said Pete, 'that there are some people who are very good at concealing their true feelings. I think they get so good at it that they hardly even know what is happening themselves.'

'Do you mean that Fred fooled himself into thinking

that he wasn't cheating on me with Natalie Hedge?' I said.

'There are people,' said Pete, slowly, 'I think mostly men, who can put things into compartments. It might have been that he thought Natalie had nothing to do with what he had with you, that they were entirely separate. So when he was with you, he could forget that she existed.'

'And the other way round,' I said.

I felt a bitterness that seemed to have taken root somewhere below my ribcage swell up into my throat. It tasted of bile in the back of my mouth.

'There are men,' said Pete, 'who have two families. Truckers and travelling salesmen, reps, that kind of thing. They have a wife and two daughters in Solihull and a girlfriend and a dog and a young son in Weston-super-Mare, and they travel between the two quite happily for years, and no one knows.'

I laughed again. I felt the bitterness subside, crawling back into its hole.

'If no one knows,' I said, 'does that make it bad? If we walk out of this room, we can't be sure that it goes on existing without us.'

'There's a men's movement joke,' said Pete. 'It goes: If a man is talking in a forest with no woman to hear him, is he still wrong?'

'There's a men's movement now?' I said. 'An actual official men's movement? What for?'

'I don't know,' said Pete. He shrugged his shoulders and turned his head and smiled over at me. There were other men I knew who would have taken offence. 'There are people who don't like change.'

20 ∫

I called Stella early the next morning, but still she had been awake for an hour and a half.

'Wait,' she said. 'I'm pressing save.'

She never minded being interrupted in the middle of something; she had faith that if a thought was worth anything it would last for a few minutes. I thought this was a cavalier attitude, but then it was one of the things I liked most in her.

'What?' she said. 'This is early.'

'I slept with Pete Street,' I said.

There wasn't a pause. She answered right back, without even a heartbeat in between.

'All right,' she said. 'I'll meet you on the corner in half an hour.'

When Stella said the corner it went without saying that it was her corner. I walked along Burlington Gardens, across Regent Street and into Glasshouse Street. I always liked that name and I wondered how it came to it.

I took a left turn up Shaftesbury Avenue, still empty this early in the day, just a few delivery trucks and men in vans on their way to Chinatown.

I slept with Pete Street. It wasn't what I had been expecting.

*   *   *

Stella was waiting for me on the corner of Old Compton Street. I could see her a block away, standing like a beacon with her white face and her red hair. I thought, with a rush of sentiment, that she hadn't changed since the day I met her. Everything changed, but through it all, Stella had stayed the same.

'Come on, then,' she said, taking hold of my arm and propelling me into the nearest coffee bar and sitting me down all in one seamless movement.

She knew the boy in there of old, and he brought us two cups of regular coffee with milk without being asked and when they were on the table and he had gone back to polishing the zinc counter, which was what he really liked doing best, Stella looked straight at me with her eyes wide like headlamps, and said, 'So, you had better tell me, from the top.'

I looked to left and right, as if I were crossing the road. I don't know what I was looking for. A place to start, maybe.

'It wasn't,' I said, 'what I expected to happen.'

'I should think not,' said Stella. 'Fucking the sugar king on a Friday night just like it was a regular thing to do.'

'I don't know about his private life at all,' I said. 'I think he was married once.'

'People like Pete Street are always married once,' Stella said, nodding.

I frowned at her. 'What does that mean?' I said.

Stella started laughing foolishly.

'I don't know,' she said. Another burst of laughter rose up in a wave and shook her shoulders. 'Sometimes I just open my mouth and nonsense comes out, I can't help it. I don't think I was ready for you to go out and start having sex without discussing it with me first. Especially with a man who could buy half the Tate without batting an eyelid.'

'You don't have to be so negative about it,' I said. I felt unsettled and defensive.

'Oh, stop,' said Stella. 'I think it's a beautiful thing. I'm just regretting that I gave up smoking that's all. It's times like this I really wish I had a cigarette.'

'Eat a bun,' I said.

Stella regarded me from under her eyebrows. I knew that look. She had been pulling that look since we were seventeen years old.

'So,' she said. 'You had better tell me. From the beginning.'

'I don't know,' I said, 'that there was a beginning. He came round to my flat. We never were on those terms before, we had a business relationship. We talked about impersonal things, we talked about art. We never discussed our private lives, and then suddenly there he was at my door saying he was sorry he hadn't come sooner.'

'Perhaps he's been waiting for this moment,' said Stella. 'Perhaps he's carried a torch for you for the last nine years. Perhaps he's dreamt and yearned and waited, and now Fred has left and his moment in the sun has come.'

'Don't be stupid,' I said. 'This is Pete Street the sugar king. It was strange, that's all. And then I got used to it and it seemed less strange and he took me to the seaside and we ate cockles.'

'Erotic,' said Stella darkly.

For some reason I didn't tell her about the hut with the picture of Olive Pleat in it. For some reason, I wanted to keep that part secret, even from Stella, to whom I told everything because she was my best friend and that's what friends were for.

'And then he took me out to supper,' I said. 'Some fish place near the Charing Cross Road,' I said. 'And we went back to my place and listened to Charlie Meldrum's last album, you know that one he did in Cuba with Ruben

Gonzalez, and it turned out that Pete Street knew all about that because jazz is his big thing and he knows Charlie for ever, they go all the way back.'

'And and and?' said Stella.

'And we were talking and listening to music and I had a bottle of rum William had left so we had some of that,' I said.

'And then?' said Stella.

I thought carefully.

'He didn't say anything,' I said. 'He got up when the record finished, and put it on to play again, and then he came over and sat down right beside me and kissed me.'

'Oh,' said Stella. 'The sugar king, who would have thought it?'

'Who would?' I said. I could feel myself starting to smile. It had been entirely unexpected, but also entirely unsurprising.

'So,' said Stella. 'Then what happened?'

'Then we went to bed,' I said.

'Yes, yes,' said Stella. 'But how did you get there? Did you suggest it or did he? You didn't do the film-cliché shuffle of clothes across the sitting-room floor, did you?'

'Certainly not,' I said. 'This isn't Channel Five.'

'Well,' said Stella. 'What then?'

I looked at her. It was curious this, because normally I was asking her these questions. For the last nine years I hadn't had any stories to tell, because when you are with someone on a permanent basis, you don't talk about the bedroom stuff. There is some unwritten rule about that. You only talk about it when it's one night or the first night, when it's new and strange and you don't know what will happen next and all bets are off. That's when you get the third degree and, mostly, you tell the truth. But if you are good and settled it would feel cheap and tasteless to exchange that kind of information. Once the relationship is over, then you can talk about it again. I thought suddenly, that now, if Stella were to ask me, I might tell her things about Fred he would rather she didn't know.

'It was me,' I said. 'I invited him into my room. And I'm very glad I did, because it was bloody marvellous.'

Stella looked at me for a moment with her mouth open and her cup of coffee stopped in mid-air and she laughed out loud.

'Oh,' she said. 'This is the best and most unexpected thing. Now I get to thinking about that old sugar king,' she said, 'he is rather sexy, with that dark rangy way he has about him.'

'He is,' I said.

'So how did you leave it?' Stella said.

'We agreed that it was just one night and it wouldn't change anything between us,' I said, rather too quickly.

Stella put her head on one side and gave me time to reconsider.

'All right,' I said. 'I told him that. I said I needed some space.'

'Because you didn't want to tell him you were using him for sex?' said Stella.

'I wasn't,' I said. 'It was very adult and mutual, but some things are perfect just the way they are.'

'And he took that quietly?' said Stella.

'Yes,' I said. 'I don't think he was planning for the future. Anyway,' I said, 'he wants to give me a job, so it wouldn't be appropriate.'

'It worked all right with you and Fred,' said Stella. 'Before it stopped working altogether, if you know what I mean. Oh dear, I'm sorry, that wasn't the right thing to say at all.'

'It's all right,' I said. 'But this is different, that's all. It's a whole other thing.'

'Will you take the job?' said Stella.

'I don't know,' I said.

I paused for a moment, and looked at her, and she looked right back, and a current of understanding and history and all the unspoken things ran between us like electricity.

'You know what I think,' I said. 'I think I need to get this charade of a show over, because now we've started we've got to finish. I need to get that done and then I can start again.'

Stella looked at me in admiration.

'I shouldn't say this,' she said, 'because it's such a hoary old sexist idea, but there is no doubt that a night with the sugar king has done wonders for you.'

'Just don't tell Jane,' I said. 'Otherwise we'll never hear the end of it and the art babies won't stop talking till Christmas.'

I left Stella, and walked up to the newsagent on the corner of Dean Street, where all the media darlings went for their periodicals, always full of spill-off from the Groucho Club and motorcycle messengers who were really poets when they weren't terrorising innocent jay-walkers, and bought a paper.

I realised that I hadn't looked at the news for weeks. When things hurt too badly the outside world recedes, and all you can do is stare fixedly at the square foot in front of you, taking small precise steps to get you from one hour to the next.

I bought my paper and took it home and read it from the front page right through to the back.

The Ministry of Defence were carrying out germ-warfare trials near Salisbury; America's most wanted man, Osama bin Laden, had gone missing from Afghanistan; fourteen people in Hungary had died in freak storms. Police were warning about China White in Birmingham, heroin so pure that it was lethal to inject. Lawyers acting for Francis Bacon's estate were threatening to sue for the return of five hundred drawings which no one would authenticate as his.

I remembered this case: there had been a flurry of interest the year before, earnest television programmes and much talk on the radio. The experts, hot under their stiff collars, didn't know which way to look. Bacon always said he never sketched: it was his great claim – that the work sprang, fully formed, on to the canvas. Then, after his death, a friend stepped forward with a huge collection of sketches and scored photographs, pages cut from magazines and painted over. At first the experts were delighted. Then, fast as lightning out of a summer sky, they changed tack and denounced the archive as a massive hoax.

People who didn't have any axes to grind either way sat back and enjoyed the spectacle. The experts spun like worms on a hook. If they were proved wrong and the archive was authenticated, they would end up covered with shame; but if they embraced the five hundred and later found they were fakes, credibility was entirely abandoned and they would never work in this town again.

And now the lawyers wanted them back, whatever they were, and everybody was refusing to comment.

Fakes seemed to be the theme for the week: reporters were exercised about actors posing as real people on daytime talk shows; a con-man had been sentenced to twelve years for flooding the market with faked contemporary art, copies of pictures by Graham Sutherland and Giacometti sketches. The copies were astonishingly good. Reputable West End dealers and venerable auction houses were taken in; phoney provenances were made up and planted in the archives of the Tate and the ICA; it was an unbelievably intricate and detailed operation; it was a sting, all right, of the old school.

I thought, We are not faking in that sense. I thought, This is completely different, this is something else, this is

Erne Malley or Nat Tate. I thought, This is post-modern and allowable.

The world, which had receded, rushed back at me. There were riots in Indonesia; a war crimes trial was starting in the Old Bailey. There was concern over pensioners becoming addicted to crack. One eighty-year-old man was quoted as saying that he had his habit under control, and that, apart from watching television, it was all he had to occupy his old age. 'It helps with the loneliness,' he said.

There was impeachment news from Capitol Hill, and outrage because a journalist had revealed a source; fury, directed away from the President, fell upon a new scape-goat. Reporters, delighted to run a piece about one of their own, were building up the story to Homeric proportions.

The weather forecast was for sunny spells.

I spent the next two days reading and avoiding the tele-phone. I finished the Dime biography and started another one, as if I couldn't get enough, as if somewhere in that dense black-and-white print I would find a coded clue to the existence of the Venus.

There were five days left until the show. In the arts pages of the evening paper there was a photograph of Damien Hirst and his son, wearing cowboy hats. There was a short, sneering article about the neurotic realists. Opposite, there was a picture of William and a paragraph about his show. The writer wanted to give him a label, but William resisted. 'I'm really a poet,' he said.

I didn't know whether to laugh or cry.

On Friday night, a week after I slept with Pete Street, I called him up. He didn't sound surprised to hear my voice, although it was eleven at night.

'I'm sorry,' I said. 'I didn't know if you'd be home.'

Pete lived in a low, wide house to the west of Ladbroke

Grove. I had never been there but I had seen photographs of it once, in a magazine. I knew that he had a drawing by Henry Moore in his study. I wondered if that was where he was sitting now, surrounded by green walls and a vivid sketch of people in the Underground during the war, sheltering from the Blitz.

I wondered what he was doing at home at eleven on a Friday night. I wondered if he was with a woman.'

'I was reading a book,' he said.

There was a pause and I didn't know what to say in it.

'Shall I come over?' he said.

'Yes,' I said.

It took him twenty minutes to get to my flat. It was a long drive, all the way up the slope of Holland Park Road, into Notting Hill Gate, along Bayswater, down the highway of Park Lane and into the dark stately streets of Mayfair, shuttered and silent, as they always were at night.

While he drove, I sat on my green sofa and wondered what I should say to him when he arrived.

He rang the doorbell and I let him in and gave him a glass of rum, and I was about to make small-talk, but then it wasn't necessary and we went to bed. It was a Friday night in a big city and I was so lonely I could feel it burning holes in me. For an hour or so I didn't feel it any more, because there was a body next to mine, and skin next to my skin, and I was wanted.

But then, when we had finished, lying back in bed, the strangeness of it hit me like a speeding car: it was the difference, how different he was from Fred. His body was much heavier, the flesh packed tight and hard into his skin. Fred had been narrow and slight, tall and angular; his skin, in certain places, was feminine, almost transparent. Pete Street was older and more weathered, he had more hair and more muscle; the power that he carried in his business life seemed to translate into his physical self.

I suddenly felt repelled by it and I was sorry that I had called. I felt that I had violated something, by asking this strange man into my bed. This was the place where Fred and I had slept naked and it was too soon and I felt all at once absolutely abandoned, and without meaning to, I started to cry, silent insidious tears, sliding out of the corners of my eyes and into my hair, so I could feel them wet and cold against my temples.

'I'm sorry,' I said. 'I am. It's not you.'

Pete stayed where he was, not saying anything, letting me cry, until I had finished.

'I'm sorry,' I said again. 'It's not your best Friday night.'

He sat up, and took my hand, and kissed me on the cheek, and smiled at me in the dim light.

'It's all right,' he said. 'Hearts get mended in the end. They can't help it.'

After he had dressed and gone I lay alone in my bed and thought of that.

21 ∫

The new Dime biography I was reading, by a Canadian man this time, had a series of photographs I hadn't seen before. There was one of Dime at the races with his wife, sometime in the early sixties. Dime's wife, Margaret, was a slight elegant figure. Hardly anything was written about her when she was alive, and now people don't remember her name. At the height of Dime's fame she stayed in the shadows, resisting attempts to make her into a celebrity. She furiously denied being his muse. In one of the scant interviews she ever did, she said that she had been at a party once and heard a woman asked what she did; this woman had drawn herself up and looked down and said, 'I am a muse.'

'I had to leave the building,' said Margaret Dime, when she told this story.

I liked that. I liked that she didn't just feel disdain and have another drink. I liked that she not only had to leave the room but the whole building.

I looked closely at Margaret's dark sculpted face. Her eyes were deep-set and close together, an intense straight gaze, coming right out of the photograph at you. She had a long uncompromising nose and a mole to the left of her mouth and she looked as if her family might have come originally from Eastern Europe, some harsh severe place, where the winters were long and there wasn't time for frivolity.

She was American, from New York originally. Dime had met her in a bar in the East Village in 1935. It was a rough area then and you still wouldn't walk down certain blocks there on your own at night now, and for a woman to be seen out in the thirties, downtown, all alone, was intriguing enough. She was wearing trousers and a black beret and playing backgammon for ten cents a point and beating everyone in the room, whatever they threw at her.

They got married in the spring and took a boat to Europe, and it was true that, whatever she said, she did inspire some of his best work. She died of heart failure just shy of her ninetieth birthday, and Dime, although ostensibly in good health himself, died three weeks later. Even the medical men said it was a broken heart.

Looking at her now, I was struck by how straight and taut she held herself. She must have been over sixty, but she looked strong and athletic. She was wearing a plain three-quarter-length coat, cut on the bias, with restrained elegance and sleeves just below the elbow to give it a night-at-the-opera kind of look.

Dime, as usual, was dressed with pin neatness, in dog's-tooth check, and looked as if he were taking time out from working on a row of figures.

I looked again at the coat Margaret was wearing and realised that it was one of Monsieur André's signature coats. St Laurent had his smoking, Monsieur André had his opera coats.

On the next page was a picture of Dime with Olive Pleat, just before he painted the picture of her that was now in the fishermen's hut. I wondered who came first. I wondered whether Dime met Olive and then started buying coats for his wife from Olive's brother, or whether it happened the other way round. I thought it was extraordinary that I was sitting in the room in which Sidney Pleat had sewn the very coat that Margaret Dime was wearing in this photograph.

There was a plate of the missing picture on the facing page: I saw suddenly, for the first time, that the Venus, in her full-throated laughter, had something of Margaret and Olive in her; that these women were similar physical types, striking rather than beautiful, strong intelligent faces, full of thought and determination and complexity, not the facile smoothness of accepted beauty. I thought it said a lot about Edgar Dime that these were the women who interested him, that he chose the woman with the trouser suit and the short hair and the fierce gambling streak, rather than some languid willing girl who would sit for him and buttress his ego and walk around his studio barefoot and compliant.

More than anything, I wondered what had happened to that picture.

Saturday morning broke with wild winds and glancing sunshine.

I called Jem early and asked him whether Olive Pleat was still alive and if she was, where did she live?

He was late for a tennis game and sounded too terse and competitive to be curious.

He gave me a telephone number and an address, and I wrote it down and sat for a long time looking at it and wondering what I wanted it for.

In the end, I didn't call. I didn't know what I wanted and I didn't know what to say, and I was afraid that she might just put the telephone down or tell me not to call again. I thought the best thing was to arrive and then see what to do. I felt a need for action, to move, travel, take a trip, make a decision.

I felt as if I had been floating through the months since

Fred left, lurching from one blind emotion to the next. I felt I was surrounded by memories and broken-up pieces of the past, of the time we spent together, of my childhood, of my mother leaving, of the dreams of my father.

I thought it was time to stake my claim, to assert myself against all these conflicting ghosts; to *do* something. I felt the fury that had been rising in me for the past weeks. I suddenly realised that it was a clean emotion, not muddied and opaque like the misery and dislocation that had preceded it. I wondered why it was that women were not allowed to be angry, why we were so afraid of it, as if it would transform us into something that people would shy away from; no longer sugar and spice and all things nice, not the way girls were supposed to be. I wondered who started that idea.

I felt this new anger surging through me like some kind of animate thing; I thought I needed to translate it into something; to go out, to take action, to *move*.

I don't know why I thought that going to see Olive Pleat was the action I was looking for. It was a whim; inexplicable and instinctive.

I wanted to go and see Olive Pleat and ask her about the lost Venus and let her tell me that she had seen Dime burn it with her own eyes and that would be the end of it.

I had a vision in my head of Olive Pleat living in a small dilapidated cottage by the sea. Her address was in Essex, and my grasp of geography was hazy, especially of the coast; I thought perhaps she lived in a small Edwardian terrace that had seen better days and looked out over the same flat sea as the fishermen's reading room. I thought that there would be a lovely symmetry to that; that it would please my searching desire for some order and reason in all this mess and contingency.

She didn't live by the sea at all. I got off the train at a stop called Chipping Ongar and took a taxi to the address Jem had given me.

It was an unremarkable white two-storey house along the side of a stretch of thick forestation, planted for timber rather than beauty, although there was something moving and stately about so many tall trees ranged so densely together; there was the sense of mystery and magic that woods always give, no matter how prosaic their intention.

A hill ran away behind the house, grazing pasture, bounded by sturdy wooden fences. A grey horse was sheltering from the wind under a group of chestnut trees. There was no garden; just a flat stretch of lawn and a beech hedge.

The taxi rattled down a single-track lane and dropped me at the gate. The driver was entirely unmoved by my journey, incurious and phlegmatic.

He told me the fare and I paid it and he drove away and I suddenly realised that I had no idea how I would get back to the station. I had a quick, violent vision of a door slamming in my face. I wondered what would happen if the address was no longer the right one. Jem had it from the time he took over the building in Bond Street, just after Sidney Pleat died in the Thames; Olive inherited the property, so Jem had dealt with her. But that was over seventeen years ago now, and people move and die and go weak in the head and get put in homes.

I thought this was a ridiculous journey and I had no idea why I had made it and I almost turned back right there and started trudging back down the lane, to the real world.

I knew Olive wouldn't be here and I thought it would be best if she wasn't.

Some cussed curiosity made me walk up to the front door. There was no bell or knocker. I hesitated. Another picture came into my head: even if she was here, she would see a stranger, ready to steal her savings or con her into buying double-glazing. If she had any sense at all she would send me away.

I knocked on the door; four short knocks. It had been painted and repainted and the surface was grooved and grained with layers of black paint.

Just as I thought the journey was going to end in bathetic anticlimax, not even a slamming door or strange face peering out, but the most mundane of all, no one home, the door opened, and Olive Pleat looked out at me.

She was unmistakable. Her skin was thin and lined and had a translucent aspect that sometimes comes with age, but she was clearly the woman in the photograph that I had looked at yesterday, the woman in the picture in that forgotten hut on the coast. Her hair was still thick, silver white now, but her eyes were open and bright and composed.

'Yes?' she said.

She didn't look suspicious or even very surprised. Perhaps people came to her door often, to ask about her life. She gave me a good sharp look up and down and nodded slightly to herself, as if she could see that I wasn't going to sell her bogus life insurance, at her age.

'Oh,' I said. 'Hello, Miss Pleat. My name is Iris Spent. I wondered if I could talk to you.'

I couldn't believe how lame it sounded, risible and blatant. If I were her I would have shut the door half-way through.

She gave me another look. There seemed to be some humour glinting in her light brown eyes, as if she were thinking of an old joke that no one else would understand.

'Are you a journalist?' she said.

'No,' I said. 'It's not that. I am interested in art. I wanted to talk to you about Edgar Dime.'

She started to smile the moment I said his name, she

couldn't help it. It came fast over her like a long-held reflex action.

'You want to talk about Edgar?' she said. 'Just like that?'

'Well,' I said, 'I know it sounds strange, but yes.'

The smile was dying on her face and I could see that she was thinking more of Edgar than me, and I wondered if that was the magic word with her, that once I had said that she made up her mind, but whatever it was, she turned and started walking into her house, and said, as if it were the most natural thing in the world, 'You had better come in, then.'

She made rosehip tea in a white china pot. She said that she didn't drink coffee any more because it made her heart jump in her chest, although she occasionally made a pot just for the smell.

'I'm eighty-nine,' she said. 'You don't want your heart to hammer too hard at that age.'

She poured the tea; her hand carried a tremor in it as it lifted the pot. I saw it and she saw me looking and she blinked impatiently, as if infuriated by the irrefutable infirmities that come with age. There was a faint rattle as the pot shuddered against the rim of the cup; the small noise of getting old.

I felt like an impostor.

'I'm sorry,' I said. 'It's very rude and uncivil of me to turn up like this, without a word of warning. I apologise. Perhaps I should go.'

She looked up with a quick, questioning movement of her head and I saw that, despite the shaking in her hands, eighty-nine years hadn't dimmed her faculties in any way at all.

'It's all right,' she said. 'I have no other plan. I was worried at first that you might be from the council. They want to move my fence. You should stay, now you're here. Stay, and we'll talk about Edgar. It's a good way to pass the morning.'

Her kitchen was square and neat. The floor was tiled and the walls were white, and it felt like being abroad in some indefinable way, something Italian perhaps in its neatness and lack of adornment. It was the kitchen of someone who knew how to cook: everything polished and functional, no extraneous elements, everything had a use and a place. I found it soothing.

We sat at a zinc-topped table and drank our tea out of thin white china cups. I remembered that the generation before Olive's had been called the moderns; all the artists and writers in Paris in the twenties, that was what they were called. Now we were post-post-modern and no-one knew what to call what would come after that. I thought that Olive was a modern: her kitchen had that idea to it.

She sat upright in her chair; she wore a dark green jersey in an Arran pattern, and the colour looked good in her monochrome room. She seemed entirely at ease, as if strangers arrived at her house every day.

She drank her tea and smiled at me. It was a reserved smile, but it had warmth in it; it was a smile of willingness, as if to say, I don't know why you are here but you are welcome anyway, for the time being.

'I think of Edgar often,' she said. 'Not a day goes by that I don't think of him. I remember him, like it was yesterday. Sometimes I think old age is like going to the cinema every day. I sit in my chair and I get the newsreel and the B-movie and the main picture and I never have to leave the house.'

She stopped and looked over at me, and smiled again.

'The old like to talk,' she said. 'I could talk all day if they let me. Or perhaps that is not a function of age; I rather think that I talked all the time anyway. That was how Edgar and I became friends. I had come to London to be a typist, that was one of the few jobs you were allowed to do if you were a woman, and all I ever wanted was to get to the city, so I took a rented room by the river, near Chelsea Hospital, which wasn't especially genteel in those days, but it was cheap and that was what mattered and I liked being close to the water. Dime lived down there although I had never heard of him. It was 1929, he was just getting his first small shows, barely even that, and anyway, I knew nothing about art. I knew the famous pictures, Turner sunsets, that kind of thing. I never really saw the point of it. I didn't care for all that Renaissance business and the old masters, and that was all you heard of if you lived in Sandwich. I never had a clue about Picasso or Braque or Modigliani, I didn't know there was something new happening. I was absolutely ignorant. But that never stopped me talking.'

She stopped for a moment, took a breath, drank her tea.

'There was a restaurant that I went to on Saturdays,' she said, 'in Chelsea. I used to have a lamb chop and a glass of sherry, and one day a man sat down at the next table, by himself, with a book, and we started talking. Or rather, I started talking, because he looked friendly enough, and I didn't know one single solitary soul in London, and after a while he said would I sit for him and I said yes. So I used to go to his studio and sit, and I talked all the way through and he said it was marvellous because it saved him the cost of a wireless.'

She stopped again and brought her eyes into focus; they had gone back into the past, you could see, she was watching the flickering pictures she had spoken of: the small restaurant room, the strange man, the high-ceilinged studio. It was seventy years ago, and she remembered it as if she was still there.

'Do you want all this?' she said. 'Is this what you want? I can tell you about Edgar till I drop. Are you writing a book?'

'No,' I said. I shook my head. 'It's hard to explain.'

'Try,' said Olive Pleat.

'I work in a gallery,' I said. 'I used to, until recently. It was contemporary art, that was what we sold. I worked with the artists and organised shows and things. It was good work, and I was good at it, and the man I was with owned it, so it was—'

'A family concern,' said Olive, smiling a little. 'I see. Nothing changes very much.'

'No,' I said. 'I suppose not. He started seeing someone else and we split up and I left my job, and I felt displaced and broken up and I didn't know what to do, and for whatever reason I started thinking about the missing Venus and then a friend took me to the fishermen's reading room up the coast, and the portrait Dime did of you was hanging there, and I live in the building where your brother had his workshop, and I don't know, I got to thinking, and I needed to do something, so I came to see you.'

Olive nodded her head like it all made sense. Hearing myself say it now I could see it made no sense at all.

'I'm sorry,' I said. 'It really does sound like a lot of rubbish.'

'Not at all,' said Olive, and I didn't think she was being polite. For some reason she seemed to see the point better than I did. 'It's entirely explicable. But tell me about Sidney. You live in his room?'

'Yes,' I said. 'It was made into a flat. I rent it from Jem Starling.'

'I remember him,' said Olive. 'He was barely old enough to go out without a note from his mother and he offered me more money than I could count for the whole building, and all I could think of was Sid dead in the bottom of the Thames with stones in his pockets.'

I wasn't sure what to say next.

'I'm sorry,' I said. 'I'm sorry for that.'

'He was always emotional,' said Olive, shaking her head. 'It makes me sad still, but I was never surprised. He took things very hard. And now you live in his room.'

'I love it,' I said. 'It feels like some hidden place in the glitter and marble of Mayfair.'

'Up in the eaves,' said Olive. 'I remember that room. Everyone was always hysterical, sitting up all night to get things finished, tiny hand stitches into satin dresses, seamstresses bent double in dim light to see better. There was every week a panic, nothing was ever done on time. But those women loved him, for a while, the ones who bought all those frocks.'

'Did you introduce him to Dime?' I said. 'Was that how that worked?'

'You mean how he ended up making clothes for Margaret?' said Olive. 'Yes, that's right. I introduced them, although at first I didn't say Sid was my brother. He was André by then, and French, officially.' She broke off and started laughing. 'He spent six months working as a waiter in a restaurant on the Left Bank of Paris to get that accent,' she said. 'But he wasn't stupid. He listened to the clientele, not the other waiters. He wanted a refined voice, top class. He'd always wanted that, ever since he was a child. So I had to say he was a friend of mine, at the beginning. Lucky I took after my mother and he looked like the spit of our father, so there wasn't any clue there.'

We finished our tea and Olive suggested we went for a walk, to see her horse. She said she couldn't ride any more, but the horse was old enough not to need the exercise.

'He's just standing in the field waiting to die,' she said. 'But he's happy waiting.'

We walked gently up the hill and she kept right on talking. She told me about London when she first lived there and how she started to learn about art from Dime, and how she began to go to the Tate and look in the windows around Mayfair, where the first of the modern pictures were starting to appear.

'I never noticed before,' she said, 'when I went to visit Sid at his shop. It wasn't what I was looking for. Once I knew Edgar my eyes were opened to all kinds of things. I was lucky to know him; things might have worked out very differently if I hadn't. I would just have been a secretary and got married to a nice normal man and had two children and done the expected thing and thought myself lucky. That's what happens to people. All those people,' she said, her voice growing fainter, 'with their lives of quiet desperation.'

She stopped talking as the slope grew steeper and she needed all her breath to climb it. She gave a sigh of satisfaction as we got to the top and walked along a ridge that gave views over a surprisingly rural scene. It seemed impossible to imagine that we were only twenty-seven miles from Hyde Park Corner.

'When it's dark,' she said, 'you can see the sky bruised orange from the street-lights in Camden Town.'

When we got back to the house it was afternoon.

'I'm going to make a risotto,' said Olive. 'Will you have some?'

She said it very matter-of-factly. I wanted to protest, but I thought that I should take her cue, and be matter-of-fact about it too.

'That would be fine,' I said. 'Thank you.'

She was an efficient and practised cook. Sitting watching her reminded me of Paco, of all the times I had sat and watched him cook in exactly this way, half bare instinct, half absolute concentration, hands moving fast and smooth, knowing exactly where everything went and the order of things.

She saw me watching and smiled another of her guarded half-smiles.

'Edgar taught me to do this,' she said. 'He had travelled in Italy and Greece, he lived in the South of France for a while after the first war, he knew about olive oil years before Elizabeth David came along. He used to buy it from the chemist – you couldn't get it in food shops in those days, not even in Soho. You had to go to the pharmacy. I always wondered what they kept it for, what medical use it served. It came in minute bottles, you had to buy ten at a time to make anything of it. Some chemists didn't like that, so Edgar went round several different ones, it became furtive and secret, like someone hoarding pills. And then he brought it home and made risotto with mushrooms. I had never seen food like that in my life.'

She cut up two small onions very quickly, before they could bring tears to her eyes.

'See,' she said. 'See all the things I learnt.'

'I wasn't in love with him,' she said, as we ate the food. 'Although I sometimes asked myself why not. When Margaret came along I was relieved, because then I knew it would never matter, it wouldn't be an issue. It's a very intimate business, sitting for someone, if you do it more than once. Even once, is something.'

'Yes,' I said. 'I did it once. I don't know what became of the artist. We were friends and I sat for him and he moved without leaving a change of address and I never heard from him again. But I think about him all the time.'

'Sometimes,' said Olive, 'I think it is more intimate than sex. You are not so taken up with *activity*,' she said delicately. 'There is more time for thought.'

*   *   *

We talked into the afternoon. I found myself telling her about my life, which was not what I had expected. She had a way of asking questions and waiting for the answers, not jumping in half-way through; she left silences to be filled, for all that she said she was the one always talking.

I told her about Stella and Paco and Jane. I told her about my mother and my aunt Ursula, and Pansy coming back after all these years with William in his elegant suits. I told her about Fred and Natalie Hedge. I went further back: I told her about Joe Goldstein and the time we saw Dr Gachet sold in New York and how Joe had lost his cattle and all those pictures he loved so, and how he lived in a small room in an unfashionable street near the Hudson River and stitched suits just like his great-grandfather.

She nodded and smiled and sometimes asked a question.

I told her about my mother leaving. I told her about Louis Winter and the Wigmore Hall and how he went to Canada and that I didn't know whether he was my father or not and how I had been wondering about it again, after all these years, in the dark nights since Fred left.

'You should go and find out,' she said.

I stopped, not sure I'd heard right.

'You should,' she said. 'I don't know a great deal about love and living with someone for your whole life. I don't know much about hearts breaking and what you do with that. But I know about life being short and curiosity being the most powerful human emotion, so it eats away at you if you don't satisfy it. It seems to me that you are at a crossroads, just now, an unexpected caesura in your life. Get on an aeroplane and go to Toronto and look him up in the book and see. People like that are always in the book.'

'Ha,' I said, the sound coming out of me half a laugh, half an entreaty. 'Well, perhaps I shall. Perhaps that is exactly what I shall do.'

'Yes,' said Olive Pleat, smiling, as if she were pleased

about something. 'Don't dream away your life in wondering.'

She made some more tea and the afternoon slid by and she
told me about the years when Dime became famous; how
reporters were always beating their way to his door when
all he wanted to do was go to the races with Margaret.
She told me how he and Sidney became friends, how Dime
used to sit in the corner of the atelier (my very room) and
sketch the women sewing, or the smart ladies being fitted
with their silks and satins, so discreetly that no one ever
noticed he was there.

'He was fascinated by women,' she said. 'I sometimes
think he loved women more than any other man I ever
met.'

She talked, unprompted, about love.

'I didn't seem to get it like other people,' she said. 'I never
found the expected kind. I never met anyone I wanted to
marry; I kept thinking about the rest of my life and I
thought, That's too long for one person. Although I used
to look at Edgar and Margaret and it never seemed long
enough for them. But people see one like that and they
hold it up and tell you it's the normal thing, the thing you
should expect, when in fact it's like a comet out of a dark
sky, it's rare and fleeting and we should look up at it and
gasp in wonder.'

She looked across at me, as if to see what I thought.

'I don't know,' I said. 'I don't think I thought enough
about the rest of my life, I thought it would just happen if
I let it.'

'No,' said Olive. 'That's no good. You have to know what
you want. You have to go out and make your dreams come
true. They say that in America, there was some study they
did, the scientific people. They said if you have a plan for
your dreams they are more likely to come true. It's not

romantic, but it's right. You can't wait on fate and wish upon a star; life's too short for that.'

'Was this your dream?' I said.

She smiled, this time to herself.

'Oh, yes,' she said. 'I had many ideas about life when I was younger and I was out in it, but really all I ever wanted was to be let alone to do my own thing. I was very cussed. I still am. Any long relationship is a series of compromises, so I thought it best if I left myself to my own devices.'

I wanted very much to ask what she did, with her own devices, but I thought it would sound intrusive and impolite.

She saw the question in my face.

'Here,' she said. She got up and led the way into the next room, a long narrow room flooded with light from wide windows and dominated by a wooden table covered in scraps of material. On one wall a quilt was hanging, intricate and thick with colour, the kind of thing that you look at and think is a precious and beautiful object, something not of our time.

'I make these,' she said. 'They tell stories. I never could paint and I never could write but I knew how to sew. Sid and I both; I didn't have his flair. I'm not sure I wanted it, although for a long time I thought I did. So I make these. You come and tell me your story and I put it in a quilt and then you take it with you and you have it for ever and you sleep under it, and I think there is something magical about that.'

She looked up at the wall.

'That one,' she said, 'was my story, but I don't sleep under it any more. I think it would give me too many vivid dreams, at my age.'

She paused and looked at her quilt. I wished I had a camera, so I could remember her face. I got the same feeling I had when Pete Street had taken me to the fishermen's hut;

I felt that if I ever came back here again, tried to find this place and this woman, there would just be a bare field, no house no forest no horse grazing under the chestnut trees, that all I would have was a hazy memory, jumbled and faded, like in a dream.

'There's something else,' she said. 'There's one other thing you should see. I'm not sure why I'm showing you this, but you've come all this way and you seem interested and I don't think you would tell anyone. I would prefer it if you wouldn't tell anyone.'

And she took me into a further room, at the end of the house, another plain room, with white walls and a high narrow fireplace, and above the mantelpiece was the missing Venus, with her head thrown back, laughing like it was the best joke in the world.

I stood staring at it for a while. I was caught in delight and disbelief; for all that I had thought it was still extant, that was mostly in my wishful mind. In my rational mind I knew it was gone. But it wasn't gone, it was here, it was alive, it was shining on this white wall in all its shimmering glory, as bright and vital as if it were painted yesterday, as if Edgar Dime were still in the room with it, waiting for the paint to dry.

I don't know what it was, something about the life in it, about the freedom and grace of the laughing figure, about her absolute defiant femaleness, but it was as if someone had physically reached out to me and touched me, filled me with reassurance and comfort. Racing incoherent thoughts ran through my head; I felt a pleasure as intense as anything I knew. In terms of pure aesthetics this wasn't the greatest work of art in the world, but it was something about thinking it was gone and then finding it here, in this hidden corner of east England, in this small white room belonging to an ordinary woman, not shown in a museum or displayed in a rich man's mansion. It moved me more than I could express, and I felt as if I were a child again and I wanted to run and sing and whirl myself round until I was too giddy to stand up any more.

'Sometimes,' said Olive, 'I laugh, when I think of the fuss over this picture, people wondering what happened to it, whether there was a conspiracy or a cover-up.'

I thought she must laugh. I would laugh too, just looking at it, out of sheer happiness.

'How did it . . .' I said. 'I mean, how is it that you . . . ?'

She looked at me again, as if considering something, but it didn't take her very long, and afterwards I thought that when you get to that age making rash decisions must go with the territory.

'I have this picture,' she said, slowly, and that glimmer of humour was back in her face, that sense of her having some private joke with herself, 'because Edgar, when he wasn't in a three-piece suit like an insurance clerk, liked to wear dresses.'

I was so surprised that I sat down abruptly. Olive laughed.

'I know,' she said. 'It's not expected, is it? Although you should really expect everything because most things are inexplicable, for a rational mind.'

She sat down opposite me and looked at me with her old clear eyes.

'Edgar was very restrained, in his life,' she said. 'He didn't drink very much, he ate in moderation, he smoked French tobacco sometimes after dinner. The wildest thing he ever did in his life, when he wasn't painting, was ask Margaret to marry him. She was not a respectable middle-class miss, she was considered very shocking when we were young. But for all that, he was restrained. He was raised like that and I don't think he could ever break out of it, except in this one way. He used to wear beautiful dresses and make himself up and put on a wig and hang earrings on his ears and walk about all evening smoking from a foot-long cigarette holder, and after half an hour we forgot it was Edgar and it seemed as if there was a woman in the room. Oh, he was very good at it, very beautiful, very thorough.'

I suddenly got it.

'And Monsieur André made the dresses,' I said.

'That's right,' said Olive. 'Edgar couldn't walk into Marshall and Snelgrove and buy a frock off the peg. There was the fear of being found out, he was very secret about it, it was never to be revealed. I think only six people ever knew at all. And besides, it was in his temperament to want the best. It was only in his thirties that he admitted to this desire, he had restrained it until then. It was before the second war, in the last days of prosperity. He spoke to Sid about it, and Sid was enchanted – it was the theatrical side of him, I suppose, the camp side, he loved dressing up. So he worked at it on his own, after the seamstresses went home, night after night, and he produced a complete wardrobe, like a trousseau for a young bride. Everything from evening dresses to tea frocks to coats; even the underwear, he made that by hand too, tiny stitches so delicate you couldn't see them with the naked eye. And you never saw Edgar so delighted, it was like watching a small boy at Christmas. So he gave Sid the Venus; that was his thanks. I think it was symbolic in a way. He painted that picture out of his love of women and all things female, and also out of his secret; there is something in that picture that almost gives the game away. Sid gave him something supremely female, in those beautiful dresses. So it was a good trade.'

She paused, looking up at the painting on the wall.

'It was a good trade,' she said, 'but of course it had to be secret. So Sid kept her in his bedroom, where no one ever went. He never took a man home after that. And when he died, I took it and kept it here. I thought about making it public, but I couldn't bear the explanations, and what would happen? The insurance bills would be beyond me and I would have to sell it in one of those awful auction houses, with everyone peering and remarking and thinking about the money and not the picture. I thought it was best left the way it was.'

'And you managed to keep it secret all this time?' I said.

Olive smiled, and this time it wasn't guarded or reserved, it was a fine smile that moved right across her face and lit up her eyes and made her look just like the girl in the painting.

'I have a few friends,' she said, 'who see me here, but they are not, by coincidence, interested in art. So they barely give her a glance. That's why,' she said, 'I thought I would show her to you. I thought perhaps it would be nice to have her appreciated for once. But I would be pleased if you wouldn't say anything to anyone. I don't want half of Cork Street on my door on Monday morning.'

'Oh, no,' I said. 'Of course not. I shan't say anything. I'm just happy I saw her. I'm happy she's here. I thought Dime had destroyed her. I thought she was just a plate from an old catalogue. I thought she was gone.'

22

Wednesday was the show. Everyone was excited and revved up about it. Stella said it was more fun than putting out a book. 'Maybe I'm in the wrong job,' she said, but in the kind of way that made you know she didn't mean it. She knew she was in the right job; of all the people I knew, she was most convinced of that.

Paco was laughing to himself and humming Louis Prima numbers under his breath.

The day before, he took me to see his club again. The builders were still in and there were dust sheets draped everywhere, but it seemed in some mysterious way to be coming along. At various intersections, men in dirty jeans were standing up triangular ladders, not doing very much.

'They'll start when you go,' said Paco, placidly.

There was plenty of room and the acoustics were just like home.

'Oh,' I said. 'It will be a big success. It will be fine, here.'

Paco smiled.

'What do you think about tomorrow night?' he said.

'I don't know what to think,' I said, which was true.

He smiled wider, like a small boy with a snail in his pocket.

'I can't wait,' he said. 'It's like a pantomime.'

*   *   *

There was a moment at five thirty in the afternoon, when I thought it was too much and too bad and I couldn't face it and what was I thinking. I picked up the telephone to call a cab to take me to the airport. Then I thought of Olive and her picture and the friends who came round and didn't know anything about art; I thought about Edgar Dime with his couture wardrobe; I thought about making your dreams come true the way you wanted; and I put the receiver down.

Jane rang the bell at six. I hadn't expected her.

'I thought I should come,' she said. 'I thought you might make a run for it if you didn't have a hand to hold.'

'Hm,' I said. 'Well, that's accurate. You can put your crystal ball away now and go back to being a normal person.'

'It doesn't take much,' said Jane. 'You've been looking shifty round the edges for some days now, if you don't mind my saying.'

'It makes me feel much better,' I said.

Jane was wearing a lilac dress that followed her shape like a faithful hound. Her hair fell round her face in waves and she looked wanton and available.

'I don't know what to wear,' I said. 'I suppose I should make an effort. I should look as if I'm having a good time.'

'Come on,' said Jane. 'The whole point of all this is for you to walk in looking pretty enough to make a grown man's eyes water, and then we have the show, and you stand up and declare that William never painted bum on a wall, and Fred is left with omelette dripping off his face on to the carpet and we all go out to dinner and you have closure.'

'Oh,' I said. 'Is that what it is?'

The place was full by the time we arrived. Aurelia Strike

had been protecting her investment by talking it up to her PR friends; they had packed the guest list with A minus personalities and liggers who at least looked pretty and people with money to fill out the mix. The art babies had wandered in as their galleries shut and were standing in a pretty gaggle in one corner looking discreetly at William to see if he was gay or not.

'We should tell them,' I said to Jane. 'Should we tell them? I don't want them to waste their time all evening.'

'I like *that* one,' she said, looking at the girl whom I had seen the day I came to talk to Fred and found him with Natalie Hedge. 'I'll tell that one, if it gets her on my side.'

Charlie Meldrum was talking to Pete in front of *Fourteen Dreams*. I looked at Pansy's bleached-out face and then at Pete, and I waved at him and he smiled his good open smile at me and turned back to his conversation. I thought perhaps things would go back to the way they were before and we would have a professional relationship again, and when I was Olive Pleat's age I would run the movie back in my head and remember sleeping with him as something distant and out of context.

The art critics were there, divided into two camps as usual; one gathered round Hayden Bustle, who was wearing a particularly interesting hat, and the other clustering around Treve Pettit. Treve and Hayden, who hated each other in real life as well as in their columns, stared at each other with narrowed fox eyes, just as if they hadn't done that at every opening they had attended for the last twenty years.

'I have a fantasy,' said Jane, 'that one day we shall discover that in fact they are husband and wife or brother and sister and they love each other dearly and meet in the dead of night and read Elizabeth Barrett Browning aloud and count the ways, and all this is just steam and sound to drum up readers.'

'I'm certain,' I said, 'that you are right.'

Fred walked over when he saw me and said, 'I didn't think you would come.'

I thought, He's used that line before.

I looked straight at him. He looked different in some way I couldn't put my finger on. I thought perhaps it was his hair. Or maybe it was just that he was having sex with someone else.

'Sure I came,' I said, as if this was nothing. 'The artist is a friend of mine.'

'Oh,' said Fred. He seemed disconcerted. He could hardly have said: I wouldn't have shown him if I'd known that; but I think that was what he was thinking.

'Well,' he said. 'I was surprised that's all. Hello, Jane,' he said, remembering his manners. 'I heard you were thinking about changing your dealer.'

He could swing from personal to main chance on a sixpence, like a black cab. I had once thought this was endearing. Now I thought perhaps it was tacky.

'I'm not,' said Jane. 'That's how rumours start. But I wouldn't come to you anyway. On account of you fucking Natalie Hedge when you were supposed to be in a caring sharing relationship with my friend Iris, I wouldn't piss on you if you were on fire.'

'Oh,' said Fred again. I could see that he wasn't having such a good time, all of a sudden. 'Well, of course you're entitled to your opinion.'

'You bet I am, buddy,' said Jane. She sometimes talked like this, if she was reading Raymond Chandler. I thought that accounted for the lilac dress: it was the kind of frock that would make a man kick a hole in a plate-glass window all right.

She sent another indiscreet look over at the pretty art baby, and Fred mumbled something under his breath and went away and I didn't watch him go.

I started to laugh.

'That was nice,' I said. 'Do you kiss your mother with that mouth?'

Jane smiled beatifically; she talked dirty better than anyone I knew. She could say anal sex and still sound like a dowager duchess.

'It was time someone told him,' she said. 'The more I think about him the more I think he was beneath you. Oh,' she said, 'and is it true that you have been sleeping with that sugar king without telling me?'

'There was sex,' I said, 'but I didn't know it was published. I was trying to be discreet.'

'There's no call for that,' said Jane, in reproof.

Pansy and Paco arrived together. They seemed to be holding hands.

'Is there something I don't know?' I said.

I looked from one to the other. They looked suspiciously clean and innocent, as if they had taken too many showers in the last week.

'I get it,' I said. 'It's all right. I'm a big girl. I can take other people being happy.'

Stella came in, looking distracted.

'I'm late,' she said. 'I got stuck and forgot the time. What happened?'

Pansy took me to one side.

'I'm not sure if it's something or if it's nothing,' she said. 'Are you sure you don't mind? He's been your friend for fourteen years.'

'He's my friend,' I said. 'That's all it is. It's not a sexual thing, it never was. So you should go ahead and make him happy. He deserves it.'

'I don't know,' said Pansy. 'I don't know. It wasn't what I expected.'

'He's good and kind and you should hold on to him,' I

said. I felt a start of despair when I said it, because across the room was someone I had failed to hold on to, and it was still too soon for me to be careless of that.

'Maybe I will,' said Pansy. She looked around and took a beer from a waiter who was standing beside her. 'What about this art, then?' she said, her eyes gleaming. 'This looks like the real thing to me. Where's the artist?'

We went over to say hello to William, but we only got a moment with him because everyone wanted a piece and there wasn't room for us as well.

He was wearing a purple suit with a green lining. He looked very glamorous and very handsome. Knowing what most artists looked like, I found the whole get-up highly improbable, but there was no doubt that he was having an effect on the room.

Pete Street's PR woman was pushing journalists towards him, thinking of column inches in her mind.

'Would you,' said a reporter from the lifestyle section of the *Independent*, 'describe your work as explicitly feminist?'

William's smile moved a little to one side of his face.

'I reject explicit,' he said. 'I reject feminist. I don't do labels.'

Stella and Pansy and I leant against the wall and drank beer and listened to the performance. William was word-perfect, you had to give him that. He was relaxed and poised and suddenly sceptical at just the right moment.

'That boy is a natural,' said Stella. 'Someone should take him up and make him a star.'

'That's what I always said,' said Pansy. 'But I don't think he's ambitious. He never was in San Francisco, although there was that one time he sat in a box for Save the Whales.'

There were questions about the zeitgeist and the *Freeze* generation and how much of the work already belonged to Charles Saatchi and whether William had ever got drunk with Tracey Emin. There were questions about black art and feminist art and polemic art. William stood and smiled through it all.

'In *The Impossibility of the Functional Independent Female in the Mind of the Traditional Male*,' said the *Independent* woman, 'are you explicitly paying homage to the work of Damien Hirst?'

'You asking if it's a plagiarism suit?' said William.

'Not as such,' said the woman, looking slightly flustered.

'I am paying my *respects* to the master,' said William. 'I never met the man, but that boy is a smooth operator. He'll do anything from fill your front room with wildlife to sell you a kebab. You have to respect that.'

They all wanted to know what he thought about Gary Hume and Rachel Whiteread and Chris Ofili and Gavin Turk and Sarah Lucas and Jake and Dinos Chapman and whether the Neurotic Realists were as neurotic as they were cracked up to be.

Then someone said the word aesthetic.

William straightened up and spoke very clearly, as if this was what he had been waiting for.

'There is no aesthetic here,' he said, 'This is not about aesthetics. This is not about beauty. Don't you think if I could do beauty like Rothko I would do it? This isn't built to last, what I'm doing here. This is trash art, this is disposable art: you look at it, you get the point, but it's not going to last for a hundred years. That's what you're getting at the fag end of the twentieth century: you're getting disposable art for a disposable age. Doesn't mean it's not worth anything. Just don't get it confused with something else, that's all.'

He stopped for a moment and stared at the room.

'I didn't know William knew anything about art,' said Jane, who had given up on the art babies and pushed her way through the crowd to get to us. 'Was he listening all that time we were talking?'

Pansy smiled to herself. 'William knows lots of things,' she said.

Stella frowned with her black eyebrows.

'Is he trashing my art?' she said. 'I thought there was beauty in *Beauty in the Eye of the Beholder*. I thought there was something of value in *The Impossibility of the Independent Female*.'

I thought William had finished but he cleared his throat and looked at the room and had another go at it. I thought he should do this more often, he was born to it.

'Listen,' he said, 'Jed Driver can take pictures of his old mum and dad and call it art; Eve Trent can stick an endoscope up herself and take pictures and call it art; a pack of students can hide in a room for a week and pretend they went to Benidorm and call it art. Artists are sleeping in boxes in public and exhibiting balls of old chewing-gum and plastering ten-foot placards with birth certificates of serial killers and making piles of garbage on the floor and creating installations of used condoms. They've always done this, this is not new. Art has been cans of shit, and pieces of felt and lard and blackboards with chalked equations, and porcelain lavatory bowls, and videos of men screaming run on a loop, and basketballs floating in tanks, and one canvas covered in black paint, and piles of bricks on the floor, and some of it matters and some of it doesn't. This is art because someone says it is and because someone is prepared to pay for it. Some things will last and some won't and you have to decide where the difference is. Do you think people are going to remember a cucumber sticking out from an old mattress or a mannequin dressed as Sid Vicious or someone's diary put out for show? Maybe they'll remember a shark swimming in formaldehyde and they'll remember twenty-five blocks of jewel-coloured resin and they'll remember a six-foot-tall egg cast of metal where they can watch their changing reflection as they move round it. And maybe they'll remember a dark-haired girl dancing like a maniac in the middle of a shopping centre and in a few years they'll think of a head made out of refrigerated blood; and even if the objects themselves don't last they'll have taken on some life of the mind and that's what will matter. And maybe they'll forget and none of it will matter at all. But if you want beauty, real beauty that will stay for ever, you haven't got that many people who are going to give that to you, and you've got to look hard for it and cherish it when you find it, and that's all I'm going to say.'

And William stood up and looked at the crowd in front of him, who didn't know what to say next, and then he walked out of the door without looking behind him.

'Well,' said Stella, 'that wasn't in the grand plan.'

I could see Fred over the heads of the critics, looking as if someone had punched him in the face. Artists weren't supposed to call their work trash then walk out of their own show, even the drunker ones.

But controversy loosens wallets. Ten minutes later there were red dots on everything in sight.

'So what do we do with all the buyers,' I said, in Stella's ear, 'when we tell them it's a fake?'

She looked straight ahead and smiled serenely.

'We are entirely charming and we give them their money back,' she said. She turned back to me. 'Isn't it time?' she said. 'This is the time, before people start to leave.'

'Yes,' said Jane. 'This is it.'

'This is the time,' said Pansy.

'This is it,' said Paco.

I could feel them vibrating with tension beside me; I could feel them lined up either side, like a gang of rough riders slouching into town.

I looked at Fred over the crowd. He had taken the bemused look off his face and was starting to realise his show was a sell-out. He was scanning the room, left to right, as if wondering why Natalie hadn't turned up. I wondered why she hadn't turned up. I hoped she had run off with an investment analyst.

I looked at his face, the face that I had known so well but which was becoming strange to me each time I saw it again. There was distance and time and changing circumstances; the fact that we had been together seemed tangibly in the past now, something finite, something that I would remember when I was old.

I didn't understand how it had got like that and I wasn't sure that I was going to go looking for the answer. There was a perceptible shift, that's all; something had split and moved away; the page had turned.

I didn't feel bound to him any more, as if everything that happened to him affected me, as if we were connected to each other in some indissoluble way. He was just a man I used to know.

'I'm not going to do it,' I said.

Jane and Paco and Stella and Pansy turned and looked at me. My eyes ran over their faces, one after the other: there were varying degrees of surprise. Mostly it seemed they were curious.

'What then?' said Stella. 'If you don't do it, what then?'

'Do you want one of us to do it?' said Pansy.

'We don't have to do it now,' said Jane.

'Maybe we don't have to do it at all,' said Paco. He started to laugh.

'That's what I mean,' I said. 'Just not do it.'

Paco laughed harder than ever. 'That's much funnier,' he said. 'When you get to thinking about it.'

'I didn't know we were doing this so everyone could have a big laugh,' said Stella. She was still smarting from William saying it was all trash anyway. She knew she shouldn't mind, but she did, a little. I knew her well enough to see it; I also knew that by tomorrow she would be thinking about something else.

'It was for revenge,' said Pansy. 'Which is a dish best served cold, after all. It was so Iris could get finished with all this and live her life like she's supposed to.'

'All this,' said Jane, looking round the crowd, which was still shivering and twitching with pleasure at being present at an act of defiance to take them out of their safe, comfortable routines, 'so you could get your heart mended.'

'I think I got it,' I said. 'I'm not sure how, but I think I did. I don't want to make a scene, not now. I wanted to hurt him and humiliate him but it doesn't seem necessary any more.'

I thought for a moment of Olive Pleat; I wondered if she was sitting in her white room looking at the Venus, laughing, the two of them together, getting the joke.

'It's the past,' I said. 'That's all.'

'Well,' said Stella, 'I think you're right. It'll just be that William has one show and the buyers will be very happy because the work will go up in price due to scarcity value and no one will ever know except us.'

'Perhaps William will turn into an artist after all,' said Paco, 'after that speech he gave.'

'I don't think so,' said Pansy. 'He once said that all he really wanted was to go and live on the Isle of Lewis and fish. Or be a poet. I can't remember. I think his father's father came from there.'

'Charlie Meldrum's great-grandfather came from Lewis,' I said.

'Well, maybe they'll end up there together,' said Jane.

She looked round the room one more time. I think she had been looking forward to a showdown, to a grand finale.

'I'm sorry,' I said, but she shook her head.

'No,' she said. 'You're right. It's your party. But I'm hungry. Let's go and eat.'

We left the bright-lit gallery, with our phoney art in it, sold for thousands of pounds of other people's money, and walked into the dark, quiet streets.

'What about the money?' said Stella.

'We can give it away,' said Pansy.

'We could invest it and start a foundation,' said Jane, who admired Peggy Guggenheim.

'We can send it by anonymous mail to sincere causes,' said Paco.

We crossed Oxford Street, empty and deflated now that the shopping crowds had gone home, and walked through Soho Square. Ahead of us, the lights of Soho were beckoning, but the square itself was bare and dark.

In the middle of the garden, an old woman was sitting on a bench, with a shopping trolley filled with plastic bags and hung with fake flowers and indecipherable bits of sacking. She was talking to herself. It wasn't wild rambling chattering, or strange insane keening; it was mild reasonable talk, as if she were in a restaurant or a taxi, making polite conversation about the weather.

The others were walking ahead of me. I fell back and stopped for a moment.

I looked at the bag lady and gave her a faint smile and she looked straight back at me and kept on talking and I couldn't tell if she had seen me or not.

What I didn't know then was that six months later Olive Pleat would die in her sleep and that a week after that the Venus would be delivered to me by the postman, wrapped in layers of brown paper, with instructions that she should go to Joe Goldstein.

I didn't know that Stella and I would pack her into a blue suitcase and smuggle her through customs at Kennedy airport. I didn't know that Joe would sit in his two-room apartment looking at the million-dollar picture we brought him with tears running down his face.

I didn't know that William would go to live in the Isle of Lewis and become a poet, and that for a year afterwards people in London would still be talking about the night he walked out of his own exhibition.

I didn't know that Natalie Hedge would leave Fred for another woman.

I didn't know that Pete Street would ask me to marry him and that I would say no.

I didn't know all this and I don't think it would have made much difference if I had.

The old woman looked away from me, her eyes cast into the future, and she turned her face back and stopped talking and looked right at me with her faded eyes and smiled, a sane, sweet smile.

I smiled back. I wanted to offer her cash or thanks or an explanation but I didn't know what for.

Then Stella called out to me and the woman fell back into her plainsong muttering and I turned away and walked out of the dim silent square, down the road, where the others were waiting, where the hopeful lights of Greek Street were shining into the night.